Courting A Cowboy

⸺⸙⸺

PATRICIA McLINN

PRAISE FOR COURTING A COWBOY

"Filled with humor, a heartwarming plot, secrets, schemes that go awry, interesting characters, clever dialogue and romance, this story is a delight. ... Do not miss it!" - *Romance Junkies Reviews*

"Sophie will steal your heart like she does all the men in the book. And you'll be waiting anxiously to see how Nate falls for her after trying hard to resist his fate. Fast paced and funny, the book will also tug at your heart." – *Kathryn Shay, bestselling author*

"OS Ranch foreman Nate Abbott needs to concentrate on an upcoming roundup. But it's hard to focus on his work when headstrong Sophie Vandercook arrives from St. Louis with her own plan - to round up a husband. Funny, winsome and brimming with passion, COURTING A COWBOY will lasso your heart." – *Judith Arnold, bestselling author*

PRAISE FOR PATRICIA MCLINN
USA Today Bestselling Author

"Breathtaking passion...(Will) have you cheering, sighing, and all choked up" – *Romance Designs*

"Fast-paced, vivid and true-to-life" – *Christine Brennan, USA Today columnist*

"One of the most entertaining and interesting western historicals I've read in a long time" – *The Romance Reader*

"Richly emotional love stories that are a joy to read" – *Booklist*

Widow Woman has "a strong woman, a dark tormented man, and a love as fierce and irresistible as the Wyoming wind." – *Mary Jo Putney, New York Times bestselling author*

"Splendid!" – *Bell, Book and Candle*

"Books you read more than once just for the nice, warm feeling" – Rendezvous

"Melt-your-heart romance." – *Old Book Barn Gazette*

"First rate" – *RT Book Reviews*

"...for writing that grabs your emotions, you can't go wrong." – *Under the Covers Book Reviews*

PROLOGUE

St. Louis, 1888

"**O**h, Sophie, did he make you an offer? What did he say? What did you say? You didn't — Oh, you couldn't have —"

"Alice, cease peppering Sophie with questions," scolded Louisa, though her expression was quite as questioning as Alice's. "You sound as skittish as one of the students."

Rather than answer her fellow instructor's questions in order, Sophie responded to the unspoken one that gathered in all the others.

"Yes, I refused him."

Alice emitted a squeak.

Louisa's gasp was controlled, and quickly followed by her own question. "Again? But, Sophie, you are not in a position to refuse respectable offers of marriage — whatever will you do?"

The last was a question she had been contemplating when Alice Drenner and Louisa Scroggins returned to the garret room they shared.

Sophie Vandercook did not flinch from facts.

She knew herself to be neither beautiful nor pretty. Her dark hair was plentiful and glossy. Her features regular, if undistinguished. She presented a neat and pleasant figure, and one attired in good taste.

She had a good understanding of literature, a rudimentary knowledge of French, a native ability at arithmetic. She had no pretensions to being as talented a watercolorist as Miss Drenner or as practiced a musician as the widowed Mrs. Scroggins, although she had passable skills in both pursuits.

Indeed, in assessing her accomplishments, Sophie held chief among them to be her willingness to scrupulously assess a situation, then to marshal her weapons and form a plan.

The first element of her assessment was that Louisa Scroggins was not entirely accurate in saying that Sophie was not in a position to refuse respectable offers. Although fairness noted that it was not Louisa's fault for drawing an erroneous conclusion, since Louisa did not possess all the information.

Sophie was fully aware of how fortunate she was to have inherited a satisfactory sum from her mother. Fortunate in comparison to her fellow instructors at Mrs. Forestell's Academy—indeed, even in comparison to the redoubtable Mrs. Forestell herself—and fortunate in that her father had been unable to squander that sum as he had all others he had encountered.

That Walter Vandercook had been unable to obtain dominion over her inheritance was thanks to the foresight of the maternal grandfather Sophie had met precisely once – and, as that occasion occurred in her infancy, she had no recollection of it.

As a result of the prosperous Philadelphia merchant's visit to St. Louis to meet his highly unexpected son-in-law, Bertram Boynton had tied up his youngest daughter's inheritance entirely for her support and for the education and support of her children.

As it happened, Sophie remained Viola Boynton Vandercook's only child. Sophie's strongest memories of her mother were of a woman continuously in a decline, right up until she faded into death in Sophie's twelfth year.

Walter Vandercook had immediately adjusted Sophie's status at Mrs. Forestell's Academy for Young Ladies from day student to boarding student, freeing himself for what he termed business pursuits, as well as freeing himself from maintaining a home for Sophie. To Sophie's knowledge the only business he had ever pursued had been trying to break Bertram Boynton's will.

He had achieved no progress in that endeavor when he passed away shortly after Sophie reached her seventeenth birthday. That left her not only an orphan, but in possession of precisely one living relative she had met: her half-brother, Gerald.

Jerry Vandercook, some dozen years older than Sophie, had figured little in her life since he had departed St. Louis – under circumstances not entirely clear to her – when she was almost nine years old.

She did not receive a reply from him to her missive communicating their father's death until a year and a half had elapsed. His letters that followed had been stilted and sparse – not unnatural, considering they had barely known each other when he left. Of late, however, that had changed, and a correspondence had grown between them that had become quite ... remarkable.

"Sophie," Alice said, still squeaking, while her kind, blue eyes filled with tears, "two offers of marriage – what if you don't receive another?"

"I don't seek the domestic life you hope for, Alice."

"But then do you plan to stay here forever, like Miss Stanley?"

Sophie looked at the packet of her brother's letters, neatly tied with a piece of rose ribbon left over from trimming her best summer hat last year. With crisp movements, she replaced the packet in the wooden box that slid precisely into the trunk at the foot of her bed.

"I don't believe I'm suited to a life devoted solely to teaching."

Upon the death of her father, Sophie had taken her immediate circumstances in hand without hesitation. She had approached Mrs. Forestell with the suggestion that she change her status at Mrs. Forestell's Academy for Young Ladies once more, this time from student to instructor.

Mrs. Forestell had not only been agreeable, but also much relieved, as Sophie later learned from a recounting by Tad, the boy who ran errands for Cook and Mrs. Forestell.

Tad had repaid Sophie for her gift of a peppermint stick by relaying an overheard conversation in which Mrs. Forestell had told her visiting sister that by adding Sophie to the Academy's staff, she had acquired a competent instructor and had avoided a potential dilemma. For she had greatly feared that Sophie might have contemplated hiring out her services as a governess.

Mrs. Forestell had seen arising before her the unwelcome choice between denying a recommendation to a young lady she felt an unusual degree of fondness toward or producing a recommendation for a young lady she felt was singularly unsuited to the position of governess. Mrs. Forestell had sufficient experience of the subdued and pliant role a governess would be expected to play and of Sophie Vandercook to know that they were not suited.

Better, far better, for Sophie to remain at the Academy, where she was one among several. Mrs. Forestell herself could head off any potential troubles that arose from Sophie's … *forthrightness*. Yes, forthrightness, which was an admirable quality, in some circumstances. Although not in Sophie's.

Far from feeling any of the pangs at that assessment that Tad had apparently expected, Sophie concurred. She had considered and discarded governess as an occupation for many of the same reasons.

Sophie found instructing pleasant, if not a passion. That, and other considerations, made her current position satisfactory for now, though not for a permanent role.

Mrs. Forestell's Young Ladies' Academy was not, perhaps, the first choice for the very best St. Louis families. But it sat solidly amid the respectable options. The young instructors at the Academy mixed not only with their charges, but not infrequently with their charges' families. Four instructors over the years of Sophie's time at the Academy had married after such an introduction. (Others had also married, but much more prosaically, and those marriages were seldom recited as talismans of hope among the remaining staff.)

Sophie's first offer of marriage had come three years ago from an acquaintance of her father's, and had occurred not long after official mourning had ended for that gentleman. Sophie, applying in her own mind Tad's colorful vocabulary, considered that the old toad had come sniffing around because he'd had an inkling of Sophie's inheritance.

If the man had understood exactly how much that inheritance would be on her twenty-first birthday, he would no doubt have been more persistent. But on the advice of her grandfather — contained in a letter written to his daughter that Sophie had found among Viola's possessions — Sophie had allowed no one to know the extent of her inheritance, including her father.

Without that knowledge, Miss Vandercook's first suitor had been disinclined to pursue the matter after her decidedly sharp-tongued response to his proposal.

Even without any knowledge of Sophie's inheritance, her more romantic-minded colleagues had understood her brisk refusal, because that individual was neither handsome nor young. But as they made clear now, they could not fathom why she had refused Harry Jenkins, the elder brother of a student and the scion of a most respectable family.

"He was far too young," Sophie said.

"But, Sophie," Alice pointed out, "he's your age. And you cannot say he is not handsome."

"And he most certainly has read a book," added Louisa, in reference to a charge against Sophie's previous suitor, "Consider that lovely bound book of poetry he presented to you."

"Precisely," said Sophie. "He's a very nice boy, but his thoughts all come from poetry, and none from sense."

She, on the other hand, had enough sense to see that not only would his family disapprove, but that Harry and she would not suit. Her refusal had been entirely different from the first. Indeed, she had tried to turn him away before he proposed, but he did not heed her hints. So she had provided a gently-worded but unmistakable refusal.

It was a fortunate circumstance that Mr. Jenkins had chosen Sunday afternoon on which to make his offer.

For three hours every Sunday evening, all three of the Academy's youngest instructors were free of any duties. Each had a small amount of additional time free during the week, as well as one whole Sunday afternoon each month, but those were rotated so at least one remained available to Mrs. Forestell. Thus, Sunday evening was the only time when the three friends could be assured of an opportunity to converse together.

When summer provided enough light, they walked in nearby Lafayette Park. Other times, they attended concerts or lectures. But on a blustery, rain-soaked March evening, they were happy to sit at their ease in the small attic room they shared. Quickly changing to wrappers to spare their dresses, they huddled together like schoolgirls, under a quilt Sophie's mother had made for her birth.

Alice sighed now. "I was afraid you had refused him, because he appeared so romantic and tragic when he departed, looking back at the house in such despair."

"You shouldn't have been peeping out the window," said Louisa.

"If one were to have a husband, one of a romantic and tragic nature would make for a very uncomfortable home," Sophie said with decision.

"But Sophie, don't you want a husband? Someone to take care of you?" Alice asked.

Sophie's most vivid early memory was of her father barreling out of her mother's sitting room just as Sophie, guided by her nurse, approached. She and Nurse had stepped back against the wall to prevent being trampled. After he clattered down the stairway with imprecations that Sophie could only be grateful she had not recognized at the time and thus could not recall now, Nurse tightened her hand on Sophie's and led her into Viola's room.

Mama had dabbed at her eyes with a scented handkerchief. She was a slender form reclining on a chaise, saying in her soft, thin voice, "All I ever sought was a man who would look after me, and cherish me. I was sadly mistaken in your father, Sophie. So sadly mistaken."

At that time, and for some time afterward, Mama's sadness had brought tears to Sophie's eyes.

As she had grown older, however, her sorrow had given way to resolution. She would not be so used. Her mother's solution had been to reside all her hopes and expectations in a husband — one roll of the matrimonial dice, as Tad would say. That was not Sophie's solution. She had no need of taking up dice of any sort, for her hands held the reins of her future.

She said, "A husband of the right sort."

"Oh, yes," breathed Alice. "One with whom you can share devotion."

"One who is responsible and a good provider," said Louisa, who might not have found it necessary to teach at the Academy if her late husband had possessed those qualities.

"One who is absent," amended Sophie.

"Absent?" they chorused, staring at her.

"Yes," Sophie said firmly.

Louisa recovered first. "But if a husband is absent, how could you enjoy the—." She colored. "—benefits of marriage."

Alice's eyes widened and Sophie could see questions trembling on her lips. She turned the conversation in a more useful direction.

"I could enjoy the benefits of marriage that are important to me. An unmarried lady–" Even one with sufficient means and of a mature age. "–is not viewed as eligible to establish her own household. Society expects her to live with other members of her family. But a wife gains many freedoms that an unmarried woman does not enjoy. And even more freedoms if she is not hampered by her husband's presence."

"But you would not have your husband's company," protested Alice.

"And so would not need to cook and clean for him and tend his wishes every day."

"That is true," acknowledged Louisa. "But how will you find such a man, Sophie? If he is mostly absent from St. Louis, won't it be quite difficult to find him, become acquainted sufficiently to elicit an offer, and marry before he departs again?"

Sophie was nodding long before Louisa completed her recitation. "You are quite correct. St. Louis is not at all the place to acquire an absent husband. I have a plan."

"A plan? But whatever will you do, Sophie?" Alice asked.

"I shall go to Wyoming."

CHAPTER ONE

Wyoming Territory

"Nothing from our Sophie?"

Before Nate Abbott answered the question put to him, he consciously smoothed out a frown he could feel tightening his forehead.

The frown plus the squeezing inside his head usually told of a storm coming. A bad one. Since he'd come west, that's the only time he'd gotten the sensations. Not like when he'd live at home, back in Ohio.

But he'd checked the sky before he and String stepped into Kirwin's Mercantile to pick up supplies for the OS Ranch. Clear as could be. Besides, he hadn't had any of this storm's-coming pressure in his head until they'd been inside awhile and he'd taken inventory of the mail for the OS. Still nothing from St. Louis.

The motion of easing his frown raised his hat brim just enough for the sun's reflection off a watering trough to slice into his eyes, so he used his free hand to adjust his hat to restore the perfect shadow.

Only then did he say, "Nope."

"But her last letter said she was sending us a surprise.

Why would she make us wait this a-way, with no letter a'tall?"

"No telling.

"It's already been longer'n ever before since she wrote. What if something's happened to her?"

"Nothing we can do."

"But she could be sick or somethin'. Maybe one of us should go back East, check on her."

"Boss isn't going to let one of his hands go off now. Maybe winter, but –"

"Winter! Winter's just ended!"

"Next winter."

"Why that's – that's–" String worked his mouth, searching for a word. "–Months off."

Nate had nothing to say to that acute observation.

The door to Kirwin's Mercantile opened, and Nate stepped clear, tugging String by the arm. String was unaware. His jaw had joined his mouth in the struggle and the toll on them made him sound half-strangled. "Next winter! Why, why there's no tellin'–"

"I beg your pardon, gentlemen," came a feminine voice.

String's struggle to find words gave up the ghost, collapsing in mouth-open stupefied silence at being so addressed.

Nate, having had broader experience and even having been raised to consider himself a gentleman, touched fingers to his hat brim and stepped back farther. "Ma'am."

But she didn't pass by.

She stayed where she was, just beyond the door she'd closed behind her, regarding him steadily. And he returned the favor.

He'd noticed her inside – hard not to. She wasn't from anywhere around here – that was certain considering her la-di-dah clothes. But it wasn't entirely that had made him notice her.

She was an attractive little thing. Small, tidy figure, a

tumble of dark curls that suggested they'd get wild given the least opportunity. But it wasn't entirely that had made him notice her, either.

"The gentleman behind the counter said that you are representatives of the OS Ranch?"

"Ma'am?" If he didn't name the suspicion growing in him, maybe it wouldn't reach daylight.

"If you are associated with the OS Ranch, then it's my hope that you are acquainted with Jerry Vandercook?"

"Jerry? Vandercook?" croaked String. "But he's – "

Nate trod on his foot. Hard.

He hadn't had time or space to make it subtle. And even if String hadn't yelped a protest, it would have been obvious something had happened, because the rowel of Nate's spur caught momentarily in the tough material of String's work pants. It tripped them both up, leaving them hopping around the narrow wood platform like a couple of toads for a minute.

"What the–?"

"Quiet," Nate ordered. String clamped his mouth shut, though he gave his foreman a baleful glare. Nate returned it with a full measure of command, and added, "No cursing in front of a lady."

Satisfied he'd stilled the cowhand, he faced the young lady who'd been watching with demurely clasped hands and an unsettling glint in her eyes. "Sorry, Ma'am, why would you be asking after Jerry Vandercook? You understand, we don't just share another man's business without cause."

"That does you credit, sir. But I do have cause. I am his sister."

"His sister!" Strong croaked. Nate only needed a look to quell him this time.

"That so, Ma'am?" He drawled it, trying to gain time.

It was an air of expectation around her – that's what had made him notice her inside. Like the crackle in the air when lightning was about to strike. Plus maybe a tingle of familiarity. And it stirred in Nate Abbott the same uneasy mix of worry and awe produced by that force of nature.

"Yes, it is so. And I have come from St. Louis to visit him."

"All the way from St. Louis, eh?" he repeated, thinking furiously.

"Yes, St. Louis," she enunciated as if he might be daft. "After my long journey, I am eager to see him. I arrived yesterday by the stagecoach, and when the gentleman inside informed me that you are about to depart for the OS Ranch, it seemed providential. I hope I may obtain transport there from you gentlemen. I understand you have a wagon you brought for supplies and I beg a seat in it and a place for my bag."

"Vandercook's sister!" String erupted. "Why, you're Sophie! You're our–"

Nate swung around on him, facing the cowhand, keeping his shoulder to the observing young lady. "Miss Vandercook, String," he said sternly. "Mind your manners with *Miss Vandercook*."

String wasn't the quickest, but he was well above Mulehead, who'd been kicked in the head by a mule three times that they knew of. String's eyes widened at he met Nate's glare, and the beginning glimmers of the complications rushing around them like a flooded creek sparked to life in his face.

"Beggin' your pardon, Ma'am," String mumbled. "No offense meant."

"None taken, sir." She stepped around Nate's shoulder, to face him once more. "On the subject of my request –"

"It's a rough ride," Nate said, with little hope that the determined figure before him would be deterred by that. He knew stubborn females, and this sure as shooting was one or he hadn't grown up with seven sisters. "And we don't take it in easy stages. We gotta get back before sundown, so there's no stopping."

"Rattle your bones," agreed String.

She smiled at the older man. A fleeting lifting of her lips that Nate could see had sent String into as senseless a state as a gallon of the strongest Cheyenne hooch.

"Thank you for your concern, but having come so far, I would be a poor thing to turn back now. And even if that were not so, my brother's letters of this past year have made me long to see the places he writes of with such eloquence."

The smile now gone, she turned back to Nate. He stifled all urge to wince at her comments.

She looked up at him, and he looked down at her. He couldn't read anything more than the request she was making in her expression, and he wagered she couldn't see anything at all in his, yet he had the notion that they were involved in some sort of showdown.

If so, he lost.

He couldn't see any way around it. Not without casting away all hopes of bringing this around.

But with an avalanche of luck and some time to think, maybe he'd see a way. Some way.

"String, get the lady's bag."

❧

From the hollow of the saddle that had come to conform to his body better than seat, Nate twitched a rein, and Sago changed course slightly. Just enough that Nate didn't need to turn his head to watch the upright little figure, which contrasted sharply with String's boneless slouch, sway as the wagon jounced over fresh ruts cut into the road by the spring runoff.

The pitch and rattle had near unseated her a couple times early on, before she'd gotten the feel of it. Still, she'd be better off if she didn't sit like she was in somebody's parlor. If String had any sense, he'd tell her —

Nate bit off the thought.

Even if String did have any sense, he wouldn't be

telling Miss Sophie Vandercook anything. The man was dumbstruck, acting like a cross between a saint and that fancy dancer they'd seen last fall in Cheyenne had landed beside him.

The snatches of conversation Nate had picked up had been 'most all her. Telling about her journey from St. Louis.

Give her credit – she hadn't complained. Not a lick. Not about the journey, not about this wagon ride.

But what a lady like her thought she was doing traveling from St. Louis to way out here on her own, he couldn't begin to figure. If he were her brother, he'd've told her straight out –

Another thought bit in two.

He wasn't her brother. And he wasn't telling her anything.

Especially not since, even after more than six hours of thinking on it, he hadn't come to a firm line of action for when they got to the home ranch.

"String! We'll get water at Bear Creek."

"Bear Creek? That's almost –"

"We're stoppin'."

They'd made two stops already. Resting the horses, he'd said. Which was true, though it was twice as many stops as usual coming back, even when it was a sight hotter than today.

So, now it was three times as many. And this last stop was only an hour or so from the main ranch, even at the pace they'd been keeping.

He had his reasons.

At the creek, he waited for String to position the wagon so the horses could drink, then before the cowhand could climb down, Nate rode up beside him.

"I'm going to ride on ahead," he announced.

"What?" String's head snapped up, full-blown panic in his eyes. "You can't leave me with –" He tipped his head to the side, indicating Sophie Vandercook. As if she couldn't see the gesture and didn't know exactly whom he meant anyway. "Nate, you can't."

"It's not far now." He wasn't sure if he was reassuring her or String. "I'll be waiting when you get there. Got to check some things with Mr. Bracken."

String's mouth opened, then closed.

"Mr. Bracken," Sophie repeated.

At least Nate thought that's what she said. She seemed to be having some trouble getting words out between lips that had picked up a coating of dust. She was lucky the ride hadn't been during a dry spell, when the dust could get thick as a blizzard.

"Yeah. Mr. Bracken, he's –"

"My brother's employer." Sophie said, coming on stronger at the end.

String swallowed audibly.

"He's owner of the OS, all right," Nate said.

"Please do give him my regards, and beg his pardon for imposing on his hospitality."

"No imposing. Out here, anybody comes by's entitled to a bed and a meal. You'll be welcomed. No fear there. I just gotta go over some things with him –" He shot a warning look at String. "– and some of the hands. So rest here a bit. Get some water yourselves, and take it easy coming in."

The final was an order to String. Hope to God, he understood it.

Nate needed time to set things up at the home ranch.

The fact that he didn't know what he'd be setting up meant he needed all the time he could get.

He touched the front of his hat to Miss Sophie Vandercook of St. Louis, gave Sago a tap on the side, and trotted away, breathing only slightly easier for the first time since he'd spotted her across Kirwin's Mercantile.

CHAPTER TWO

"**H**ey, Nate!" Edith Bracken leaned over the railing on the front porch of the OS Ranch main house, her pale braids swinging out in front of her. "What're you doing getting in so late? Thought for sure you'd stayed over to tomorrow."

"Something came up." And to make matters worse, Sago had picked up a stone. Nate had stopped to get it out, then walked the horse a good mile before he was sure the hoof was going to be okay. That had cost a lot of his lead time on the wagon. "Where's your pa?"

The fact that Edith was on the porch meant Frederick Bracken was away from the home ranch. It was the ironclad rule of the OS owner that his young daughter stay in the house when both he and Nate were gone. It was Edith's interpretation of the rule that made the furthest possible inch she could stretch over the porch's railing still count as the house.

Nate couldn't decide if it was good news or bad that Bracken was gone.

"What? What came up? Something wrong with the wagon? Or did —?"

"Will you quit jabbering, girl, and tell me where's your pa?" It was said with affectionate exasperation.

"Over to Shrieves' place. Rider came in not an hour after you and String left, and said they were meeting there about the spring roundup. Pa went right off. Remember, you said I could come this year. Not just to visit, but for the whole thing."

"Never said the whole thing," he responded absently, working out how this might just work.

"You did! You said the whole thing. And I can rope the whole time, too."

He lifted his head to meet her gaze.

"Some," she amended.

He kept looking at her.

"At least one, Nate. You gotta let me rope at least one. You know I can. Why, you taught me, and there's nobody better at teaching roping than you, so you gotta let me."

He'd admit that for a scrap of a girl she was more than half decent with a rope, and well above that on horseback. He relented. "We'll see. But roundup's a ways off still. Right now we got another matter to talk about."

"We do?"

"We do. You're the lady of this house, Edith Bracken, and you've got a guest coming to stay."

Her eyes had rounded at being called the lady of the house, but that was forgotten in the excitement of a guest. "You mean a real guest? Like somebody who'll stay in the house? Who? Who's coming?"

"Nobody you know. She's a young lady from —"

"A lady," Edith breathed, as if he'd announced Queen Victoria herself were about to ride up to the porch steps. "From England?"

It wasn't entirely outlandish, since some titled folks had had ranches back in the early days. But most had sold up as time went on, and he hadn't heard tell of any remaining around here after the winter before last.

"Not from England. From St. Louis."

"St. Louis," she repeated in exactly the same tone.

He needed to hurry this along. "The fact is, she's Jerry Vandercook's sister."

That brought her back to ground. "But Vandercook —"

"I know. But she doesn't."

Edith recoiled. "I'm not tellin' her. I don't know her. I don't know about things like that. I'm not—"

"No, you're not telling her. Will you be quiet for a shake and let me get a word out?"

Damned if the girl didn't shut up and stare at him with the expectancy of hearing golden words flow from one of those oracles that old book of Ma's had said they had around where the Pyramids were.

And damned if he could think of a word to say.

That state of affairs might have continued, if Edith hadn't looked over his shoulder and let out a whoop. "There's the wagon! There they are! I see her, I see her."

He twisted around to see the wagon closing in on them at a pace that should have been impossible for that old team. Although he had to admit there was just the possibility that it was a trick of his mind, like a sun-sick cowpoke thinking he saw water in a field of dust.

He sidestepped Sago right up to the side of the porch, reached out to catch Edith by the shoulder, and leaned in to speak directly into her ear.

"Here's what I'm saying to you: Don't talk about Vandercook. Not a word. You leave it to me, Edith. You hear? You leave it all to me."

"But—."

"If you can't follow orders, you won't be on roundup. And this here's an order. You leave it all to me."

Her mouth stayed open, but as he eased away from her he saw the threat had taken hold.

His turn had brought him facing the bunkhouse and barn. Hands were accumulating like filings to a magnet. Some instinct always told them when a supply wagon was coming in.

The rule was they had to wait until the supplies were unloaded at the house by Doughy and Mulehead before they got their hands on any personal purchases. But when they saw that the wagon held a passenger of the attractive female variety, he wasn't entirely sure that discipline wouldn't break down.

At least Tinhorn wasn't around. He would have broken ranks for sure, and made his way straight to the wagon to make the acquaintance of Miss Sophie Vandercook. Jasper Tinton considered himself every young lady's dream from here to the Mississippi River and back. To Nate's disgust, the young ladies seemed to agree.

Nate made the introduction between Sophie and Edith in quick time, ordered String to see to the lady's baggage, and rode toward the bunkhouse.

He might just be able to get this thing in hand.

With Bracken gone, and Sophie parked with Edith for now, that left him only every cowhand on the OS Ranch to get into line before any of them opened their mouths.

⚮

Deposited on the front porch of a spare wooden structure set slightly apart from other, even plainer, wooden structures, Sophie considered the girl before her. String and the wagon were already disappearing around a corner of the building.

"This is Edith," Nate Abbott had said by way of introduction. Then he'd instructed the girl: "Look after her. Give her something to drink."

For a moment, the promise of liquid distracted Sophie.

Distracted her from the peculiar appearance of this building — as well as the others that apparently formed the headquarters of the OS Ranch — as if scrubbed of every last vestige of moisture that surely must once have formed sap when the logs stood upright in the forms of trees.

And distracted her from the oddness of the version of

nature that surrounded her.

This day's travel had confirmed what she had merely glimpsed from the stagecoach – Wyoming Territory was as unlike St. Louis as a rock was from moss. On the stagecoach, she had been wedged in the center, with other passengers, their hats and packages combining to allow only slices of views. Driving with String, she had enjoyed a view interrupted only by his slight, bowed form and the figure on horseback that paced them most of the way.

From that vantage, she had observed trees huddled thirstily along creeks, mountains that rose with abrupt suddenness to the west, with brighter green vegetation banding the inclines before giving way to snow-whitened peaks. In between were rolling, dun-colored swells and dips that went on and on, with no distinguishing characteristic other than their pervasiveness. They appeared as desiccated as she felt.

With that thought, the urgency of her thirst rushed back.

"A drink –" she started, but no sound emerged from her lips.

"And don't talk her ear off like you always do," Nate, the OS foreman – one of the facts she'd wrested from String – had added before riding away.

"I don't!" the girl protested to Nate Abbot's back, before turning to Sophie and pouring out her brief history.

The daughter of Jerry's employer was of that particular age when a girl recognizes that she's approaching womanhood, while those around her still consider her a child. Sophie suspected that that was particularly the case for Edith Bracken, who, as she was in the process of informing her guest, was surrounded entirely by men.

"Mama died eight years ago, when I was practically a baby," Edith confided. "He never says so, but I'm sure that's why Papa came out here from Connecticut to run cattle. He didn't want any reminders of his *Tragic Loss*."

Sophie managed a sympathetic murmur.

She was prevented from needing to conjure anything more elaborate, because Edith's eyes narrowed as she surveyed Sophie from head to toe and back, taking in the traveling suit beneath a duster now coated with the reddened dirt.

"That's a mighty pretty dress, Miss."

Despite her thirst and dust-dried lips, she smiled. Wyoming might appear an entirely alien land, but clearly the feminine interest in fashion needed no translation.

Sophie considered the girl's calico Mother Hubbard, worn into a state even more shapelessness than most of its kind, and so short that it showed not only the top of her boots, but a portion of her unstockinged leg. Sophie licked her lips twice, and this time sound emerged.

"It's quite past the height of fashion, I fear, but it is sturdy and so served me well."

The traveling suit was in itself entirely practical, with a modest bustle that was easily accommodated, even in the most crowded conditions. What Sophie now regretted was the vanity that had pushed her to wear a stricter corset than the traveling one she could have chosen. She might have more readily taken advantage of opportunities to sleep during her travels, and she certainly would have been more comfortable.

Edith's eyes widened. "You mean there are clothes more fashionable than that?"

"There are, indeed, and I would be happy to discuss them with you if I might have a glass of water?"

"Land sakes! Of course you're wanting a drink – what was I thinking, keeping you standing here? You sit right down." Edith pointed to a rough bench covered by a much-mended cushion. "I'll be right back."

She was as good as her word.

The water in the pitcher and glass Edith brought to her on a tarnished silver tray was tepid and not entirely clear, but Sophie didn't think she had ever experienced anything quite so reviving. She allowed herself to lean back as much as she could, considering the constraints of the corset, against the front of the house where the bench was set, to listen to the flow of Edith's tale about another girl in the neighborhood who apparently lorded it over Edith on matters of appearance and sociability, and to feel the moisture seep back into her parched body.

After some considerable time and a second pitcher of water allowed her to feel significantly revived, Sophie became aware of the tall figure of Nate Abbott surrounded by a growing number of men similarly clad in the attire of cowhands. They gathered at the far end of the open yard, near a rough rail fence beside a long, low log building.

She could not be certain after all this time, but she did not believe that any of the men there was her brother.

An odd flutter in her midsection beset her. Excitement. But also uneasiness.

She fully realized that she would not be feeling either if it had not been for the letters of this past year. These letters had revealed to her a brother she could admire — which was the cause of the excitement. The uneasiness came from the question of whether he would feel a similar regard for her.

She had debated during the monotonous hours of her journey whether or not to confide her plan to Jerry. She had resolved to await their reunion to make a final assessment, but all in all, she was inclined to not.

First, because explaining her plan would require telling him about her inheritance. She had kept that information to herself for so long that it would take a great deal of consideration before she told anyone. And to tell her half-brother could be particularly uncomfortable since he was excluded in this matter.

In addition, men were frequently not as practical about such matters as women.

The group of men was too far away to hear what was being said, even if Edith's stream had ceased. But Sophie began to imagine that she could hear her name being spoken now and then.

Surely it was her imagination, she decided, for the name she thought she heard was *Sophie*, rather than *Miss Vandercook*.

"Edith," she slipped in, when that young lady paused for a rare breath, "do you know my brother's whereabouts?"

The girl choked.

Sophie poured her a glass of water, instructing her to take slow sips until she had regained her composure.

"Swallowed wrong," Edith said.

She nodded. "I'm relieved to see you are recovered from your paroxysm. I'm certain you will forgive me for repeating my question, since you no doubt have forgotten if, indeed, you heard me at all."

But apparently Edith had heard her.

"You have to ask Nate. Nate'll know. Me, I don't know a thing. You ask Nate."

The girl's faith in her father's foreman was touching, though it occurred to Sophie that Nate Abbott could have informed her about Jerry at any time during the long hours of their journey, if he had been inclined to such a courtesy.

She kept silent on both matters.

A new arrival from the direction of the corral beyond the barn changed the tenor of the discussion among the men, she thought. She was weighing how, exactly, when Edith erupted from her seat with an exclamation.

"Oh, Pa's back! He was over at the TS."

"The TS?"

"The Shrieves' place. Next ranch over," Edith said. "We weren't sure he'd be back today or not till tomorrow."

"From your next door neighbor?"

"It's a piece, and there's some rough country between. Once took Mulehead near a week to get back, but that was in winter, and of course it was Mulehead," Edith said, with no apparent recognition that Sophie was having trouble assimilating this. "Wonder what they're all talking about over there."

Sophie put aside geographic wonderment and contemplation of something – or was it someone? – called Mulehead, to focus on the girl's final comment. Yes, what were they all talking about?

"With your father returned, I believe we should go to greet him so that I may thank him for his hospitality. I do not want to be thought backward in my courtesies to him."

The notion appeared alien to Edith, but she was perfectly willing to be guided by Sophie in the matter, so they descended from the porch and started across the open space.

CHAPTER THREE

They were buzzing as bad as a nest of bees around a honey pot.

Nate looked at the faces of the men surrounding him. Some barely sprouting fuzz, others tanned as leather. A few with book learning, others with honed cow sense, a few with nothing more than a strong back. Every one of them carrying near his weight in dust and grime after the long winter.

Bees? More like buzzards.

But buzzing all the same.

All over a walking headache named Sophie Vandercook.

He'd gladly wish to God he'd never heard the name if that meant he'd never have had to lay eyes on her. But in his experience, the Almighty didn't deal in such bargains.

"So she don't know?" demanded Mulehead. "She really don't know?"

Since that's what Nate had just told them, he might have been tempted to answer sharp if it had been anyone else. But Mulehead couldn't help that some of what mattered had leaked out of his head each time the mule had kicked him. And he hadn't had much to spare to start.

"She doesn't know," he repeated. "And that's how it's going to stay. Everybody clear on that?"

They were.

"You'd best get back to helping Doughy, Mulehead, or he'll have your hide."

Once he'd shuffled toward the kitchen door, Nate turned to the others.

"Every last one of you's got to watch what you say or this isn't going to come off right."

"What are you gonna do, Nate?" String demanded.

"Send her back."

A moan rose from the men.

Nate shook his hand at the wordless plea. "It's the only way. She don't belong here."

"Our Sophie's a lady," Dally Hodges confirmed with mingled pride and regret.

"That's right. So she's got to go back to Grayley and take the stage –"

"The stage!" erupted from several throats.

"By herself?"

"We'll get her to the stage –" *Somehow*, Nate added to himself. "– and then she'll get herself back to St. Louis."

"But, Nate, a gentle-reared lady like our Sophie, shouldn't ought to be traveling alone like that," said String.

"How, by all that's holy, do you think she got here?" Nate demanded.

"Still," String said stubbornly. "She's just a bit of a thing. Like a good breeze might blow her over. A man's got to look out for a lady like that."

"You don't have any sisters, do you," Nate muttered. It was the only explanation for how String could have missed knowing what that upright figure and stubborn chin meant.

Trouble.

And here it was, starting all ready, with the buzzards

buzzing in full agreement with String. Not listening to a word their ramrod said.

"She can't go by herself on no stage," pronounced Hodges, capturing the mood of his fellow hands. "One of us'll –"

"Or two," slid in young Gunner.

"– have to take her to Fort Laramie where that railroad spur gets to now. Or Cheyenne."

"*Cheyenne!* Why not waltz her on back to her front door in St. Louis?" Nate demanded.

"Well, now that –"

"Ain't happening." He glowered around the circle. "You – every one of you – know what this round-up means to Mr. Bracken. A lot of you would have been trading in your saddles for town jobs if it hadn't been for him keeping you on this winter when there was barely enough for a flea to do. We got cows to wrangle – not ladies."

The buzz shifted to a low rumble of discontent.

"Unless you don't want jobs. I can find other hands a sight faster than you can find other jobs," he reminded them.

"Stage won't run for another week," noted Hodges. He'd been with the OS even longer than Nate. "So from now until then, it makes better sense for her to stay here. We could have a dance –"

"A dance," other voices picked up eagerly.

"Saturday night."

"We could get the word to some of the other outfits."

"Nah, don't want any of them horning in."

"String can play the harmonica, but we need a fiddler."

"I can fiddle some," Royal King offered.

"No fiddling. No harmonica. No dance." Having gained their attention, Nate lowered his voice to its normal pitch to add, "The only dancing we're any of us doing is with those cows at roundup. And till then we're going to use every minute getting ready. And Sophie Vandercook is going back to Grayley soon as possible."

He raised his voice again to carry over the rising mutter of unhappy men.

"It's the only way. She'll be more comfortable at the hotel there, with other ladies around."

"Well, leastwise we can take her to Merachade's and get her picture took," said Royal. "Only one we got is near worn out."

That was true.

And it was true that Merachade, a carpenter who also served as undertaker – since he had the necessary skills for making a coffin and anybody could dig a hole – had obtained a camera nearly two years ago. He'd traded for it with some poor homesteader who'd been heading for Oregon, and Merachade had been selling likenesses just about ever since.

He'd started by photographing his customers – the dead ones. Said they never complained about staying still so long – and families bought the final remembrance of their departed. This past year, he'd graduated to live subjects.

"That's right – one picture for each of us. So nobody can go getting his dirty hands all over it and smudge up her hair like –"

"That's enough," Nate ordered. Lester and Royal had come to blows over that infraction three times during the winter. Another go-round was the last thing he needed right now. "And how, exactly, would we be explaining to Sophie why she needed to have her picture taken so many times?"

With no responses other than boots scuffing the ground, Nate relented enough to say, "I'll get Edith to ask her to have her picture took. Okay?"

That drew some smiles.

"And we get to meet her, right?" said Gunner.

"Yeah, we all meet her, just like you and String done – that's only fair," Hodges said.

Nate wanted to say no. Only because keeping the men from saying a wrong word would take every bit as much attention, experience and alertness as it took to prevent a stampede.

Yeah, he wanted to say no in the worst way, so the taste of it on his tongue turned from sweet to sour as he swallowed it down and said instead, "I suppose."

A new buzz lifted among the men.

Nate raised both hands, tamping down the air to settle them. "But nobody says anything to her – not a word. Not about Vandercook, not about the –"

"What's going on here?'

Nate swore under his breath. He'd been so focused on the hands, he hadn't noticed the arrival of Frederick Bracken, the owner of the OS Ranch. Neither had the boys – even though most faced the way Bracken had come.

They'd been so dazzled by the prospect of Sophie that not a single one had given him a warning, even though every last one of them, right down to Mulehead had had it drilled into them – especially this past year – that this was bunkhouse business. Not to be breathed about in front of Bracken.

Last thing he needed in this instant was the complication of a moral, upright owner breathing down his neck.

The men automatically stepped clear, allowing Bracken an open path to join Nate at the center of the circle. After a quick look around, no doubt to gauge the tenor of his cowhands' mood, he focused on his foreman.

"Well? What is it?"

"Nothing to worry about," said Hodges from the second row, while others buzzed agreement.

At nearly the same time, Nate said, "String and I got the heck of a surprise in town,"

What did they think? They were going to hide her in the bunkhouse without the owner knowing? No, they needed Bracken to take her in to stay in the house. For tonight, anyway. Maybe two nights before they could get her on her way back to St. Louis where she belonged.

It was just that Nate would have far preferred to pick his own time and place for this discussion. Because it would take some persuading to get Bracken to see things the way Nate needed him to see them.

It would also take some skirting around the truth.

Bracken looked from the other men to Nate and back. "What kind of surprise?"

For the absolute silence that descended on the other men, they might have been holding their breath. Waiting for Nate to speak. Leaving it up to him.

"It's Jerry Vandercook's sister, come to visit him from St. Louis."

"Vandercook's sister?" Bracken's sandy brows shot up. "But he's dead."

Nate nodded solemnly. "Yes, sir, he is."

"Died last spring," Bracken continued, as if to be sure they were speaking of the same person.

"Yes, sir. Just about this time last year it was."

"Dead alright," someone in the circle murmured.

"But then why would she come to visit, after you wrote to her, telling her of her loss and how her brother had died?"

Nate couldn't decide if it made it better or worse that there wasn't a trace of suspicion in the man who paid his salary.

"The thing is …" started String, then sputtered to a stop.

He looked at Nate.

They all looked at Nate.

"The thing is," he took up, drawing in a breath, "Miss Vandercook thinks her brother's alive."

"Alive?"

"Yes, sir." He paused, but the owner didn't plow into that opening with recriminations, so Nate felt his way a little farther forward, like a blind man on a tightrope. "We didn't want to break it to her so harsh – Your brother's dead. Like that. Not with her being a gently reared lady and all. A teacher at a young ladies' academy."

"A real lady," came the surrounding chorus.

Bracken nodded slowly. "I see. But –"

"Thought we'd ease into it, you know. Maybe tell her Vandercook wasn't feeling well. Get her sort of used to the idea."

Bracken nodded again, then frowned. "But when the letters stopped coming from Vandercook she must have known something was seriously wrong."

Nate nodded, as if appreciating that his boss had cut straight to the heart of the matter.

"You're right, Mr. Bracken. She surely would have."

"And then she would have written to me, asking after her brother."

"Most likely," Nate agreed. "Makes sense. She'd write to you. Or maybe to me."

"But she hasn't," Bracken pursued. "Written, I mean."

"As it happens, she has. Regular, too."

"She's kept writing, without receiving a reply – how extraordinary."

Here they were. Where the track divided and it was go one way or the other, because there was no going back.

"Thing is," Nate said, "she did receive replies. She's been writing to her brother every week, sometimes more, and as far as she knows, he's been writing back to her, a letter every week. Sometimes more."

A groan or two rose from the listeners, but most were too busy holding their breath to make a sound.

"But how on earth – ?"

Nate said it straight out because Frederick Bracken wasn't one to pick up the finer points on his own. "I've been writing letters to her and pretending to be Vandercook."

Murmurs rose from the men that let it be known that

Nate hadn't written those letters alone, that they'd all had a hand in it.

Nate wasn't sure that distinction got through to Bracken.

And there sure wasn't any point in muddying the waters by going into details about how the letters that had been arriving for the past year from St. Louis addressed to Nate had each held inside the envelope a letter for "Gerald Vandercook." No sense confusing the man more than he was already twisted around.

Movement caught Nate's eye from the direction of the house, and Nate knew they didn't have much more time.

"Sir, I'm sorry, but there's a young lady – a young lady who appears to be heading this way this very moment – and we need to be deciding what we're going to tell her, and soon."

Every face in the circle swung toward the house, then snapped back to their foreman and their boss in the center.

"I won't lie," said Bracken.

That was no surprise.

Bracken was an honest, upright man to work for. His rules were simple but firm. No drinking, no gambling, no illegal activity. That ruled out the shenanigans some of the boys in other outfits got up to, which often led to fights or even gunplay in the bunkhouse.

And he was no hypocrite. He lived by an even stricter code than he set for his cowhands. He didn't do more than frown when the boys got to town after fall roundup and had a time with some of the sporting girls there. But he certainly never indulged himself.

In fact, Bracken was so straight-laced, the question in Nate's mind was how he'd ever come to father a child, much less that wild girl Edith.

"No sir, no sir," Royal agreed miserably. "You won't lie."

Nate straightened. It wouldn't be pleasant, but it would get the job done. "We'll just tell her flat-out that her brother's dead, and her trip out here's been wasted."

"No!" came the appalled chorus. "You can't do that to *Our Sophie!*"

"Well, she's going to have to be told some time," Nate said.

"We need to break it to her gentle-like," Hodges said.

"Can't be telling her when she's tuckered from that long journey." String looked over his shoulder at the visitor and Edith Bracken approaching, and spoke faster. "You know what it's like when you trail a young heifer hard, then try to wean them sudden, Nate – er, and Mr. Bracken. They go into a decline. Drop to their knees and just sink into the dirt."

Bracken's eyes widened in alarm. "Perhaps, the young lady does need to, uh, get her bearings before you inform her of her tragic loss."

Nate didn't miss that it had become his duty to tell the visitor that Vandercook had died. When the time came. And since Bracken had already declared his stance on the matter, Nate knew it also fell to him to feed her the lie for the time being.

He wished to God he'd never learned to write.

CHAPTER FOUR

Sophie saw Nate Abbott look toward them over his shoulder, and felt an odd catch in her breath. No doubt because she was trying to read into his gesture a confirmation that the discussion being held among the tightly clustered men had something to do with her, which gave her every cause to intrude on the gathering she had not been invited to join.

Away from the sheltering porch roof she became instantly aware of the sun's fire. On her shoulders beyond the scant shade provided by her hat – which she had naturally put back on, along with her gloves – and on the bottom of her feet, where it rose up from the ground through the soles of her sturdy shoes like water in a puddle.

Occupied with that sensation, it was not until they were practically upon the men and Edith had stepped back to let her lead the way that Sophie came to wonder if she would be left stranded on the outside of this tightly gathered circle of bewhiskered males.

Instead, the men nearest her stepped back, one snatching his hat off his head, and inclining it. Others followed, large hat after large hat being removed as they parted before her, allowing her step by step to proceed to the center. Some of the men cast their eyes down, a ruddy color in their cheeks, others stared, but with no malice.

And so she found herself in the center of this gathering, with only one hat still on its head – Nate Abbott's.

"Miss Vandercook," he said. "This is Mr. Bracken, owner of the OS Ranch." He nodded to his companion in the circle's open center, a fair-haired man wearing work pants and shirt similar to that of the men around him, but topped with an embroidered vest of good quality and a well-tailored coat. "Mr. Bracken, this is Miss Vandercook. Uh, Jerry's sister."

"How do you do?" she inquired.

Mr. Bracken reached up, as if to tip his hat, only to discover he had already removed it. With a jerky motion, he extended his free hand toward her.

She responded by putting hers out, though she hoped he would be satisfied with the brief, polite resting of her gloved fingertips to the side of his top finger, as Mrs. Forestell taught was acceptable for a modern female. Despite Mrs. Forestell's advice on accepting it as a compliment, Sophie found she did not care for having her hand kissed in the continental manner, which was adopted by a few of her students' fathers. Furthermore, she believed that any lips that encountered her glove at this moment would come away with a mouthful of dust.

He bypassed her light touch, grasped her hand, and pumped it. It was an odd sensation. As if her arm were a rag being shaken out on the back step of Mrs. Forestell's.

As abruptly as he had begun, Mr. Bracken dropped her hand, apparently to obtain a firmer, two-handed grip on the brim of his hat.

"Welcome to the OS Ranch, Miss Vandercook."

"That's my pa," Edith informed her from over her shoulder.

"Thank you for the welcome, Mr. Bracken. Mr. Abbott and Mr. ... uh, String, assured me you would accept my unannounced arrival without rancor."

"Without what?" someone in the back of the circle whispered, and was roundly *shush*-ed.

"We are delighted to offer you whatever hospitality the OS can extend, Miss Vandercook."

"Thank you, indeed, sir. As Mr. Abbott mentioned, Gerald Vandercook is my brother."

Another mutter came from the crowd around them. "Half-brother."

She looked up, searching for the speaker, but could not identify him. She smiled. Jerry must have spoken about her to his friends.

"That's right. He is my older half-brother, and we have not seen each other for a very long time. I am not convinced I would recognize him immediately ..."

"He's not here," Nate cut in.

She was unsure if he meant it as a kindness to end her doubt or as a reproach to point out her ignorance.

She was even less sure of how she felt about that turn of events, beyond the disappointment of not making the adult acquaintance of the relative she had come in this past year to hold in high regard. Through his letters, he had revealed himself to be an acute observer, practical-minded, yet with a touch of the poet to him that surprised her.

In her thoughts about coming to Wyoming, she had sometimes envisioned her brother offering his assistance. Sometimes his neutrality. Sometimes his disapproval. She had prepared herself for each of these eventualities.

It required an adjustment to adapt to his absence at the overture of her venture.

"Not on the OS Ranch anymore," someone said.

"Yes, he is," disputed another voice. Followed by a faint "Oof."

"Not right now," added a new speaker.

"That's right," said String. "Vandercook's away."

"Over at the TS." It was the same voice that had offered the information that Jerry was not on the OS Ranch at the moment. This time she traced the speaker to the second row back. A dark-haired man who seemed to be peeking out at her from between an oversized hat and an overgrown beard.

"The TS – Oh, yes, the neighboring ranch."

"Not like neighbors you're used to," Nate Abbott said.

She recognized that he was annoyed, but she found herself unable to assess at what.

She arched her brows at him. "Having only met today, your knowledge of what I'm accustomed to cannot be extensive, Mr. Abbott." She held his gaze as she would that of a student who needed reminding of her authority. "However, Edith has informed me that the ranch belonging to the Shrieve family is some distance and can require a day's ride or more."

"That's when the weather's good," supplied String. "The track can get wiped clean out by snow or rain or rock slides."

"Ah, but the path must have been free of any of those encumbrances now, because Edith informed me that Mr. Bracken –" She smiled at him. "–returned from there just today, and in a shorter time than she might have expected."

It seemed to Sophie that several faces turned what might have been called an accusatory glare on Mr. Bracken.

Edith had informed her that Nate, as the girl called him, was the *ramrod* for the OS *outfit*. He did have an air of authority, and String and the other men certainly appeared to heed his words. So much so that it seemed a bit odd, since Mr. Bracken was the owner, and thus the ultimate authority.

Nate Abbott, his fierce frown now seeming to be applied impartially to the darkly bearded man in the second row and to her, said. "Vandercook's over there working on a project for them for a while. We do that out here – help each other – and he's been promised to the TS Ranch for a week." He paused, then added, "Maybe more."

"A week?" she repeated in some dismay.

But even as the words came out, she recognized that a week without her brother on hand could serve her purpose. She had little experience in the matter, but had been informed by others that an older brother's presence could be inhibiting. As for her disappointment at being deprived that week with him, she needed to be practical. She had a limited time in Wyoming, and an object to achieve.

"I see," she said, her thoughts aligning in a new sequence. "Then if I might accompany whoever goes into town tomorrow, I will hope to find accommodations there. I shall further hope that Jerry might join me there after he has completed his task at the TS Ranch."

The town of Grayley had been small, yet active, with any number of riders coming in and leaving, even in the short time she was there. She could see that it could meet her needs quite well, surely better than the OS, since it would not have Nate Abbott glaring down at her.

"We don't go to town but every other month," said String.

"Except for winter, when we don't go at all," added the dark bearded man.

"You'll have to stay here," came from a younger voice.

"Yeah!" agreed a chorus.

"Oh." Sophie felt a trace dizzy with the speed with which she was being required once more to adjust her plan. Or perhaps from twisting around the circle to look from speaker to speaker.

"We could make an exception –" Nate Abbott started, but was interrupted by his boss, who spoke for the first time since their introduction.

"You'll stay with us in the main house, of course, Miss

Vandercook," said Mr. Bracken. "It would be our pleasure to have you as a guest as long as you choose to stay on the OS."

"That is very kind of you, sir, but in my brother's absence, to impose on your hospitality that way –"

"Nonsense. There's a code out here in cattle country," said Mr. Bracken. "No one gets turned away."

"Oh, yes, Mr. Abbott told me of that."

The ranch owner nodded in confirmation, then added with an air of rusty gallantry, "And certainly no one would turn away a lady as young and lovely as you, Miss Vandercook."

Sophie thought she caught, under the shading brim of his hat, a grimace on Nate Abbott's face, but the other men murmured approvingly.

"I shall be honored to accept your kind invitation, sir."

Mr. Bracken smiled at her, and Edith clapped her hands.

"And you can tell me all about the clothes in St. Louis!"

◦◦◦◦

"We could send a couple hands to take her back. She could stay in town till the stage comes," Nate said to Bracken. "The hotel's perfectly respectable with the Lavoyes running it."

"Perhaps, though I hate to think of such a gentle-bred young lady being alone."

"You could write an introduction to Mrs. Lavoye and that schoolteacher who came last year. They'd take her in, introduce her around. She'd have plenty of company."

Especially once the hands from close-by outfits heard there was a new, unattached female in town. They'd be finding excuses flimsy as a cloud to go into town. Heck, he'd have to watch for that happening with the OS boys, even out here. They were going to need every last hand capable of getting astride a horse when it came time for roundup.

"We can't spare a man," Bracken said from beside him. So his thoughts had followed a similar trail. Though the result appeared to sit better with the owner than it did Nate. "Not with the roundup coming. You know that."

Unlike a number of other owners, Bracken hadn't sold up after the disastrous winter before last. Not only had he held onto as many head as he'd had left, but he had bought up more from those leaving the cattle business. Before that killing winter before last, he'd been more cautious than most, so he'd had the capital to do it. But now he was stretched. He couldn't afford to miss a single head in this roundup.

"Doughy says suuuupppppeeeerrrr!" Mulehead's shout from the kitchen door could probably be heard clear down to Texas. "Suuuupppppeeeerrrr!"

Hands were already streaming toward the open kitchen door.

"Besides," Bracken added, clapping him on the shoulder as they headed toward the door, because nobody kept Doughy waiting, "having Miss Vandercook here will be a pleasure – you wait and see. She'll be good company for Edith."

It wasn't Sophie Vandercook keeping company with young Edith that had Nate worried.

Though right this second, he couldn't say precisely what was gnawing at his gut in addition to the usual ready-for-supper hunger.

CHAPTER FIVE

Sophie stood on the porch, her hands shading her eyes, to better watch the molten ball of the sun as it disappeared behind the silhouette of the mountains. After the trial of supper, Sophie was glad of a moment of solitude.

The food had been plentiful and hot. The stew was more than passable, the biscuits heavenly.

Everyone sat together at one very long table along the front wall of the house's kitchen. In addition to a number of benches that the men pulled up to the table, chairs were retrieved from other rooms and crowded into every cranny of space.

The cook grumbled about cowhands who spent all their time in his kitchen and no time at all with cows.

She could attest that was not true, for there was a distinct scent of cow about the gathering, and it surely emanated from the closely gathered men, along with other odors she chose not to identify.

Before the meal began, she was aware of every pair of eyes on her except for Nate Abbott's and Mr. Bracken's.

Once the food was served, each man – again with those two exceptions – never looked up from his plate.

No one spoke except for Edith, with occasional contributions from Mr. Bracken. In fairness, Edith left very little time for anyone else to speak. Questions stumbled over statements, interrupted by exclamations. As accustomed as she was to young girls, Sophie still had difficulty untwining the jumble into anything she could address.

It hardly mattered, because as soon as she produced part of an answer, Edith was off into further questions.

And that was just as well, for Sophie was not entirely convinced she could have upheld a normal polite conversation as she observed the end of the meal in astonishment.

As each man cleaned his plate – after every one of them consumed seconds – he rose from the table without a word, carried his plate, mug and utensils to a dish bucket by the stove, and walked out the door.

In barely the time it would have taken to serve the first course in polite society, she, Edith, Mr. Bracken and Nate Abbott were the only souls remaining at the long, empty table. Quickly after, Nate muttered something to Mr. Bracken about talking to him in the office when he was done, and he, too, departed.

The ranch owner offered a few polite remarks amid Edith's stream, but Sophie became aware that he was stealing surreptitious glances at his pocket watch.

The next time his daughter took a breath, Sophie addressed him. "I am certain that my arrival has interfered mightily with your routine."

"We are delighted to have such delightful interference," he said gamely.

She shook her head with a smile. "Having been away, you must have a great many matters to attend to. Please, sir, if you wish to make me truly comfortable, you will treat me as you do Edith."

He smiled back, and she could see the younger man he'd once been. "Thank you, Miss Vandercook," he said simply.

He left them, and Sophie completed her meal – she was remarkably hungry – amid the undemanding flow of Edith's words.

In the end, the cook had shooed them out of the kitchen, reminding Edith that if she was going to take the apple peelings to Beauregard, she'd best get to it.

And Sophie had found her way to this solitary bit of porch to contemplate this extraordinary day.

Boot heels sounded on the wooden surface, approaching from the side of the house. Nate Abbott.

She knew, without looking around.

He apparently felt no need to announce his presence, no concern that she might prefer to not share his company at this moment.

"Good evening," she said with cool politeness.

"Evening," he mumbled back. Then stood beside her, saying nothing.

Without moving her head, she slid her gaze toward him, seeing from the corner of her eye that he, too, was looking toward the sliding sun. With his head tilted slightly down, the brim of his hat gave his eyes the necessary cover she had to provide with her hands.

She looked back, and saw two mountain peaks piercing the lower curve of the sun. Its descent seemed to gain speed, the mountains rising up to meet it, their dark solidity overwhelming the liquid fire of its light.

When the top rim disappeared from view, she released a long-held breath. Then pulled it in again, for while the sun had disappeared, its light splayed sweeps of orange and yellow so fiery it seemed the mountains themselves must ignite.

The clouds were ablaze for certain – drifting bands of flame that produced no smoke.

"Remarkable," she said.

He grunted agreement. "The sun don't turn tail and run out here. It puts up a fight."

"In reply to a question I asked of him, my brother wrote that Wyoming Territory has its own peculiar, harsh beauty. I didn't understand when I read that. How can beauty be harsh?"

He shifted, then grunted again. "Harsh is right. If you want soft green grass and trees overhead every step you take, go back east – Ohio or St. Louis."

She glanced toward him, then returned her gaze to the ever-changing sky. "Ohio? Is that where you're from?"

"Yup."

"Do you miss it?"

She sensed more than saw the tip of his hat that indicated the blazing sky. "Don't see that in Ohio."

She smiled. "Trees get in the way."

"Trees and buildings and ..."

He mumbled the last word, but she thought it might have been people.

She straightened the line of her mouth against the tug of a fuller smile. "You don't care for people, Mr. Abbott? Is that why you came to Wyoming Territory?"

"Question is, why'd you come to Wyoming Territory?"

"Ohio is farther than St. Louis. If you came that distance, why should I not come the lesser distance?"

He turned his head toward her. She continued to look out. "You came here for good? Leaving your –" He swallowed something before continuing. "– life in St. Louis behind?"

"No. I shall return to St. Louis. I teach there. I have friends. It is my home."

"So why're you here?"

"Is it so strange that I should want to see my brother?" She shifted to see him better. He was watching her closely.

"You don't know him." Just as she turned toward him, he faced back to the horizon. "Mean to say, you said it yourself – you wouldn't know him to see him."

She, too, faced the horizon again. "True. We have not been well-acquainted. We are children of different mothers, and quite separated in age. He left our home in St. Louis when I was still a girl. We have, however, corresponded since our father's death." She considered that. "Sporadically at first, but very regularly in the past year."

"And you think you can get to know somebody through letters?" He made no effort to hide his skepticism.

"Yes. Not all letters, certainly. Some correspondence would give you no clearer view of another person than passing by on the street and saying good morning each day. But these marvelous letters –"

His boot heel skidded noisily on the porch beside her, and she caught herself.

What was she thinking telling such things to this stranger – betraying her brother's confidences. She did not know how Gerald might regard Nate Abbott, no matter what esteem the other cowhands she had seen might hold him in.

"For example," she picked up in a more prosaic tone, "he has written to me so vividly of the marvels and oddities of Wyoming Territory and this ranch, as I indicated earlier, that I was compelled to journey to see it myself."

"Oddities, we have for sure."

She smiled, then let her breath out in small increments as she considered the sky. "And marvels."

They watched in silence. The darkness of the mountains overtook the valley in long, reaching shadows. The blaze gave way to embers, then mere wisps of glow caught in the clouds, while the sky darkened to dusty lavender.

"Harsh beauty," she murmured. "My brother was exactly right."

Nate Abbott expelled a short breath. Before she could ascribe any meaning to it, he tugged at his hat brim, said,

"Good night, Miss Vandercook," strode down the steps, and into the dimness beyond.

⚬⚬⚬

In his customary corner, Nate leaned his chair back against the bunkhouse wall, trying to pin down what had been gnawing at him all day long.

But the excited voices of the other men, gathered near the center of the room, kept intruding on his private considerations.

They were mooning over that small, smudged, faded photograph of Sophie that had come nearly two years ago, well before Vandercook died. You'd think they hadn't just spent a considerable amount of a day gawking at the real, live person, the way they were taking on over her likeness.

It was *our Sophie* this and *our Sophie* that. Got to be as hard to ignore as a toothache. And it sure cut into the work that had got done today.

"By gosh, Nate, we forgot about that," announced String from the center of the group.

Nate had lost the thread of their conversation some time ago – if it ever had a thread. "Forgot about what?"

"Them scissors we bought at the Mercantile."

They'd been among a couple dozen miscellaneous items they'd picked up along with the main supplies for the ranch.

"What about them?"

"We need 'em."

The pair they'd used to keep their hair to a decent length between trips to town had broken years ago. The patch repair had broken down for good this past winter, leaving all the men except him and String – who'd indulged in a visit to the barber during their trip to Grayley – with hair past their collars.

"If we didn't need them, we wouldn't have bought them."

50

"We need 'em for tomorrow," String said.

"Tomorrow? Why?"

Doughy clicked his tongue impatiently. The cook's nickname had started as Sourdough, and had more to do with his temperament than his biscuits, good as those were. "Weren't you listening, Nate? We're going to do our spring washing and get cleaned up tomorrow."

"In honor of Sophie – Miss Vandercook," said Gunner.

"Now wait a minute. We got work to do –"

"Nate, you were saying just before you left for town that we look like a band of heathens, and to plan the clean-up for when you got back," said Doughy.

"Be sure to get it in before roundup starts," added Mulehead, who had an uncomfortable habit of repeating Nate word for word at the least opportune time.

"We got all our clothes set, and Doughy's going to set out the tubs first thing," said Hodges.

Nate grumbled, "Heaven forbid we get anything like work done around this place."

That appeared to be sufficient benediction for the hands. They went back to their discussion, before sending String off to the main house to find the scissors to be ready first thing.

Was what was gnawing at him as simple as that? That the arrival of Sophie Vandercook promised to make his job of keeping the men on their chores not just harder, but nigh onto impossible?

That would wear off, surely. Look at the way that two-headed calf over at the Bar J had caught everybody's attention for almost a week last year. Why every man jack on the ranch had found some pressing need to ride over to the Bar J. But once they had, once they'd seen the two-headed calf, they'd settled down.

Gunner's voice rose, seeming to respond to Nate's thoughts: "Even seeing her picture, I never thought she'd look so good, not judging by Vandercook."

"Good? She's a beauty," someone on the far side of the group said.

"Aye, and smart as a whip. Did you see how she's learned all our names so fast?"

"And the way she got down from the wagon? Neat as you please!" added String. He was making the most of having encountered Sophie well before his fellow hands. "Nice trim ankle, too."

"Now, don't go talking about our Sophie like that, String," scolded Doughy. He didn't always join them in the bunkhouse of an evening. But tonight he'd hurried over right smart so as not to miss any of the conversation. "She's refined, our Sophie is."

"Manners fit for a queen," agreed another voice.

"She's a lady."

"She's right smart."

"She's a beauty."

"She's an angel."

Nate pushed off the wall, bringing the front legs of his chair back to solid connection with the ground with a thud that turned the heads of the other men to him.

"She's plotting something."

That was it. That's what had been gnawing at him from the moment Miss Sophie Vandercook appeared in his line of sight.

"Plotting! How can you say such a thing about our Sophie? She's an angel."

"You said that before, Lester. And how I can say it is I know females, and that one over there –" He dipped his head in the general direction of the main house. "—is plotting something."

"What makes you such an expert on females," sneered Jasper Tinton, who fancied himself the most popular OS hand with anyone who wore a bonnet.

"Seven sisters," Nate said.

"Seven sisters! I never knew you had sisters back in the States!" said Gunner.

"Never knew he had a mother or father, neither," said String. "Close-mouthed as all get-out, that's Nate."

"I got a mother, and a father for that matter. I also got seven sisters – five older and two younger."

Each one more hard-headed than the next. They'd made his life a misery, too, what with their feeling free to meddle in his doings at all times, but refusing to listen to any word he had to say to them, including about their dealings with men. The six that had married so far had seemed to do okay, but who knew for sure, not this far away. Leastwise it wasn't his concern anymore.

As for their meddling in his life and talking, talking, talking over every detail at him from sunup to sundown, he'd had to come all the way to Wyoming Territory to get clear of that, but he'd succeeded, and these eight years had been the most peaceful of his life.

So peaceful, in fact, that for the first time he'd found himself thinking these past months that he might consider getting married in a few years, after he had his own place. For a long time he'd been certain he'd never take to having a woman in his life permanent. He'd thought that attending half a dozen dances a year with the respectable ladies and visits twice that often to some decidedly unrespectable women would do him just fine.

But lately, he'd been thinking maybe that might not keep on being enough. Maybe it wasn't even enough right now.

If a man was thinking he might like to have his own ranch, and some sons he'd pass it on to someday, well, that naturally led to thinking about taking a wife. The right kind of wife. One soft and quiet. Who looked up to him and listened to him, and never gave him any trouble.

"And I'll tell you something about my sisters – every one of them. When they got a kind of glint in their eyes it was sure as shootin' that they were plotting something."

CHAPTER SIX

"Good morning, Mr. Ickles."

"Morning, So – Miss Vandercook." The cook, who even inside wore a red-banded hat that Edith informed her was his trademark, looked around from his stove with a smile that fled as he saw her putting on her hat. "Where you going?"

"To become better acquainted with my surroundings, and to work up an appetite for what will clearly be another of your excellent meals."

"Oh, you can't go outside, Miss."

"It appears to be a fine day."

"It is. But ..." He cast an imploring look at Mr. Bracken, who had just walked into the kitchen, followed by his daughter. The owner cleared his throat.

"You see, Miss Vandercook, it would not be, uh, seemly for you to go out."

The door the men had come through the evening before for supper opened at that moment, admitting the foreman, Nate Abbott, who gave a slight nod, which the unparticular could interpret as a greeting.

"Especially that door," concluded Mr. Bracken.

Sophie looked around at the other four people in the room. "Whyever not?"

"Go ahead and let her," the foreman said.

"Nate!" The cook sounded scandalized.

"No, no – unthinkable. Perhaps later in the day, exiting from the front door. And with a parasol. Yes, definitely a parasol –"

Edith dropped into the same chair she had occupied last night, and interrupted her father. "Everyone's in their altogether out in the yard. It's the big wash-up after winter, though I 'spose it's cause you're here, because none of 'em's been in any hurry before this. Even though I told Gunner he was smelling more'n ripe, just the other day. But now they're stripping off all their clothes to wash those and themselves. That's why you can't go out. Me neither."

"Either," Sophie corrected automatically, even as her cheeks heated with embarrassment at the idea of the men she had encountered ... no she would not think of that.

Nate Abbott chuckled as he hooked his hat on the post of his chair then took his seat, and Sophie found that under that sound her embarrassment fled, though heat remained in her cheeks.

"Don't worry, Miss Vandercook," he said with not the least measure of reassurance in his voice. "It's not the whole outfit out there dancing around naked –"

"Nate," admonished his boss.

"– at once. We run 'em in shifts. With some cleaning out their bunk and things from the winter, others washing clothes and bedding, and another group washing themselves. So it's only a third of the boys in their altogether at once."

She looked down at him. "And why not you?"

Without the hat's shading brim, his blue eyes looked right at her. "In my altogether?"

A flare sparked in his eyes, and she felt the burn of its

heat in the center of her chest like a coal had landed there, before it expanded rapidly up her throat and into her cheeks.

Her cheeks might do what they will, but she had dominion over her eyes. She would not look away. She would not give into this heat that was neither embarrassment nor anger. "Bathing and washing your clothes."

As soon as she said it, she recognized that she knew the answer, for she had been fully aware of his clean scent, so unlike her fellow passengers on the stage, from those first moments on the walk in front of the Mercantile.

"Cleaned up in town." He looked away, and she found herself pulling in air. "I'll be doing the rest just like any other hand."

"Nate's worked quite an efficient system," Mr. Bracken said, then launched into details of the orderly rotation.

Sophie listened as she took her chair, glad to discover that the heat lodged in her chest had subsided.

The meal passed much as the previous evening's supper had, though with approximately a third of the men not in attendance. Those who were there were dressed as they had been previously. Edith informed her that the absent men would have their breakfast while covered as best they could be as soon as the two females left the kitchen.

"More work for me," grumbled the cook, Mr. Ickles.

She could not dispatch her food at the rate the men did, but she did not linger over the meal.

Edith led her to a parlor she had not previously seen. It sat across the entryway from the office and faced away from the bunkhouse and other work buildings.

"Look, I found some drawing things I had as a girl," Edith announced. "You can draw me clothes like you seen in St. Louis."

"Saw."

"Saw," Edith echoed cheerfully.

"Ah, here you are."

Mr. Bracken's voice intruded at exactly the wrong moment. A line showing the volume of the sleeve hadn't been correct. Sophie had just rubbed it out, knowing exactly where she would place it to get it right ... until the moment was broken.

"Hi, Pa," Edith said, without taking her gaze from the point of Sophie's pencil on the drawing.

"I have been a very poor host, Miss Vandercook. I plead the press of business as my excuse. With the hands devoting the day to their cleanup, I have been using the time to catch up on my bookkeeping."

Sophie banked a sigh that threatened to escape, and put down the pencil. With the drawing nearly correct, she had promised Edith she would do her best with the aged cakes of watercolor to enhance the illustration.

"Press of business, indeed, sir. And far more important than an unexpected and uninvited houseguest."

"An unexpected delight," he corrected gallantly.

"You are very kind. I hope I may impose on your kindness further by asking you to not stand on formality with me, sir, but rather to make me feel less of an encumbrance by continuing on with your usual duties — such as your bookkeeping."

"It will be our pleasure to treat you with a lack of formality as you ask —"

"Like one of the family." Edith nodded decisively.

"Still," Mr. Bracken said, "I must apologize for leaving you to your own devices so soon after your arrival, Miss Vandercook. And for the entire morning. It's nearly time for the mid-day meal."

"Not at all, sir. We have been very well, and happily, occupied here, as you can see."

"So, what is it you two young ladies have been doing?"

"Sophie's been drawing me clothes like they wear in St. Louis. A cuirass bodice, that this one's name, and this is an overskirt they call a waterfall, because of the way all that fabric comes down and down and down, one layer right over the other. It's like magic watching them appear from under her hand there on the paper. Oh, and this one, Pa, the one she's working on now, it has a woman walking next to a man in a – What's it called?"

"Frock coat." Sophie supplied.

"Frock coat. But it's the lady that matters. It's the very latest fashion – a tucked bodice with bishop sleeves that Sophie drew, just from remembering things she seen – saw – walking in Lafayette Park with her friends. And, look, she's drawn the trees – oh, and steps like you'd have inside, only this is outside in this park. Lafayette Park. That's a place in St. Louis."

"Is it indeed," he asked solemnly. Mr. Bracken held out a hand for the paper.

Sophie hesitated, but Edith didn't, sliding it quickly from under Sophie's reluctant hand and handing it to her father.

He took the paper with a slight smile, then held it closer and studied it.

"This is excellent, Miss Vandercook. Truly excellent."

"Mere sketches, sir. And only passable at that. My fellow instructor, Miss Drenner, is a fine watercolorist. My skill is limited to such quick sketches."

"You've caught the mood – why I believe this person could walk right off the page. Haven't seen anything like it since Mrs. Bracken and I …" His expression of wistful memory shifted with a throat-clearing. "Well, certainly nothing like it since I've been in Wyoming Territory."

Edith protested, "I draw. I gave you that picture of Beauregard."

He gave her an affectionate smile. "Yes, you did, though I wasn't sure if it was Beauregard or the mule."

Edith's face crumpled for just a moment before she

drew herself up into the best posture Sophie had seen from her.

Her father regarded the girl with surprise, a flicker of realization, and a hint of sadness. Sophie had seen that expression on the faces of her students' fathers. For almost certainly the first time, he was seeing in his daughter something other than his little girl – he was seeing a wisp of the woman she might become.

"Maybe Sophie could teach me to draw better." Sulkiness dampened Edith's usual cheerfulness.

"It would be my pleasure," Sophie said instantly, and saw the girl brighten. "Instruction benefits any young lady aspiring to draw."

"I'm not sure we should impose on Miss Vandercook."

"Impose? Not at all, sir. I should be glad of a way to repay your generous hospitality."

"We would pay you – you are a teacher, after all."

"Indeed you will not pay me, for then I should have to insist on paying you for my room and board here, and we should be right back where we started." She smiled, and slowly he smiled back.

"It's extraordinarily gracious of you, Miss Vandercook. We're very grateful."

Edith snorted, a child once more. "Better wait to see if she can teach me good enough so you know a horse is a horse."

⚜

Nate was plenty ready for a break when Mr. Bracken called him aside not long after dinner.

As at breakfast, a third of the boys had been absent for the mid-day meal, waiting to eat until the ladies were no longer at the table. The remainder were divided sharply into the washed and the not-yet-washed.

Those who had washed, had also been shorn.

String had started in the role of barber, but there'd

been howls by the first victim when he cut close enough to gather in some scalp.

"Oh, quit you're hollerin'," String had snapped. "It'll stop bleedin' eventually, and cuttin' it short'll keep you from needing to do it again any time soon."

Called in to serve as referee to the dispute, Nate had found himself pressed into wielding the scissors himself. He'd warned them he had no experience, but they'd preferred that to what they'd seen of String's work.

At least Nate hadn't drawn blood.

But he'd found the work amazingly tiring, considering it was just making the scissor work while standing over whichever boy's turn it was to perch on the chair they'd brought outside.

Bracken had three items on his sheet of bookkeeping he wanted to check. They retreated around the corner of the bunkhouse, out of the noise and shouts of the wash-up and well away from the heat of the laundry fires.

Nate answered them quick enough, but the ranch owner lingered.

"Miss Vandercook is quite a fine young lady," he said.

Nate kept silent, figuring that was safest when you didn't know what direction someone was heading.

"It's nice to have a woman about the place," his boss said.

A curse crossed Nate's mind, but not his lips. "It's a rough life on a woman out here. And we've done real fine without any females on the OS."

Not to mention there'd been a dozen or more good women who'd set their caps at Frederick Bracken, only to be ignored right into despair. Women who knew this life, several of them widows who had been working ranches beside their men for years. Bracken could have married any one of them any time, and not a soul wouldn't have thought it was fitting and proper.

But Sophie Vandercook from St. Louis? Surely, Bracken couldn't be thinking of such a thing.

There wasn't a female less suitable this side of New York City – hell, this side of Paris, France.

Nate didn't stop to examine why he felt so strongly about the matter. A lot of cow sense was paying heed to what your gut told you, and his gut was saying this was a bad idea. A damned bad idea.

"Perhaps. Perhaps," Bracken muttered, then roused himself. "Certainly, it is a difficult life for a gently reared lady. However, you're wrong in one particular, Nate – there is a female on the OS. My Edith."

"Well, yeah. Sure. I meant – a woman. Edith, why, she's not half grown yet and already she has the makings of –"

He'd been about to say a good cowhand. Just in time he'd recognized that might not be the right thing to point out in this conversation.

"More than half grown, Nate. I know we're all accustomed to seeing her as a child, but she is not that entirely now, and soon she won't be at all. If only ..."

Nate knew that look. The man was thinking of his dead wife. He seldom spoke of her, but he got that far-off look now and then.

After a spell, Nate shuffled his feet, and Mr. Bracken blinked hard, and tugged at his hat.

"Yes, well. My point is that Edith is coming to an age when she would greatly benefit from a woman's influence."

Nate felt a claw at something like panic in his gut.

"Wouldn't do to jump into anything hasty, sir. That could be worst thing of all for young Edith. You don't really know much about Miss Vandercook."

Certainly not what Nate knew of her, first from the more general letters funneled through Vandercook's avaricious hands, and then much better these past months through her letters to him – to them, all of them. All the hands of the OS, though she didn't know it.

Nate mentally shook his head – what did he know of

her, really? Marks on a piece of paper. Could be lies in every word and space for all he knew.

That's when it came to him, what he needed to be saying.

"She is, after all," he said, watching his boss, "Jerry Vandercook's sister."

That struck home with Bracken.

The ranch owner had found Vandercook even more objectionable than Nate had. The only reason Bracken hadn't fired Vandercook had been Nate's interference, which had been entirely on account of the other hands' devotion to Sophie through her letters to Vandercook.

"Perhaps a cautious approach is called for."

Nate nodded. "Wouldn't want to risk getting tied up in anything that could do Edith harm. Expose her to the wrong sort of influence."

"No. No. Absolutely not. That—"

Bracken broke off as Gunner came around the corner at a run.

Nate would have liked to have tied off the knot on what Bracken had been saying, but there was no chance of that when Gunner skidded to a halt in front of them and started shouting.

"Nate, come quick. There's trouble."

"Should I—" started Bracken.

"No," Nate and Gunner said in unison, already moving.

Nate arrived by the twin tubs the hands were using for bathing to find Lester and Hodges squared off. Lester wielded a dolly stick still dripping water from where it had been snatched from stirring clothes in the laundry tubs. Hodges countered with a washboard held up as a shield.

Near as Nate could tell, the battle raged over a nub of soap.

Horses, cards, saddles, ropes, hats, females, money, food, which day it last rained – he'd broken up fights over all those and more. First time he'd had to break up a fight over soap.

Both warriors were hampered by the fact that the soap was wet, and thus slippery, while Hodges was further hindered by wearing only his long johns and Lester more deeply handicapped by being naked other than his boots and the shirt he clutched to his privates with the hand not shaking the dolly stick.

"What is going on here?"

"If he don't give over that soap he stole from me, I'm gonna plug him a good one," declared Lester.

"He's hogging the whole thing, Nate," said Hodges. "Like to use it all up afore any other soul gets a chance at it."

A grumble came from the witnesses.

"Just cause you don't have the least bit of acquaintance with soap, and don't know I'm using it proper –"

"I'll show you where to use it –"

"Quiet!"

The whip-cracking tone Nate rarely employed did the trick.

With combatants and spectators quieted, Nate pushed the back of his hat up to rub at his neck. It also had the effect of tipping the brim down so low nobody could see his expression. If they saw his grin, he'd never get a hold on this soap stampede.

Slowly, he resettled his hat into its proper place.

"Hodges, give me the soap." He held out his hand. "Now."

The last word did the trick.

With the slick lump in his hand, he felt like Solomon. Though if he offered to split this baby in two, he'd have two dozen more wanting a piece of it.

"Hodges you're in no position to be using soap yet. So Lester is going to get it now. And he can use as much as he wants. But –" He interrupted both a solitary whoop and a chorus of bellows. "So can everybody else – use just as much as they want. Thing is, if there's anybody at the end of the line today who doesn't get to use this soap as much as he wants, then every soul who went before him and got to use the soap, has to pay a whole dollar to each of the ones that got no soap."

Into the silence as each of them figured out this twist, came the voice of young Gunner. "I'm going last!"

Mulehead turned to him. "Why?"

"Cause I'll either have all the soap I want now, or enough money to buy all the soap I could ever want next trip to town."

CHAPTER SEVEN

Supper was a subdued affair.

Mr. Bracken had returned to his bookkeeping in the afternoon, and by the frown he wore it had not been a rewarding task.

The last few hands were still out in the bath, but all at the table now were freshly scrubbed. And that seemed to have them on their best behavior. Nate had even heard Gunner ask for a dish to be passed instead of just reaching for it.

Or maybe they were as tired as he was.

Turning out his separate room in the bunkhouse, gathering his bedding and every stitch of clothing he hadn't had with him in town, toting the water, stoking the fire, stirring the contents of the laundry tubs, wringing each item out and hanging up the tough, water-weighted work clothes, and all on top of his barbering duties, was a day's work.

Especially with his mind worrying over Sophie Vandercook and what she might be up to. Along with the added complication of what Mr. Bracken might be thinking.

At least the lady in question showed no sign of trying to catch the ranch owner's attention.

She appeared as tired out by this day as any of the rest of them. Of course she'd just completed a long journey the day before.

Never complained, either. Not on the wagon ride here, not once they arrived. Too bad. Because one of those delicate ladies who'd've demanded to go to her room to rest as soon as she'd arrived, and who'd've stayed put there for the duration would have been a sight easier to deal with.

Wouldn't have stirred up the boys in the bunkhouse. Or the ranch owner. Or –

"And Sophie said she could show me how to make these clothes. Isn't that the best thing you ever heard?"

– Edith, who was the solitary soul at the table burning with enthusiasm.

She'd been going on from the time she sat down about Sophie this and Sophie that. To hear her tell it, the works of art their visitor produced today should've been hanging in one of those museums back in the States.

"Just from the drawings she made. The *magnificent* drawings she made that're just like you said, Pa – like the people could walk right off the paper. And now I can have some of those clothes. I couldn't believe it when she said, but she said for sure that she could. Didn't you, Sophie?"

"Yes, I did."

"We'll go into town and buy some fabric at the Mercantile – it won't be like St. Louis, but Sophie can –"

"Edith," Mr. Bracken said in what passed for him as a stern voice. "Perhaps another year. This isn't the time to be spending money on fripperies."

"But I won't have Sophie any other year."

A few utensils paused on the way to mouths down the row of cowhands. They were fond of young Edith. Didn't like her being disappointed. They also knew the edge the

OS Ranch was up against.

"We can remake some of your existing dresses," Sophie said smoothly. "With your father's permission, of course."

"That's fine."

"But they're all old and worn out, and there's nowhere near enough material like you were saying those skirts need."

"Some of the styles do not require as much material. We shall make a style for which we have sufficient material."

"But I like that waterfall skirt. It's just like the waterfall up in the mountains. Of all of them, that's the one I want." Edith slumped. "But it takes so much material, and I don't see – Oh! I know. We have trunks up in the attic with old clothes and such. We could –"

"No!"

Every face along the length of the table turned toward the remarkable sound of Frederick Bracken shouting.

He scraped his chair back, muttered an "excuse me" and left the table.

"Finish your meal," Nate quietly ordered the men.

As he turned back to his own plate, his gaze met Sophie's.

She glanced toward Edith, then raised her eyebrows. He gave a slight nod.

He saw the questions that remained in her eyes, but most of all he saw understanding.

She didn't need it spelled out that not only didn't Edith have a woman here to mother her, but that Bracken didn't allow such things as memories to soften the lack.

Sophie Vandercook wasn't stupid. He'd admit to that.

That, he figured, was part of the problem.

The gushing over Sophie's likeness had recommenced in the bunkhouse just about as soon as they'd parted from the live version.

Nate couldn't take it.

He grumbled something about having a smoke and left – without a single one of the fools putting it together that he rarely smoked.

He'd leaned against the outside of the bunkhouse a while, but he could still hear them buzzing again. So he ambled along the path that led to the creek that looped a wide horseshoe around the buildings of the OS Ranch.

There, under the cottonwoods, the sun announced the day's end with the last of its slanting warmth sparkling the water.

This was what mattered. Not some fading picture. And not the female whose likeness it bore. Both had been trouble right from the start.

The day that picture of Sophie had come, Vandercook had offered it to the highest bidder. Before the auction – or the bloodletting – had begun in earnest, Nate had stepped in and declared that wasn't happening.

Vandercook had shrugged and slid the picture back into the envelope.

A low, pained howl emanated from the men.

Nate had reconsidered. Taking Vandercook aside, he'd dickered with him on the price, then declared there would be equal shares to make up the amount, and there'd be equal shares in ownership. That wasn't entirely true. There'd have been too many who couldn't put up a share if he'd divided the real price. So he'd made up the difference himself.

Vandercook had given him a mocking smile and carelessly flipped him the card with the likeness on it.

It landed perfectly in Nate's palm, the small face of a young lady. Soft masses of hair was barely tamed by being coiled at the crown of her head. Her eyes were direct and alert, looking at something before her. Her skin looked like it would feel as soft as a newborn chick. And saving all that softness from floating away into nothingness, had been that firm, sharp chin.

It was the chin that got him.

That and the letters.

But that was before he'd seen her – the live Sophie Vandercook – standing in front of him out front of the Mercantile. Had he known right off? Had he not wanted to know? So different in life from that photograph. Not still, not containable, not safe ... and sending his gut into an uproar.

He knew what that meant. Trouble. The worst kind of a trouble a man could know.

He had to get her out of here. And soon.

The thought had no more formed in his head than he heard rustling from the part of the path that came from the house and he knew. He knew.

The one place he came to think that wasn't in the saddle. And that was an entirely different kind of thinking – half watching all the time what the land and sky and animals were telling him. Here at the creek, he could let his mind go where it wanted, not where it needed to go. And now she'd found it, too.

She went straight to the water. Only noticing him when he stood from the log where he'd been sitting.

She started, and swung around. But she didn't run toward the house like a sensible woman would do.

"Oh. Mr. Abbott," she said in that calm voice. "You startled me, appearing like that."

"I was here first. If there was any appearing, it was accomplished by you. You shouldn't have come out here – " He stopped himself from calling her Sophie. "Miss Vandercook."

"It's a warm evening."

"You'd be safer back where you belong."

"It is perfectly acceptable for a young lady to be abroad in the early evening hours. The sun has not even set yet."

"Perhaps in St. Louis, but the wild critters don't give much heed to etiquette here in Wyoming Territory. When the wild cherries ripen –" He jerked his head toward bushes across and down the creek a way – "the bears will be here regular. Specially this time of day."

Her eyes darted to the side, perhaps looking for wild animals.

"Elk come around sometimes, too, and they're not any friendlier," he added.

She stood her ground, and lifted her chin. "You're here."

"I have a gun. And I wouldn't be near as tasty a morsel as–" He snapped his mouth shut before it said some other fool thing.

She turned so he had only her profile. "Then I shall rely on you to shoot any animals that attempt to devour me."

"Shouldn't rely on me – shouldn't rely on any of us out here. Don't you know this country's full of desperados?"

"Desperados," she scoffed. "You have all acted as perfect gentlemen."

"Acting's another way of lying, ain't it." He deliberately roughened his voice. "That's why I said you shouldn't have come out here – not just to the creek at night, but to Wyoming," he added as she opened her mouth. "See that's what don't sit right with me. What I keep turning around in my head. You, acting like such a lady, but coming out here. All this way. By yourself. To country every soul knows is rough as all get-out. And I've got to ask myself what you're doing here?"

"Have you forgotten so quickly, Mr. Abbot?" The slice of her voice was light, delicate. It cut just the same. "I have come to visit my brother."

"Without ever telling him you were coming."

"You can't possibly know that."

His mouth twisted. "I'm about as positive about that as a soul can be. Not many secrets in the bunkhouse.

Specially not about a thing like that – a hand having a visit from his pretty young sister from back in the States. Why that topic'd carry conversation for a whole winter in a bunkhouse out here."

"Perhaps I wanted to surprise him."

A shimmer of something in her voice had him peering at her in the waning light.

"Perhaps you weren't sure he'd want to see you," he said slowly.

She shot him a look, then just as quick had herself facing forward again, that chin up so it nearly pointed toward the stars showing their first light to the east.

Now, why had he said that? And not harsh or mean like he could have to push her on her way back to St. Louis. That's what he should've done. That's what he needed to do.

"Perhaps you are right, Mr. Abbott." She said it slow, but straight out. No fluttering or twittering. "I don't know Jerry well."

"Thought you'd been writing letters back and forth for years."

She flicked another look toward him.

"Like I said, no secrets in a bunkhouse," he said.

She seemed to accept that. "Yes, we have written for quite some time. I suppose it's natural that for most of the course of our correspondence there was a distance … a stiffness. Perhaps you are aware that Jerry is my senior by some dozen years?"

He made a neutral sound.

"Our father's first wife passed on when Jerry was a child. I believe he was raised by his mother's sister. Some years later, our father married my mother. By the time I was of an age to reason, Jerry was a young man. And then he left St. Louis to seek his fortune in the West." She looked at him over her shoulder, with the hint of a smile. "I am aware that he has not fully succeeded in that endeavor."

He dipped his head, and she appeared to accept that as acknowledgement, for she gave a nod, and turned to the creek as she spoke once more.

"Since, as you say, there are no secrets in the bunkhouse, would you tell me something?" She didn't wait for him to say no. "Has my brother changed markedly? In this past year, I mean."

He swallowed, thinking there wasn't much bigger change than alive to dead. He was thankful she wasn't looking at him, instead being back with that chin-pointing at the stars. "Changed?"

"Yes. You see, it's these last letters that made me decide to come to Wyoming Territory. In this past year, it seems my brother has become a man with an eye that sees beauty around him in this strange land, while at the same time he has gained a steadiness that engenders respect. These letters ... His letters –" One hand started a movement that might have been a flutter, quickly roped in. "– have deepened. They are the reason I have come to meet my brother at last."

He couldn't get a word out.

She faced him full-on. "Mr. Abbott?"

He felt like a prairie dog frozen in the open with a coyote bearing down on him.

He dove for cover.

"Ain't noticed anything like that in your brother, Ma'am. Now, it's late, Miss Vandercook. And what you need to do is get back to the house. Right now. Mr. Bracken'd have my hide if he knew I let you be out here like this."

He escorted her back. Only because he had to.

And all the while, he told himself that what he needed to do was stay far away from her. Far, far away. Until he could see that she was far, far away, back in St. Louis.

Sophie wrote quickly and confidently, assuring Alice and Louisa of her safe arrival at her destination.

She had written them from Cheyenne of the trip west on the railroad.

Now, she added an unstinting account of journeying north to the furthest extent of a newer line. Through an acquaintance of Mrs. Forestell's sister in Cheyenne, she had arranged for a horse and buggy to carry her to connect with yet another line. That, too, stopped short of her destination, however. For the final leg, she had shared the rough accommodations of a stage, which appeared to run only when its driver had succeeded in packing every square inch of it with paying customers.

Louisa would enjoy this portion of the letter tremendously, having warned that Sophie would be miserable.

Briefly, she told of her great good fortune in encountering the foreman and a cowhand from the OS Ranch the morning after her arrival in the closest town. She knew she would astonish them with what was considered "close" in Wyoming Territory.

Tiny sketches accompanied descriptions of both the home ranch and Edith.

There she paused.

She had learned many things in the days she'd been here. The necessity of wearing a wide brim hat at all times out of doors. How the sun could beat down like a fire overhead, only to leave a cool in the evenings that felt like spring water.

That Nate Abbott had not precisely lied about the bears coming to the creek, but that he *had* misled her. A question to Mr. Bracken ascertained that bears visited no closer than a mile from that spot behind the house with the stepping rocks that reached the other side. Mr. Bracken had added that if she were concerned about such an unlikely occurrence as a bear venturing so near the house, that her best option was to make considerable noise before approaching the area, thus encouraging any wildlife to depart before her own arrival.

That method also appeared to work on ranch foremen. At least twice, she had caught sight of him heading back toward the ranch buildings as she approached the creek.

The matter of the bears, as well as her conclusion that Mr. Abbott had raised their specter to discourage her from visiting the creek, she did not feel compelled to disclose in her letter.

Her brother's absence, however, had to be mentioned.

The effects of it were more difficult to convey.

There was the uneasiness among all the occupants of the OS Ranch whenever the topic arose. In addition, she realized now, it never arose unless she brought it up. Everyone else appeared quite content to never mention Jerry.

There had been that awkward moment three nights ago by the creek when she had asked Nate Abbott about him.

She had clearly mis-stepped.

She had gathered, especially from some of the more lurid tales young Tad had recounted to the staff from his reading, that there was a strong code among the cowboys of the West. Perhaps she had run afoul of it unknowingly.

It had certainly discomfited Nate Abbott, a man who seldom appeared to be discomfited.

She pursed her lips and gave a small shake of her head. What had she been thinking of to seek his counsel? She had not come so far – in life or on this journey – to discover that she was truly her mother's daughter in relying on the first broad-shouldered male she encountered.

No. She had come with a plan, and she would follow it.

Though it was rather odd that she found herself in need of explaining in her letter to her friends at Mrs. Forestell's Academy for Young Ladies why she had not advanced her plan one whit in these past days.

CHAPTER EIGHT

"**N**ate! Come quick," String shouted as he rode up.

"Now what?"

"You're needed back at the home ranch."

"What for?" But he knew what for.

Sophie.

It was what he'd been called to tend to a dozen times a day in this week since her arrival. No matter how he tried to avoid her, there he was, dealing with her. Didn't matter whether the living, breathing female was there or not. She was always at the bottom of whatever trouble rose up.

Getting the hands away from the home ranch was like driving a dry herd from a water hole. And the work had slowed as a result.

There was a dust-up near every day over who got the prime seats at meals — those near her and those with the best view of her. There'd been a near riot the night before when she dropped her napkin, with boys falling over each other to get it for her. And he'd had to stop a fistfight when Tinhorn Tinton and Royal King both got inspired to bring her cuttings of arrowhead, fleabane, Indian lettuce and sweet root at the same time.

Only good news out of that was their tussle had flattened the patch of wildflowers so thoroughly that nobody else could get the temptation.

More than half a dozen times, he'd sworn to anyone listening that he was ending it right then by telling her the truth. But each time, he had a near stampede on his hands from the boys, groaning and wailing that she'd leave if he did.

Didn't he know it – it was the one thing he kept holding on to.

The mess wasn't made any easier with Bracken calling for him every other minute to do something for Miss Vandercook, or answer some question for Miss Vandercook, or put up a swing on the porch for Miss Vandercook.

Here he was, a respected cowman, trying to ride herd on a bit of a female.

The only good side of it was she hadn't had much of an opportunity to work her wiles on Bracken. All they'd need would be to have her here permanent as the owner's wife.

Nate supposed he had to be grateful to Vandercook on that score, since the reason Bracken kept out of her way instead of doing all these chores for her himself, was his fear that he'd be forced to decide between telling her the truth or an outright lie.

Though Nate also had a notion the OS owner had realized that a man who couldn't even consider having his daughter go through his dead wife's trunks was a long sight from being prepared to let any other female into his life.

Some of the hands grumbled – Tinhorn the loudest – that Nate got to see so much of Sophie. Though not a one of them volunteered to take Nate up on his offer to tell her flat-out that her brother was dead, which would end his spending time with her for sure.

They were all too busy falling into near-faints at her feet, with only Edith and Bracken falling harder or faster than the OS hands.

Nate seemed to be the only one with the sense to see the willfulness in her. In a letter-writer that trait could be viewed with some indulgent fondness. In a flesh and blood girl waltzing around the OS like she was the Queen of Sheba, it was another matter entirely.

From that evening by the creek, she'd been cool as ice to him. Wary. And he'd been the same to her.

That was good. They knew where they stood.

He just wished she stood in St. Louis, Missouri.

"Doughy says to tell you, she's talking to Bracken," String said.

"So let her talk."

"She's askin' *questions*." He waited, but that didn't appear to have the impact on Nate that he'd expected. "Bracken said to get you. Right away."

Nate sat another moment, looking toward the mountains. Then he allowed himself one curse, turned his horse, and galloped back toward the home ranch, and the biggest, sharpest, thorniest burr under his saddle he had ever encountered.

Except for possibly her brother.

Nate figured what said the most about Jerry Vandercook was that everyone on the place had called him Vandercook.

Any other hand with a name like that would've been Van or Vandy or even Cookie. But a nickname required the name-finder having some sentiment about the person getting the nickname, and there wasn't anyone on the OS Ranch who had a particle of sentiment toward Jerry Vandercook.

The lack of feeling was entirely mutual. Only thing

Vandercook cared about was money. And as far as Nate could tell, Vandercook had never met a way of making money he didn't like, unless it involved work.

If Vandercook had devoted half the time to tending cattle that he did to trying to get out of chores he would have been a passable hand. If he'd devoted half the time to cattle that he did to trying to put more jingle in his pocket by any method (other than working), he could have risen to a downright decent hand.

As it was, he'd been a never-ending irritant to Nate, once it became his chore to make sure Vandercook didn't succeed in schemes to avoid work or to drain the resources of the other hands.

He played cards, of course. He bet on horse matchups, too. That was to be expected. He also bet on the darnedest things – how many head before a brindled steer would pass through the gate. Or what color hair the first woman they spotted in town would have.

And having taken a goodly share of his fellow hands' wherewithal, he'd lend it back to them till payday with a stiff added payment due at the end.

There were small things, too, like charging hands who didn't read or write for using his skills in those areas. When Nate learned about that he'd put an end to it by simply doing the reading and writing himself for nothing. Wasn't like most of the men got a lot of letters, and they sent even fewer.

All except Vandercook.

Got to be they'd all sort of hold their breath each time mail came in to hear Mr. Bracken call out Vandercook's name. He never seemed that taken with the letters he received. Not, that is, until some of the men started asking questions.

Who was that writing him? His kid sister, Vandercook had said without interest. Where'd all the letters come from? St. Louis. As the men had exclaimed on letters coming from such a big city, Vandercook had started to get what Nate thought of as his money look.

When String asked, "What's she saying in this letter?" and several others took up the question, Vandercook's most reliable source of income was established.

He'd charged the men of the OS Ranch to read his sister Sophie's letters aloud. Although that task soon fell to Nate, because he didn't rush through the letters like Vandercook did, or refuse to repeat parts. After a letter came, the only topic for days on end was whatever had been in it. And after that wore out, they'd start on when they might next hear from Sophie.

A second revenue stream resulted from Vandercook letting his fellow hands contribute to the letters he wrote to her. Bits about the ranch, the land, the horses, and, of course, his "friends."

Unfortunately all this cut sharply into Vandercook's already limited time for doing work. Bracken started noticing.

He'd mentioned the matter twice to Nate. The third time he talked about it, he came as near as giving Nate a direct order to take care of the matter as he ever got.

That presented Nate with a quandary. He couldn't tell his God-fearing boss that with the exception of his daughter and himself, every soul on the OS was involved in lying to some girl in St. Louis; a lie that was lining the pockets of Jerry Vandercook. Frederick Bracken didn't hold with lying, and if he found out about the letters to and from Sophie, he'd feel obligated to fire the entire outfit, which would leave Nate running the place single-handed … unless he got fired, too, for letting the lying happen.

On the other hand, if Nate made the boys quit the letters coming and going with Sophie, they'd all up and quit, so he'd be in the same predicament.

He'd come no closer to finding a way out of that box canyon when Vandercook presented the solution.

He got himself killed.

They'd gone looking for him when his riderless horse came wandering into camp last spring.

Could have been a snake or something else that spooked his horse, and he got thrown. That could happen to the most careful rider.

Jerry Vandercook was not the most careful rider. It was even money he'd just fallen off and landed the wrong way with no spooking involved.

Nate couldn't help but think, as he looked down at Vandercook lying in the dust a year ago, that it was the only time the man had come close to doing a kindness for another soul during his four years on the OS Ranch.

"You sure he's dead?" Gunner had asked, looking a little green.

"He's dead all right," Nate said.

String spat, adding his confirmation.

No neck that was still put together the way it was meant to be could turn a corner the way Vandercook's had.

"What are we gonna do?" String asked.

"Bury him."

"Not about him – what are we gonna do about our Sophie?"

"Somebody'll have to write to her and tell her he's dead."

"We can't – it'll break our Sophie's heart!"

That began a refrain that dinned in Nate's ears for days, through the burial and beyond.

Vandercook had been one of Merachade's few customers who'd had no takers for a picture. The bunkhouse was unanimous that no remembrance photograph of the departed was desired.

That had seemed the right thing at the time – no sense adding any expense for Mr. Bracken, who'd insisted on paying for the burial, even though Vandercook was overdrawn on wages. Even when Nate presented Bracken with the cache of Vandercook's sideline earnings, the owner had refused it, saying Nate should send it on to that sister of Vandercook's he'd heard mention of.

That presented Nate with something of a dilemma.

He couldn't very well send Sophie her inheritance until she knew of Vandercook's passing, and he'd been delaying that duty.

It had reached a crisis the evening String and Hodges came thundering up to where Nate was riding back from a two-day stint of moving a section of the herd higher up the mountain.

"You gotta do something, Nate." Hodges shouted while they were still nearly out of hearing range.

"About what?"

"Young Gunner let something slip about Sophie not knowing yet that Vandercook's dead, and Bracken says he's going to write to her himself – says it's his duty."

"Good. 'Bout time somebody tells her."

"But then the letters'll stop."

"Yup." Also a good thing, to Nate's mind.

"No!" They both wailed. Then String continued in a solo: "We all talked about it last night, and we agreed – you gotta tell Bracken you'll write to her, Nate. Then we can just go on with the letters like before.

"Ain't like Vandercook's been much of a brother to her anyhow. Why he wouldn't remember from one letter to the next the name of her friends or that time she got so sick last winter. We're the ones that worry about her and all, so it's right we should be the ones writing to her. We'll just pick up writin' like we've been doin'. Only now we don't have to pay to do it."

"You're forgettin' that none of you know how to write," Nate said.

"You do," said Hodges. "We'll even pay you. We'll pay you more'n we paid Vandercook, because you'll do it nice-like. We all decided that last night, too."

"You're all loco. Even if I agreed to this – and I'm not agreeing – the first time a letter came back from Sophie addressed to Vandercook, Bracken would want to know what the hell was going on."

Stunned silence greeted this statement. Clearly, that aspect had not been part of the previous evening's discussions.

"Could be a problem with the mail getting through," Hodges offered.

"Not for more than a letter or two," Nate retorted.

"Nah," said String, slowly, "what you're gonna have to do is tell Sophie to send the letters to her brother's friend Nate Abbott and he'll be passing them on from now on."

He'd said no.

Lot of good that had done him. Because he came right back to that problem where they all got fired or they all quit, and either way he'd be trying to run the OS single-handed.

Not that he took the boys' money. He wasn't about to do that.

If he was entirely honest with himself, he'd come to like writing the letters. Putting in bits the hands offered, sure, but with all the parts in between coming from him.

Gave a man a chance to get out some things he thought but couldn't say to the boys in the bunkhouse.

And it got to feeling, when he was reading her letters out loud, like she was writing back to him. Just to him

Could have kept going on that way, too, if she'd just stayed in St. Louis.

CHAPTER NINE

"I could begin to believe that my brother does not wish to see me."

Mr. Bracken seemed to gargle the coffee he'd just swallowed.

"Wouldn't say that, Miss Sophie," said the cook, Mr. Ickles, whom the cowhands called Doughy.

Has he been informed of my arrival?" She directed the question at Mr. Bracken, as the weaker link in this chain.

She had let this situation go on far too long. A recognition she had been forced to acknowledge when she sat down to write Louisa and Alice a second letter from the OS Ranch. While it had come to seem somewhat natural to drift through pleasant days with little thought of the brother she had come all this way to see, explaining it to her friends had been impossible.

Time to face facts. She was dilly-dallying, and that needed to stop.

"Informed?" interposed Doughy, as Mr. Bracken's gargle threatened to become choking. "What do you mean by that?"

She frowned at the man. "By informed? I mean has someone communicated with my brother concerning the fact that I arrived at this ranch more than a week ago?"

"Can't say as anybody's done that. Not to say communicated with him."

Sophie stared at Doughy, forcibly closing her mouth. For an instant she couldn't think of anything to say. But that instant passed.

She turned to her host. "Mr. Bracken, I am greatly appreciative of the hospitality you and Edith have shown to me. Nothing could exceed your generosity and warmth. However, I am beyond understanding how it is that no one has communicated with my brother that I have arrived here. If he had been on some journey beyond reach, I could understand that –"

"You could say that," muttered Doughy from behind her.

She kept her focus on Mr. Bracken, even when the outside door opened. Even when she recognized the figure entering as Nate Abbott. "—but that no one has gone to this neighboring ranch ... I know it is some distance, I do realize that, but I have come an even more appreciable distance, and you did say you would help me in any way you could."

"Can't help you with this," Mr. Bracken said. The words were so strangled that it took a moment to untangle them into sensible syllables.

"Whyever not?" It was not, perhaps, the most civil of questions. Mrs. Forestell would have scolded one of their charges for being so forward. But this entire situation was so extraordinary that Sophie felt she must be excused.

Nate closed the door sharply, the sound drawing her gaze around to him. The door opened again immediately, and what appeared to be the entire staff of the OS ranch filed in quietly behind him. They spilled out at either side of his unmoving figure, and then farther, until they encircled the room, with her and Nate Abbott facing each other in the center.

The foreman did not heed them. He looked directly at her, his gaze holding hers.

"Because Jerry Vandercook's dead."

She made a sound. It wasn't quite a word.

"That's why nobody's gone to the TS ranch," Nate Abbott said. He said the words clearly, slowly. "That's why nobody can inform him you're here. Because he's dead."

"Dead?"

"Dead. He's been dead these 12 months near enough."

"Oh, lord, she's going to faint," said String. "Why'd you go and say it so bald, Nate?"

"I'm not going to faint. I never faint, Mr. String," she said, although her voice sounded far away to her own ears. Then she rallied. "This is nonsense. You say Jerry has been dead all these months, yet I have received letters from him – many letters – in that time."

She looked around at the men's faces, prepared to see that her logic had unmasked their joke – though why they should joke about such a matter she could not fathom.

Instead, what she saw as she looked from face to face was, first, sheepishness, and, second, a shifting of their eyes to the side. Gradually, she became aware that all the looks were directed toward one individual.

Nate Abbott.

She looked into his eyes. A hint of sheepishness showed there, as well, but no shifting. He looked back directly at her and said. "I wrote those letters."

"You! You wrote the letters from Jerry?"

"The ones since he died."

"Oh." She had a sudden memory of telling Alice and Louisa how much improved Jerry's writing had become, both in legibility and in content. Quite insightful, in fact.

Then she had stopped telling them about the letters in any but the vaguest terms, holding them to herself, reading each one over and over.

It was remarkable, she had marveled to herself, that

without otherwise experiencing it, she had recognized her burgeoning sense of connection with and affection for her correspondent as a sister's love for a brother. A brother who had left behind his early stark, awkward communications to come to write letters with an extraordinary mix of keen observation, wit and warmth. Surely that was the result of his feeling the same familial connection and affection –

"Oh, dear!"

"She's going to faint for sure!"

"Catch her!"

"Don't let her fall!"

"I'm not going to faint," she stated firmly, shaking off a dozen hands that reached to prop her up.

Oh, heavens, the things she'd said to him at the creek about Jerry's letters – his letters.

But there was no time for missish embarrassment. She needed to know the truth of this matter.

She forced herself to look at Nate again. "Jerry's truly gone."

The brother she had thought she had found in the letters – letters he hadn't written.

"Yes, ma'am."

But he wasn't gone, because he'd never been. Jerry had been a figment.

"And you wrote the letters since – oh, yes, I see, ever since the request to send my letters to your keeping."

No, not a figment. Jerry had been those early terse letters. The later ones, the ones she'd read so many times had been from –

"Yes, ma'am."

Nate Abbott.

Anger rushed up through her like a laundry fire catching hold of a nightshirt hung too low. She dearly wished she'd listened more closely to Tad so she had the vocabulary to express the molten fury inside her at this moment.

Instead, what she did have at her disposal was the chill, haughty backbone of Miss Sophia Vandercook of Mrs. Forestell's Academy for Young Ladies.

"So, from that time, everything I read as being my brother's words and everything I wrote believing was for his eyes alone has been written and read by you."

He said nothing.

He had confirmed her other statements – or did they qualify as accusations? – yet remained silent now. Though he did not look away from her.

She became aware of the sound of feet shuffling. Many feet shuffling.

"Don't be blamin', Nate," said a voice she recognized as String's. "Nate wrote 'em, but we all told him bits to put in."

That statement opened a torrent of words from all around her. She turned and twisted trying to keep up with each speaker, but the fragments came too fast and from too many directions.

"We'd been readin' your letters since way back—

"—like we knew you so well–"

"—that worried when you were sick—"

"—throwed by his horse—"

"—how could we tell you he'd—"

"—didn't want you to feel lonely like–"

"—selfish, too. Didn't want you to stop writing–"

"—not that different from what we'd been doing–"

"—'cept Nate didn't want money from us like–"

"—shut it! She don't need to know–"

"—always been Our Sophie."

The spate of words wound down to absolute silence. She looked at those surrounding her, but one by one the gazes dropped to the floor.

All but Nate's.

She addressed him. "My brother died in a riding accident?"

"Near as we can tell. His horse came in without a rider,

so we went searching. Didn't look like anything except a bad fall. It's rough country out here. Fall the wrong way …"

"When?"

"Like I said, a year ago and some."

"The date?"

He frowned. "Don't rightly know –"

"The twenty-eighth of April," said the young one they called Gunner. He hiked his chin up and looked around a bit belligerently. "My birthday's the next day, so I recall."

She gave a slow nod in acknowledgment of his contribution.

"Where is …?"

"Up on that hill, back of the creek." Nate tipped his head in the direction. She had noted a ridge rose slightly beyond the creek. Presumably that is what he meant. "He's not the first."

She swallowed. "I should like to see where my brother is buried."

Mr. Bracken spoke for the first time since Nate's arrival. She had forgotten he was here at all. "It would be my honor to accompany you, Miss Vandercook."

"Thank you, sir, but if someone would direct me, I should prefer to be alone."

Nate Abbott gave the straight-forward directions. "Take the path to the creek. There are rocks to step across on, and you'll see the path picks up the other side. Just follow that up the hill. There's a pair of pine trees up there. You'll see a few graves by them. Jerry's is farthest to the west." She inclined her head.

Without look up, she walked to the door, bypassing him. The other hands stepped aside for her, opening the way. In no hurry, she took the wide-brimmed hat Edith had given her to wear from its peg by the door.

As she followed the path to the creek, she was aware of a cluster of men following at a discreet distance.

But when she crossed the creek and began the ascent

up the hill, they remained on the house side of the creek.

Exactly as Nate Abbot had described, there were twin pine trees and a handful of graves, marked by simple wooden crosses in varying states of diminishment.

In the newest, the letters spelling out Vandercook already had softened from the intervening winter. The ground revealed only the slightest swell. If the cross had not been there she wouldn't have noticed.

Though her eyes stung, she shed no tears. She could not be entirely certain if that was the result of fortitude or because the dry wind up here blew them away.

She had never known this man who was her brother. Now she never would.

Sadness surrounded the thought. Though, in fairness, she did not know if she should be sad. His letters – the letters he had truly written – had given no hint of a man she would have admired. There was every chance that he had been like their father.

Perhaps the one man she could truly say she believed she would have liked to know was her mother's father, who had dispensed such sensible advice.

But he was gone. They were all gone. Every soul she could possibly lay claim to – gone. She was utterly and completely alone.

A shiver took hold of her shoulders. It teetered for an instant, threatening to become a sob.

Instead, she turned it into a shake of her shoulders, which sifted resolve right down her backbone.

She was no more alone now than she had been an hour ago, when she'd been perfectly happy if somewhat peeved at her brother's continuing absence.

She was a sensible, modern woman.

She found as she came down the steep path – aware of the watchful knot of men retreating as she advanced – that her sorrow had transferred to determination.

Good.

It was time to get on with her plan, with her life.

She safely crossed the creek, then turned around to face it and paused.

Ah, yes, her plan. How would she need to adjust her plan in light of her new circumstances? Should she pursue it still?

As she stood, contemplating that question in the glittering slide of the water, she became aware of the rumble of male voices from behind her.

The rumble gradually rose to the level of recognizable words.

"See if she's okay."

"Somebody's got to ask her."

"She shouldn't ought be alone like that."

"Get Edith, then." That was certainly Nate Abbott's grumbling voice.

Objections arose in snatches about Edith being too young and not used to the sensibilities of a lady from the States.

"Go on, Nate, go on."

So she was not startled when Abbott appeared in her peripheral vision, some half a dozen yards down the course of the creek.

"You okay?"

She heard the words, though she might well not have for the distance, the sound of the creek and his decided lack of enthusiasm for the question. So she accounted no obligation to respond.

He edged closer.

"You okay?"

Even knowing he was there, she had to stifle a start at the volume. It was near a shout.

With great dignity, she turned her head toward him, while looking well beyond him. "I prefer to be alone, Mr. Abbott."

He came up to her now, apparently as at ease as if she had issued the most cordial of invitations, and spoke in his normal tone. "We've gone round that corral already. A lady shouldn't be alone out here."

"It's full daylight."

"Still." There was nothing in that syllable for her to grab on to, to exercise her reason on in order to display his utter lack of reason. Insufferable man.

"I am thus forced to say that it is, in fact, a matter of my not caring for your company."

"Why?"

Beyond insufferable. "For the very good cause that a gentleman would not have participated in deceiving a lady, as you have done."

"Never said I was a gentleman," he muttered.

She sailed on as if she had not heard that less than an excuse – indeed, an indictment. "A gentleman would not have pretended he was someone else in order to obtain a lady's confidences. To wheedle them out of her," she added in a significantly less lofty tone.

"I never wheedled anything out of anybody, including you – especially you, Sophie Vandercook."

"Miss Vandercook."

"Miss Vandercook," he repeated in a tone that indicated the words felt like ground glass in his mouth.

Satisfied with that state of affairs, she continued. "I don't know that I shall ever be able to forgive you."

"Fine, because I'm not asking you to forgive me, because there's nothing to forgive." He kicked at the dirt, sending up a plume of dust between them.

"There most certainly is! You obtained my confidences under false pretences. You –"

"Not just me. All the hands. So why're you so all-fired mad at me?"

The question made Sophie's breath catch beneath her ribs as if the strongest hands imaginable had just given a tremendous yank on her corset ties.

If Nate Abbott had stopped there, she might have been forced to contemplate the question with her usual rigorous clear-sightedness. So she was much relieved when he continued immediately.

"I'll tell you why – because you know that I know what that expression means."

"I have not the slightest idea what your meaning could be."

He spun toward her, setting up more dust. "I'm informing you, Miss Vandercook, that I know what that expression means."

"Expression?"

"That –" He flung an arm toward her. It brought his open-fingered hand to just under her chin, as if he intended to caress it. He jerked his hand way. "– expression. On your face."

She drew herself to her full height, her hands folded in front of her, and turned to face him. A dignified and sedate posture marred only when eddies of dust stirred by her movement reached a level that made her sneeze three times in quick succession.

A chorus of muted "bless you's" came to her ear, though a quick survey showed no visible forms. She decided she was justified in not acknowledging the interruption.

She continued to gaze at him levelly as she again asked, "Expression?"

"That expression," he repeated. It appeared to take him an effort to rouse himself to add, "That butter wouldn't melt in your mouth. But it means the direct opposite. It means you've got a plan working in that head. A plan that can't be any good for anybody else."

"My goodness," she said mildly, though her heartbeat sprang to a canter. "And you can tell this from my expression?"

"Yes, I can. I grew up with a passel of sisters, and I know."

"Ah."

Wariness flickered in his eyes. But it came too late. He had opened this trap, and she intended to spring it.

"There you have the advantage over me," she added, and she would have been a saint not to revel, just a little, in the knowledge that although he didn't know how, he did know full well that he didn't have the advantage – not at all – even before she added, "Not only have I never had a sister, and not only am I an orphan, but now I have lost the sole sibling I could lay claim to. I am quite alone in the world."

Around them arose a rusty "Awww."

Then a single, rough voice called, "You're not alone, Sophie! You have us!"

The sound of Nate Abbott grinding his teeth in frustration was not the least bit musical.

She enjoyed it immensely.

CHAPTER TEN

The buzz in the bunkhouse that night was unbearable. But there was no way on earth Nate was going back to that spot by the creek. Not after he'd seen her heading that way after supper.

Not because he'd been watching particularly where she went, but because it was his job to know everything that happened on the OS.

Supper had been enough to make him forget to eat, with the hands casting worried looks at Sophie every other second, while she and Bracken discussed the possibility of Wyoming becoming one of the states.

After supper was worse.

Barely out the kitchen door, and he got jumped by a dozen hands demanding if he thought Sophie would leave in the morning?

If she has any sense.

Wasn't there a way to keep her here ... at least a little while?

Nope.

But wasn't he going to do something?

Nope.

Out of sheer exasperation, he'd set the next one who asked a Sophie question to sorting old bridles. After that, anybody who asked a question got handed a chore to be done right that minute. Took a bit for them to catch on, so Doughy would be tickled the wagon had had its rough cleanout already and pleased with the extra firewood piled up.

By the time Nate reached the bunkhouse, they were steering clear of him and questions. But they were still talking the topic to death.

He cut String out of a clump of hands filing into the bunkhouse by shouldering him to one side.

"What's that for?"

Nate jerked his head, and didn't answer until they were out of earshot. "Got something for you to do."

"Ain't repairing harness all night, if that's what you got in mind."

"Go down to the creek and keep an eye on Sophie."

String's eyes started and his Adam's apple bobbed. "Talk, you mean?"

"Repairing harness looking better, String?"

"I'm not much of one for talking with ladies."

Nate took pity on him. "No need to talk to her. Just be sure she – hell, I don't know – doesn't fall in and drown."

"More likely to crack her head than drown," String concluded after a bit.

"Fine, then make sure she doesn't crack her head. If she got injured we'd never get her out of here."

"Why?"

"Why? Because everybody'd treat her like some fancy china doll –"

"Why do you want her to leave?"

Nate swore. "I've had enough questions tonight. Just go down to the creek, String."

The older man shrugged, and ambled away.

And Nate had enjoyed a full half hour of peace, out

here, leaning his forearms against the corral fence's top rail, watching the clouds rush to their next destination as the dying sun turned them more colors than a rainbow.

He had wondered what Sophie was finding to do so long at the creek, and if String might have worked up the nerve to say more than "Evenin' " to her. Or maybe String had hidden himself away, so she never caught sight of him.

Not that he cared one way or the other. As long as she didn't cause trouble, and he didn't have to answer questions.

From the corner of his eye, he saw young Gunner emerge from the bunkhouse, look around until he spotted Nate, then make for him with purpose in his stride.

And, damned if he didn't come right out with a question first thing.

"You think Sophie's okay?"

Nate kept looking at the clouds. "Sent String to keep an eye on her."

"String? You think he's ... I mean, he's a good hand and all, but she's a woman in mourning."

"For Vandercook? She'd be the first."

"Well, she doesn't know what he was like."

"I wouldn't be surprised if she has a fair idea. She's not stupid."

"No, of course not." Gunner sounded insulted at the thought. "It's just ... It's hard on a lady, especially one with refined sensibilities, as Sophie has."

Nate shrugged.

"I think I'll just go see that everything's okay. You know, see if I can help in any way."

"Suit yourself."

Needing no further encouragement, Gunner left Nate with only his own thoughts for company.

I wouldn't be surprised if she has a fair idea. She's not stupid.

He'd surprised himself a bit with that. When had he come to that conclusion?

The first second he'd laid eyes on her.

Nah, that made no sense.

More like it was from her letters over the years.

Vandercook hadn't said much, except one comment about her probably being as silly a skirt as her mother had been. More proof the man didn't have much except avarice in his head.

So it hadn't seemed right, not right at all, that she'd had that lost look on her face when she came back from his gravesite.

He could have told her some sharp truths about the brother she was mourning, but ... well, no sense running down a man to his sister when he'd never have the chance to show himself any different.

When she'd corrected his using her name, there'd been half a breath right then when he was this close to turning on his heel and leaving.

But he hadn't.

I grew up with a passel of sisters, and I know.

Ah.

For an instant after that syllable he almost thought – but he knew better. If not from his experience with his sisters, then from a sinew-deep instinct that read the glimmer in her eyes and understood that in some way he hadn't yet fathomed, he'd already lost that go-round.

There you have the advantage over me.

And then what sounded to be every last fool hand on the OS making noise like a bunch of bawling calves, before Hodges – damn him – piped up with "You're not alone, Sophie! You have us!"

The glint in her eyes then – oh, yeah, his guts had flipped at that. And he'd known for sure then that Sophie Vandercook was the furthest thing on this earth from stupid.

He became aware now of a commotion behind him. He turned, leaning back at his ease against the corral fence.

The hands were pouring out of the bunkhouse. Young Gunner was bringing Mr. Bracken and Edith and Doughy out of the house. And everyone was converging around String and Sophie, as they emerged from the path to the creek.

Gunner ran toward him. "Nate, come quick! You got to hear this."

Nate pushed off from the fence and walked slowly toward them.

Everyone swirled around. Doughy slapped his red-banded hat against his thigh before clapping String on the shoulder, while Bracken shook his hand. Edith squealed and grabbed hold of Sophie's arm.

"What is this?" Nate asked, but his gut knew.

"You won't believe it," Gunner said. "You purely won't believe it."

"String?" Nate did not look at Sophie.

The hand looked up. "The thing is, Nate ... Well, see, we was talking, and she was going to leave and the thing is – we're gettin' married."

❧

S ophie woke so early the sky was barely gray.
... you know that I know what that expression means.
Or perhaps she had never slept.

It had not felt like excitement that had kept her awake. Well, perhaps excitement would be too much to ask, after all. String was very kind, but not the sort of man to disturb one's rest.

And she had not misled him.

He had asked if she'd be leaving right away, and she had honestly said there was no attachment to hold her at the OS any longer. She had not said, absolutely, that she would be leaving, because she had not determined that yet.

He'd blurted, "If you married somebody – somebody on the OS ..."

Then he'd sputtered out. She'd waited, but there had been no more. She'd picked up the thread. "Yes, that would be an attachment that would stop me from departing immediately."

"Keep you here."

"Yes, it would. At least for a while, Mr. String."

"Jes' String."

"Jess? Your Christian name is Jess?"

He'd waved a hand. "No. String. Only name. No mister."

"Ah, yes. Well, String, as I was saying, marriage would, indeed, keep me here for a while. But, eventually, I would return to St. Louis. It is my home. Would you have a desire to live in St. Louis?"

"Good God, no! Beggin' your pardon, miss."

"No pardon required, String. So, I would return to St. Louis in due course, and you would remain here in Wyoming Territory."

"If we got married, like, you mean."

"Exactly. So it appears to be an arrangement that would suit us both."

"If you say so, Miss."

"Sophie. I believe you should call me Sophie now."

His expression lightened for the first time. "Our Sophie."

She found that slightly odd, yet endearing.

I'm informing you, Miss Vandercook, that I know what that expression means.

So, no, excitement was not to be expected among her mix of emotions. Nor joy. But satisfaction. Yes, satisfaction certainly should be hers.

Yet the success of all her plans had produced a sensation inside her that she had not experienced since … when? The death of her mother? No, that was silly. Surely this was an occasion for joy, not sorrow.

She'd been so young at that time, how could she accurately recall her emotions from all those years ago.

It means you've got a plan working in that head.

It was more like when she'd had the influenza winter

before last. She'd been fortunate to have been spared a severe case, yet even so she had been left with the belief that she would never again be able to swallow food, the belief that her skull would crack open at any second, and the belief that her ribs had tightened around her lungs in a decidedly uncomfortable way.

A plan that can't be any good for anybody else.

Why she should feel that way now, when String had provided her with exactly the solution she desired, she needed solitude to discover.

With Edith indulging in wild flights of delight – as she had well into the night – no solitude would be found in the house. So she slipped out, stepping soundlessly down the stairs and out the door, as she had learned to do as a student at Mrs. Forestell's Academy, After a glance told her no one was in sight, she hurried across the dusty open ground.

Once outside, she hesitated. Mulehead would be using the path between the house and the creek at any time. He drew water from there to give to the chickens.

She could take the path from the back of the bunkhouse instead. Surely whatever activity there might be among the hands would be at the front of the building. She skirted the other outbuildings, avoiding the open center area, and reached the side of the bunkhouse.

A low rumble of male voices came, but she didn't pause to identify them. Not until she was just about to pass the back corner of the structure and venture into the short open area before the cottonwoods would give her shelter, when she heard "… Sophie …"

Instinctively, she stopped.

Only then did she realize that the voices came not from inside the bunkhouse, but from a porch across the back.

An open door masked the speakers from her view, and she from theirs. But if she had gone any farther she would have been entirely visible. Besides, she knew the voices now, and caught the words by listening carefully.

"You have nothing to explain to me," Nate Abbot said.

"Feels like I should. Feels like you have a right to hear," String responded, in a low mumble.

It wasn't precisely polite to listen like this, but in her years at Mrs. Forestell's Academy for Young Ladies, both as a student and – especially – as a teacher, she had found that being over-nice in one's qualms about what one happened to overhear left one at a decided disadvantage.

Indeed, she had more than once remarked to Louisa and Alice that the primary means of communication at the school was eavesdropping. To set out to listen to conversation not intended for one's own ears would have been an entirely different matter. But when one happened to be walking in the vicinity and heard one's name …

"Since you been the one writin' the letters to her, Nate – least mostly you, with the rest of us puttin' in stray bits here and there, and you puttin' it all together so it sounded real letter-like."

Sophie was still digesting that when Nate's voice, came, gruff and off-hand. "It doesn't matter."

She stifled a gasp. Though why she should, she couldn't imagine. Of course it didn't matter to Nate Abbott. She had known that full well.

A man who had deceived her, lured her into thinking he was an entirely different kind of man from what he actually was – by pretending to be her brother, she meant. By giving her an image of her brother that wasn't true.

So his *doesn't matter* declaration could only make her more secure in the knowledge that she'd been wise to follow her course.

"It does matter," pursued String. "Because if there was anyone what had a right to be askin' Sophie to be his bride it's you, Nate. So –"

"I'm not asking any female to marry me, not now and maybe not ever, and now or ever, it certainly wouldn't be Sophie Vandercook nor any female one bit like her. Thought never entered my mind."

"That so?" String said, sounding unsure, though how he could be Sophie couldn't imagine when, to her ear, Nate had covered the subject beyond thoroughly.

"Yeah, that's so." The sharp sound of boot heels on the wood floor of the bunkhouse porch indicated Nate was moving, and when he spoke again, his voice sounded different. Clearer and more certain. "So don't give it another thought, String."

Sophie shifted to the side, and realized that she could see him in the gap between the partially opened door and the doorframe.

"Well, I am giving it another thought. Because it don't seem right, somehow," String said, using more words than she had ever heard from him. "I can't puzzle out exactly how. But I started talking with her meaning to say to Sophie about you and her not speaking so sharp to each other – not that she speaks sharp, but she gets that look in her eye, and she stands up tall – tall as a bit of a thing like her can – and she starts shooting those big words at you like bullets, but all the time so polite and she looks so –"

"Prim? Know-it-all?"

"Nah, Nate, that's not it at all. You know it's not. And I know for a fact you know it, 'cause I've seen –"

"You're off course, String. You were saying you went to the creek."

"Was I? What ... ? Oh, yeah, I figured long as I was keeping an eye on her the way you told me, that I might as well see if I could set that right a bit. So I started hanging back by the trees, but then I went right on up there by the creek to talk to Sophie about you and her, and then ... and then I don't rightly recall exactly how it happened, but then, well, we was promised to each other. Engaged, she calls it."

"I'm not surprised you can't recall exactly how it happened," Nate said in that drawl that usually went with crinkles at the corners of his eyes and sometimes made Sophie want to laugh and other times – as now – made her want to strike him.

As the urge to strike him ebbed, she realized his words were as clear now as if he were speaking directly to her. So clear, in fact, that she looked anxiously at the open door, but no one was visible beyond its edge.

"The thing is, Nate, I don't know how I came to be askin' Sophie to marry me," String said in a rush.

"I don't suppose it was your doing at all, String. If you ever come to recall exactly who said what, I suppose you'll discover it was Sophie that did the asking."

She wasn't entirely certain she succeeded in stifling a gasp at that, even with both hands pressed over her mouth, but she was too angry to be concerned. She spun on her heel and hurried toward the barn, then the protection of the other outbuildings until she reached the path that connected the house and the creek.

If she met Mulehead, so be it.

Far better to raise questions in his simple mind than to tell Nate Abbott exactly what she thought of him.

CHAPTER ELEVEN

"Thing is," came Nate's drawl from just behind her, "there's a hitch in this plan of yours to marry String."

The insufferable man must have practically run to be at the creek this soon after her.

"String and I will certainly overcome any obstacle."

"No preacher to do the marrying."

That brought her around to look at him, a reaction she immediately stifled by turning back to the creek. "There is a minister in Grayley. I met his wife."

"Oh, his wife lives in town all right. Him, too, come winter. But this time of year, he's out to the distant ranches and settlements. Won't be back to the closer-in ranches like the OS until the weather turns. So you'll have to stretch this engagement right through the summer into fall, if you can hold on that long."

She eased her clamped jaw to say, "When String *asked me to marry him* I'm certain he took that into account."

"Ah." He stepped over the log and showed every sign of preparing to sit next to her. She turned her back to him. He sat anyway. "My ma had a saying."

"I don't care for your company, Mr. Abbott."

"Nope, that wasn't it." From his spot to her immediate

left, he skidded a stone into the creek. "In fact, she seemed to like my Pa's company just fine."

She preserved a rigid silence. But that didn't send him away any more effectively than her direct statement had.

"The saying was something about those who listen in on other people's conversations don't hear any good of themselves."

Her backbone stiffened, far less by the boning surrounding her ribcage than by the anger and mortification roiling inside.

"For the future, should you consider going into the line of spying on folks, you might want to remember that if you can see someone through a crack, there's a chance they can see you, too."

She maintained a coldly severe silence.

"Especially when you're dressed like a cardinal bird."

He stretched a foot out and just brushed the hem of her skirt – with only a hint of red in it to pick up on the color in her bodice – with the toe of his boot.

She twitched her skirt away.

He chuckled.

She rounded on him.

"You, sir, may have permission to lecture someone else on any matter pertaining to conduct or propriety when – and only when – you have acknowledged your base breach of trust and propriety."

"Base? Breach of trust and propriety?" He was no longer smug or self-satisfied. "Where do you come up with that hors– hogwash?"

"From your own actions, Mr. Abbot. Fully acknowledged."

"This unforgivable whatever it is you're saying I did, doesn't seem to have stopped you from getting String to ask you to marry you, so it must not have been so unforgivable of him!"

"He wasn't the ring-leader," she said. "You were."

"Ring-leader? It wasn't my idea to keep writing those

letters to you."

"Perhaps not." Now that he was ruffled, her calm tone perfectly threaded disinterest into a weave of dignity. "But you are the leader of these men, under any circumstances. Regardless of who put forth the idea, you could have snuffed it in a moment, if you had exercised your influence."

"Good G—gravy. You make me sound like a preacher and a politician all rolled into one. All's I am is the ramrod." But his protest held the sullenness of one who knew his foe's argument was strong.

"Exactly."

"And what about you?" he rallied.

She wasn't about to aid him by asking *What about me?*

He didn't falter for the lack of that assistance.

"You swung your loop out and dropped it over the head of the most unsuspecting fella on two legs. Why, I've seen rustlers with more compunction over roping in a steer than you had over dragging that proposal out of String."

"You think – you accuse me of – of *roping* him into offering for me?"

"Yeah, I do."

"How dare you!"

"I dare because I know females. Know their ways and their tricks. How they don't ever come at you straight on, with what they're really after, but always come at you sideways, and –" His hands made a peculiar gesture. "— Twisty."

Her anger cooled immediately and completely at the abrupt change in the heat of his.

A memory came to her. Holding Lizzie Wendersham on the day word came of her brother's death, how she'd ranted at him, calling him names Sophie wouldn't have guessed gentle Lizzie knew.

And all the time she'd heard the anger in Lizzie's voice, she'd felt the pain in her body – in her soul. That had been the first lesson, but over the years Sophie had dealt with enough of the girls in moments of trouble and sorrow, to recognize now that the fuel under Nate's fire was pain.

"What happened, Nate?"

"Nothing happened," he snapped. Immediately, he gave his words the lie, adding, "It was a long time ago when I was a stupid boy."

"Nate–"

He stood before her extended fingertips did more than brush his sleeve.

"Nothing to do with you."

He turned on his heel and strode away.

True. Absolutely true, she told herself as she cupped the hand that had reached toward him in her other palm.

⁂

In the week since her engagement, Sophie could write to her friends that Edith was progressing well with her drawing.

And that she and her pupil spent fair-weather mornings capturing scenes around the home ranch. Oh, and those fair-weather mornings were glorious, with air so clear you thought you could touch the mountains on the horizon.

As the broken, red-earthed hills and ridges became distinct, identifiable landmarks, she informed her friends that she had been wrong to describe this land as barren. To the observant there appeared the massed white willow mixed with wild cherry and other berry bushes along creeks. The stunted pines and junipers on the higher hills formed fantastic shapes she tried to capture in her sketches.

Sweet-songed meadowlarks proudly presented yellow throats decorated with a black cravat, flanked by dark and light stripes that formed almost a herringbone pattern on their backs. They offered never-ending variation for sketching. She wished she could capture the song as well in the sketch. Of all the birds, they were her favorite.

Among the wildflowers she could make no such distinction. The bright red of the Indian paintbrush, the rich blue set off by the white center of the blue flax, the white daisy-like bloom of the short plant dismissed as mule ears, and so many more that Edith identified and named in such a cavalier fashion that Sophie was forever asking her to repeat the name and point more closely.

Even grass was not simply grass. Buffalo, wheat, grama grass – each unlike the shorn carpets she was accustomed to. And where the grasses did not grow, there was sage to add pungency to the air when their skirts brushed it, or the men's boots crushed it.

She breathed it in deeply, determined to recall this scent when she left Wyoming.

In inclement weather she and Edith sketched Doughy in every attitude of washing up and preparing dinner, unless he shooed them out of the kitchen.

The afternoons included projects to remake Edith's clothes – although the girl was correct that there was barely enough good fabric left in any of them to suffice. To supplement their discussions, Sophie sent Edith searching through newspapers for items about current fashion and through books for past fashions. In this manner did she slip in a modicum of history, current affairs and geography to extend the girl's education.

Some afternoons Edith disappeared, leaving Sophie to entertain herself with writing letters, reading and preparing her next disguised lesson. From the girl's bright eyes, heightened color and dusty skirts and boots, Sophie surmised that she went riding.

On those occasions, Sophie frequently had to pull herself away from staring out a window at the expanse of open space under a sky with blue that reached seemingly impossible heights.

Her evenings were spent on the front porch in the company of String.

Now that they were engaged, Mr. Bracken had decreed it acceptable for them to spend this time alone. When they were alone, the time was mostly silent. This had allowed Sophie to keep her clothing – which suffered many more indignities here than in St. Louis – in good repair, mending almost the moment it became necessary.

In practice, however, they were rarely alone.

Nearly every hand nearby found a reason to discuss some topic with String on these evenings.

But any given night several of the hands would be absent. For they were increasingly spending nights away from the bunkhouse in groups of two or three or more, sometimes one night, frequently more. Preparing for the roundup, they said. Further informing her that this year the roundup was to be closer to the home ranch than ever before.

Edith asserted that she was going on the roundup, as well, though Sophie noted she save those assertions for times when her father was not among her listeners.

Early on, Sophie noticed a missing button from String's shirt, and volunteered to sew it on. She set to showing Edith how to accomplish this – Sophie had full evidence that neither the girl nor String knew the proper method. Soon the men of the OS Ranch would bring their necessary mending with them when they came to the porch, including Doughy and Mr. Bracken.

All except Nate Abbott.

String played the harmonica, and soon someone – usually Jasper Tinton, who did have a fine voice, though not quite as fine as he appeared to believe – began to sing.

Frequently she sketched the faces of the men, to their embarrassment and delight.

They were very companionable evenings.

Sometimes she noticed, only because her favorite seat happened to face that way, that Nate Abbott sat on the porch of the bunkhouse. Alone. Other times, he followed a route that likely took him to the creek.

Tonight, he had started on the porch, tilted well back in his chair. When Jasper Tinton began to sing "Love's Old Sweet Song" which had become quite popular in the past few years, the front legs of Nate's chair thudded against the porch floor loud enough to be heard all this way. Then he rose and, without looking toward the house, headed toward the creek.

"What are you thinking?" Edith asked.

Blinking, Sophie realized that she had stopped with the thread fully extended and the needle poised in the air, staring out to the horizon, that Tinhorn had ceased singing and that everyone was looking at her.

"How lovely that song is, of course." She smiled at Tinhorn. At his broad and knowing smile in return, she shifted quickly. It had not evaded her notice that while he had flirted with her from the start, he had made no true attempt to fix her interest. Now, that she was spoken for, his flirtation had begun to push beyond what was comfortable. She added to Mr. Bracken, "And how very much I would like to see more of the OS. I have been here all this time, and have hardly ventured past this porch."

Mr. Bracken clapped his hands on his knees. "Well, now you're going to stay and marry String, it's only right you should see the ranch."

"**M**iss Vandercook has expressed a desire to see the ranch," Mr. Bracken said the next day at breakfast.

"You have to ride to see the ranch." Nate didn't look up from his nearly empty plate.

"We could hitch up the wagon for her," Bracken said doubtfully.

Nate made a dismissive sound. "Won't see much and she'd get her teeth rattled out of her head for the effort."

"I ride," Sophie said.

It was one of the activities that gave Mrs. Forestell's Academy for Young Ladies an advantage over its competitors. All the young ladies received riding lessons. Sophie had excelled.

It took a moment before both men turned to her, Bracken smiling, Nate frowning.

"Including jumping, of course," she couldn't resist adding.

"I knew you would." Edith beamed at her. "If you didn't bring a split skirt, we can remake one of mine."

"I have a riding suit."

"Really? They make suits special for riding? Most ladies wear split skirts. Elsewise, I just take my skirts and bunch them up like, either side of the saddle."

"Either side – ? Astride? Oh, no, Edith, I ride sidesaddle."

"Sidesaddle!" The girl's eyes widened. "You can ride like that? And jump? I wouldn't want to try that, and I'm not afraid of anything on a horse, am I, Pa?"

"No, you're not," her father agreed.

But Sophie barely heard him because of the brief, under-his-breath comment by Nate Abbott: "St. Louis ridin'."

He dismissed her ability and her in those short syllables.

Worse, she saw the line of his shoulders relax. He was relieved. He thought he could keep her in this house, never to venture beyond it, and that suited him just fine.

She turned her shoulder to him and addressed her host.

"I am accounted a more than creditable rider, Mr. Bracken," she said. "And as Edith notes, sidesaddle is generally held as more difficult than astride, so I am satisfied that I would be able to withstand the challenges you – or anyone else – should extend to me."

"I'm sure you would, Miss Vandercook," soothed Bracken.

"We don't have any sidesaddles," Nate dropped into

the conversation with unmistakable satisfaction. "Not a one."

"That's true," Bracken said. "We've had no need for them, since Edith has refused to learn – as I know she should," he added quickly, as if Sophie were about to criticize him for failing to insist his daughter learn that ladylike skill.

"I wish I had learned now, so'd we'd have a saddle for Sophie," Edith said. "Not that I'd ride that way, because it's like being all twisted up on top of the horse. Why, when Charlotte Shrieve comes ridin' in to a party or such, she looks like – Pa! That's what we'll do. We'll send to the TS and ask the Shrieves to lend us one of their sidesaddles for Sophie."

Mr. Bracken was nodding before she finished. "I'll write a letter right now, and Gunner can take it over."

From behind her, Sophie heard Nate's sibilant exhalation of breath, and allowed herself a smile.

"Gunner's barely broke to bridle, sir. I'm thinking he shouldn't –"

"Nonsense, Nate. You're always saying what a good head he has, and what a hard worker he is. Let the boy stretch his legs a bit. Should be back in two, three days."

Sophie turned to the girl, adding the final punctuation. "Thank you for that excellent solution, Edith. It will be such a delight to explore your ranch with your father and you."

CHAPTER TWELVE

The sidesaddle arrived in four days, along with the TS Ranch owner, his wife, two daughters bracketing Edith in age and a young son. The elder son, they were told, was left in charge while the rest of the family came to meet the visitor from St. Louis.

Sophie's widened eyes when Gunner rode in ahead of the others to deliver the news displayed her surprise at this large a party traveling two days to meet her, with the prospect of a return journey of two more days.

Just showed how little she knew of Wyoming Territory.

Nate, on the other hand, counted himself lucky the entire outfit wasn't showing up.

He figured Newell, the TS foreman, would be setting up nights with a shotgun to keep his hands from all slipping away to the OS for a chance to see the young lady from St. Louis.

To give her credit, Sophie immediately recognized that common sense dictated that with such a long a journey, the Shrieve family would stay overnight. She got right in there with Edith, doing whatever it was females did to get ready for guests. Doughy, he could understand. He was cooking up a storm to uphold his reputation, and the reputation of the OS Ranch.

When Bracken declared they'd hold a dance that night to entertain their guests, Nate swallowed a groan.

But he didn't hold back in chewing on Tinhorn for delaying departure to meet with two other outfits' reps headed to another roundup. Gave him hell for making the other reps wait a day and more, just so he could do some dancing.

Without leaving off admiring himself in a bit of mirror, Tinhorn gave back a line of palaver about how he couldn't deny the ladies the pleasure of having one decent dance partner.

That didn't get more notice than a gnat from Nate, but then Tinhorn pointed out the other two reps were on the back porch of the bunkhouse that very moment washing up for the night's doings. Somehow they'd decided to show up here instead of going to the meeting place.

When three hands from the Double S showed up and Oscar Johnson from town said he was passing this way so he brought their mail, Nate knew the word was getting around by more than a whisper on the Wyoming wind.

For Nate's part, he did his best to keep every OS hand as busy as he could all the rest of that day. It was a losing battle, as they slipped off soon as his back turned to clean up and put on their best clothes. On top of that, boys he'd've expected to stay out on the range overnight or longer started showing up with one lame excuse or another. Not a one admitted that somebody was spreading the word – for all they'd tell their foreman, they'd had no idea in the world there was fixing to be a dance that night at the home ranch.

Still, Nate kept trying to keep the OS boys' hands occupied with what needed doing – wasn't much he could do about their heads – because there'd be darned little accomplished tomorrow, either. And roundup was coming up on them like an avalanche.

Soon came the time when he was the only soul left who wasn't in the main house.

No sense being a martyr.

He put on a clean shirt, his good vest and gave his boots a swipe. That would have to do for ... whoever might notice.

"Nate!" Doughy called from the other side of the kitchen as he stepped inside. "We gave up on you."

He could see that. The table had already been pushed against the wall, and the chairs with it. And through the doorway he could see the office and parlor had received the same treatment. It allowed a careful dancer and his partner to promenade from one side of the house to the other.

Mr. Bracken was doing exactly that, with Sophie at his side, followed by Mr. and Mrs. Shrieve, their daughters and a couple of hands, then Edith and Gunner. Cowhands, lined up in each room, clapped and whooped in time to String's mouth organ.

Sophie wore the red top he'd likened to a cardinal bird. Now she looked even more like one, with more red swooped and tied around her skirt and over a bigger bustle than she'd worn before.

She looked more distant somehow, yet with her eyes shining, and her face glowing with pleasure, it was like she was calling to him to close that distance.

"Saved you some supper," Doughy added, pointing to a cloth-draped plate on the back of the stove. "And there's cake and such."

The *cakes and such* loaded the table as much as any dinner.

"You've done yourself proud, Doughy," Nate said. "And thanks for the supper."

He ate in the corner by the stove, watching the gaiety, moving when the heat got intolerable. Got that way for the dancers, too, so doors and windows were thrown open.

While Tinhorn partnered Sophie, with a hand clasped tighter at her waist than necessary, Nate decided it was a good time to move through the rooms, passing a few words here and there, reminding the hands from other outfits that there'd be no drinking this night, and having the satisfaction of seeing a flask get slipped back into a pocket of a jacket hanging over a chair.

Mr. Shrieve had brought his fiddle, and he soon retired from the dancing to join with String. They sat on the steps of the stairway, a nice solid seat, out of the way of the dancers and with plenty of elbow room.

Mrs. Shrieve sat out a dance or two, then started up again. There was no sitting for any of the other ladies, even little Hattie Shrieve.

Six or seven dances in, Nate found himself standing next to Mr. Bracken, and passed a casual comment.

At the end of that tune, the OS owner held up his arms, and shouted, gathering attention.

"It's been pointed out that it isn't right that our affianced couple doesn't have the chance to have a dance together."

Cheers, catcalls and whoops drowned out the rest of what he said, but soon enough a hand from the TS pulled out his own mouth organ and took String's seat, while String stood before Sophie.

"If you're going to look like you're going to your own hanging, String, I'll dance with her myself," shouted Tinhorn.

That was greeted by boos and comments that he'd already had his turn, and everybody got to dance with Sophie once before anybody got a second turn. It also prompted String to tighten his mouth and take hold on Sophie like a maverick he expected to have to fight to the ground before getting a brand on it.

The music started – not half as good as String's, but that was all right.

By some unspoken agreement, only Sophie and String

danced, everyone else encircling them and watching. Nate, too.

Sophie looked up to String's face, said something low, and smiled.

Nate let out a long breath. And even then it was only a slice of how long he'd been holding it.

He'd wondered, some of these evenings, with those cozy gatherings on the porch, the music, the easy laughing and all … Listening to it as he had from a distance, not seeing what was on their faces.

But now he saw what was in her face.

And he knew he'd been right. Sophie might take String as her husband, but it wasn't for anything like love. Oh, she liked him okay, but something else drove her to get String to offer for her. There he was– right back to that question of what was it that drove her?

This was a better time than most to study her, trying to figure that out. He wasn't taking any time from work. And everyone else was watching, too.

So he watched her, even as String returned to his playing and her new partners swirled her away. Dancing. Laughing. Talking. … Sparkling. Like sun on snow. Until it was near blinding.

Every male in the place was close enough to moonstruck as Nate ever wanted see. The two Shrieve girls fell right in line, too. That might have been surprising, considering they were females who – unlike young Edith – liked being the center of attention, and here was Sophie taking that spot.

But Nate could excuse that as Sophie having all the news to tell them about the latest fashions and such – they couldn't afford to give her dagger looks when they wanted what was in her head.

Thing was, Mrs. Shrieve, a sensible sort of woman, also seemed taken with Sophie Vandercook of St. Louis. Went so far as to corner Nate at one point and say, "Are you sure she's Vandercook's blood?"

"Seems so," he said.

Though if it came right down to it, he didn't know that for sure, either.

When Sophie laid a hand to her throat and begged Gunner to give her a moment to catch her breath before claiming his dance, Nate was watching.

And when she slipped through the other dancers forming up, passed the stairs cluttered with cowhands keeping the musicians company, and made for the hall that ran alongside the stairs toward Bracken's back bedroom, he did, too.

Was she up to something? Was she going to –?

"Oh!"

Nate supposed that's what she said, though it was more a sound than word.

She'd stopped outside Bracken's bedroom, facing away from its closed door, looking into a mirror that hung there over a little table. Her hands were raised to her hair, one hand holding up a curl that had been bouncing against her shoulder for half the night and the other poised with a pin to secure it.

Only the sound she made had kept Nate from walking right into her in the shadows.

Over her shoulder, his gaze met hers in the mirror. Its crackled surface minutely fragmented her image, so even here, in this unlit corner, she seemed to sparkle and shimmer as she had out in the brightness of the parlor.

He reached, because he couldn't not reach.

His fingertips gathered in the bottom of the curl she held, curving his hand around it so the softness nestled into his palm.

Without looking away from the reflection of her eyes, he was aware of a new pattern in the rising and falling of her chest, in the shorter, shallower breaths he heard coming from her parted lips. He could smell the clean dampness of her from the exertion of dancing.

She would taste that way. Clean and warm and

dazzling.

He needed that taste. Needed it now. Needed it –

"For mercy's sakes, Nate, what're you doing blocking up the hall?" Edith arrived in a breathless swirl of motion and skirts. "Pa said to open his door and window to get more cross-breeze with the front door."

Nate stepped to the very back of the hall to let Edith past. Before he could do more, he heard the window flung open, and the girl was back.

"Sophie? Is that you? What're you doing?"

"Repinning my hair –"

"How on earth can you see back here to – Oh, so you finally made it, Arnie. Land sakes you're slow. Told you I'd have the window open and be back before you could stir yourself."

The young hand from the Double S ranch hurtled down the hall toward them, peering in an attempt to adjust to the same abrupt plunge into dimness that nearly resulted in Nate running over Sophie.

Arnie homed in on Edith, an angled shaft of light catching her in the open doorway, while shadows obscured Sophie and Nate.

"But you're not back," he said, "so I get to claim a forfeit."

Edith's eyes were bright, her cheeks glowed with color. Something like shock prickled through Nate. He'd known she was growing up. A man with seven sisters couldn't miss that. But this – this was something he had missed. The girl would be a beauty someday. And someday was coming fast.

"What forfeit?" she demanded.

"Oh, I got some ideas."

Nate's focus snapped to Arnie at his tone, and he saw the cowhand's gaze was latched onto another consequence of all the dancing Edith Bracken had been doing – she was breathing hard, straining against the buttons of a too-small bodice that was trying to contain her gently swelling bosom.

One stride brought Nate out of the shadows and squarely between Arnie and Edith.

Even in this light, Nate saw Arnie's eyes flare and his cheeks darken. He immediately backed up two steps, his hands raised in innocence, placation and surrender.

Nate was forming words that would drive home his point to the hand without stirring Edith to either recognition or – heaven help them all – rebellion when the girl pushed him aside.

"That's okay, Nate. I'm not giving up no forfeit. I won fair and square. So you'll get me that lemonade like you promised, Arnie, and that's that."

She punched the cowhand in the shoulder as she passed him and headed back to the dancing, entirely unaware.

Nate held the younger man's gaze a second more with his glare. "And that's all. Ever."

Arnie gulped and nodded before following Edith. But not too closely.

Nate meant to walk away then, to follow Edith, maybe. But as he turned, his gaze tangled with Sophie's again, though in an entirely different way and with no mirror between them now.

She spoke. "Her father needs to–"

He shook his head.

"Then someone –"

"If you think I'm going to – No. I'll drive off the rustlers, but ... no."

She sighed.

And he heard himself say, "Thank you, Sophie."

Sophie Vandercook danced all night.

Stopping only when Doughy served a breakfast that did the OS Ranch proud, just as the sky lightened slightly behind a curtain of bulky clouds.

He would have danced with Edith or any of the others if they'd lacked for partners. But Nate Abbott wasn't a man to stand in line waiting.

That's what he told him himself, standing on the front steps, after handing up Charlotte and Hattie to the wagon while Mr. Bracken performed the same service for Mrs. Shrieve. Mulehead and Gunner brought rocks Doughy had heated in the stove to help the travelers fight the chill, unseasonable for even this hour of the morning. Most of the hands had headed out as soon as breakfast was done to put in their day's work, fully willing to have forfeited a night's sleep for the pleasures.

The Shrieves in the wagon called out their thanks and invitations to come to the TS any time. Edith and Bracken and Sophie and the remaining boys on the porch behind him returned the calls. The calls stretched out, harder to hear as the figures in the wagon grew smaller and smaller.

Nate heard the others troop inside, but he watched until he couldn't make out the wagon, leaving the others time to sort themselves out inside before he went in to tell Mr. Bracken what he and Mr. Shrieve had discussed about the roundup.

He turned and reached the top step before he saw Sophie.

She'd apparently dropped into the nearest chair, sitting almost sideways, her head propped against the wall of the house, her arms wrapped around herself against the morning chill.

Sound asleep.

He looked toward the door. Somebody would notice she wasn't inside. Somebody would come through the door any second, looking for her. Somebody who'd take care of the situation. Somebody other than him.

No one did.

The chill wouldn't lift for a while yet, maybe not at all with the day's clouds.

He made the scolding sound he gave the young horse he was training up when it went wrong way round on a skittering heifer. Then he walked to where she sat, took off his vest and set it around her.

She seemed to ease from its warmth, arms relaxing, the dip between her brows disappearing.

He tucked it better, only because it looked to slide off her any second.

When he realized he was standing there watching her for no good reason, he spun away and headed down the stairs. But he didn't hit his usual stride until he reached the packed earth beyond the porch, where the ground would muffle the thud of boot heels.

The sidesaddle brought by the Shrieves appeared to have been broken-in well before Sophie had been born. However, having been kept in good repair, it was serviceable.

There was no thought of riding on the day the Shrieves left, as every soul on the OS did both that day's work and filled in gaps left by the previous day's gaiety. Setting the house back to rights fully occupied Sophie and Edith.

That is, it did once Sophie woke from her nap on the porch.

She was startled to discover herself snuggled under a vest she immediately knew to be Nate's.

She could not imagine how it had come to be there, holding off what was an unusually brisk breeze.

In addition to that mystery, she quickly realized that it presented her the problem of how to return it.

Last night's vision of Nate, caught in the mirror beside her image arose. The lack of light had carved his face to essentials, with only his eyes bright and clear. They had looked into hers through the reflection and she had felt —

No. She had been tired. All that dancing. And in the

dark, she could not have seen, she could not have felt ... Anything.

She shook her head, clearing it.

She needed a plan for returning the vest to its owner.

Going to the bunkhouse was out of the question. Even Edith knew that was not the place for a young lady to visit.

Nor did it seem right to retain it until he asked for it back. Such a request from him, no doubt in front of others, could be ... awkward.

She was, after all, promised to another man. And to be asked to return an article of clothing, even though she had not requested its loan, and even though it was an article of outerwear ... well, not precisely outerwear, since it had clearly been close enough to his skin to carry a scent that she– Not that it mattered. Yet, it would be awkward to return it in front of others.

So she folded it and put it beneath the cushion on the porch swing to await an opportunity. It came not long before dinner, when Doughy went to tend the chickens, while Edith was helping Mr. Bracken return chairs to his office.

She entered the kitchen and put the vest over the back of Nate's usual chair. Then she brought in the last chairs from the porch, arriving back in the kitchen in time to take her seat as the men began to enter.

She was wishing String a good day when Nate came in. His gaze went to his chair and he flicked her a look. At least a flick was all she caught of it before she looked away.

The sound of his chair pulling in tugged her gaze back to him. This time she didn't look away.

And in his eyes, she somehow found the scent and the warmth of his vest – of him – again. It sank into her.

Sophie cast about for something – anything – that would make him look away, so that she might, too.

"I am so looking forward," she heard her own voice say, though in a high, brittle tone she could not like, "to exploring the OS, now that I have a sidesaddle."

That succeeded better than she could have ever hoped.

He dropped his gaze to his plate, and did not look at her again during the meal. Nor when he finished, stood, and put on his hat.

He reached for the vest. His hand hesitated. Not even half a heartbeat, yet she knew it. And it made her wonder –

From under the brim of his hat, his eyes met hers again as he slowly slid first one arm, then the other into the vest. A burning in her chest spread in pulses down her, leaving her limbs weak and weighted.

It was the same burning she had experienced last night in front of the mirror.

But she was not tired out from dancing, and it was not a dark hallway where she could be mistaken in a look.

She knew she was not the only one who felt this burning.

⚬⚬⚬⚬

Sophie had to curb her eagerness to ride, as rain fell with resolute concentration the next afternoon. Maddeningly, it ceased that night before bringing another day of rain today. And now it appeared to be following the same pattern, with the sky lightening just in time for the sun to set.

"And did you see the way she simpered at Gunner? About made me sick."

Edith had spent a good portion of the past two days divided between deriding the behavior, clothing and looks of Charlotte and Hattie Shrieve and lamenting that she could never look so fine.

"Which she?"

"Hattie, the younger one."

"Ah."

"It was the older one – Charlotte – who kept trying to get Nate to dance with her. You should have seen Tinhorn's face when he realized she was trying to set a

124

loop over Nate and not him! Lester said she was like a female dog in –"

"Enough!"

The girl blinked at her. Sophie assumed her best classroom manner. "Edith, do you truly want to be more ladylike?"

Wariness settled on the girl. "Maybe." That emerged slowly, but her next words came in a rush. "But not if it means I can't ride and rope and such. I don't want to be like them that way. They can't hardly do nothing–"

"Anything."

"Anything except female things."

"Nor can I."

"But you're – you're a real lady."

Smiling, Sophie said, "Thank you. If you care for it, I can share elements that are suited to the more mature young lady you are becoming – nothing that would interfere in your other activities," she added hurriedly.

With that assurance, Edith agreed.

Doughy grumbled some at their raiding his kitchen, but then cooperated by contributing not only salt and baking soda for Edith to brush her teeth regularly, but also borax, butter, egg whites and even the rind of an orange, which he heated and squeezed to release several drops of fragrance.

Sophie combined these ingredients with grated soap and some of the scant store of lotions she had brought with her in varied quantities for Edith to cleanse her face, then to apply to both face and hands each night.

At the same time, she set elementary rules for Edith: The cleansing routine every day and night, neat hair, neat clothes, gloves as well as the hat at all times when outdoors, and proper language.

After cleansing, the girl was so taken with her reflection as Sophie braided her hair neatly, that she agreed readily.

Edith arrived at breakfast the next morning with an air of expectation that disintegrated to crestfallen as not a single face turned her way except for Sophie's.

Sophie smiled encouragingly, and said, "Your father has good news, Edith."

"It's a fine day, and as soon as you've finished up the meal and are ready, we shall head out, and Miss Vandercook will finally have the chance to use that sidesaddle."

Edith finished eating almost as quickly as the fastest of the hands, and was nearly out the door.

"Edith?" Sophie called.

"I know – hat and gloves!" the girl scooped up the items and was gone before Sophie could say more.

Sophie went upstairs to change her attire. At Mrs. Forestell's Academy, she and Alice and Louisa would help with such matters as tightening corset ties, though she could certainly manage without help – she refused to be such a slave to fashion. Now, wearing her traveling corset – and with even that looser than she would usually employ – she entertained a notion that her casualness might shock her friends.

She hesitated only a moment before discarding the jaunty hat that went with her riding suit for a broad-brimmed hat Edith had so generously given her, using three hat pins to ensure it would remain in place.

CHAPTER THIRTEEN

The kitchen was empty. Outside, she discovered Nate Abbott standing in the yard, hugging the shade of the house, and holding in one hand the reins to a horse she recognized as one of his usual mounts, and in the other hand the reins to a gray-muzzled animal she felt sure Edith would categorize as a plug.

"Good day," she said carefully.

He tipped his hat, and said nothing. She looked past him, surveying the yard for her host.

"You ready to go finally?" Nate asked. Not with any patience.

"Yes. As soon as Mr. Bracken arrives, we'll depart."

"He's not arriving. He's left. Said to ride out with you and show you the operation."

"Oh."

"Course if you'd rather not …"

She regarded him steadily. "I was, naturally, anticipating the pleasure of Mr. Bracken's congenial company for this outing. However, seeing portions of the ranch beyond this immediate vicinity is an object worth any inconvenience —." She let that linger an extra instant to let him draw his own conclusions as to her meaning, before adding. "—even forgoing Mr. Bracken's company."

She regarded the horse, and decided that it was even older than the saddle. Sophie certainly need have no fear about this ancient equine rearing or bolting. It would be getting the animal moving that would test her horsemanship.

But, she consoled herself, at least that would make mounting no difficulty.

That consolation evaporated as she realized she and Nate Abbott appeared to be the only persons in the vicinity, which meant he would have to help her.

As if recognizing that fact as well, he glared at the sidesaddle, and mumbled, "Real practical this is for this country."

He bent his back, lacing his fingers together and presenting them as a cup for her foot.

Staring at the crown of his hat, she didn't budge.

She was most accustomed to mounting with one groom holding the horse's head, while a second assisted her into the saddle. That precaution taken for restive horses clearly was not necessary here. And, indeed, she had experience mounting with only a single assistant. Yet she found herself hesitating.

"I can mount from a block." Her words came out in a hurry, as if she had only breath for one word so ran them all together.

He straightened, then made a show of making a circular survey of the area. "No mounting blocks here, Miss Vandercook."

"I can use the steps by the house," she said. "Or that log behind the shed. Or the lower rail of the fence."

She wasn't at all sure of the third option, but trying it struck her as preferable to relying on him.

"There won't be any steps out on the range. If we can't get you into this saddle, the two of us, then you can't ride." He said it flatly, but beneath there was a hint of satisfaction.

Discovering that relying on him was preferable to – what was the phrase he'd used about the sun that first evening? – turning tail, she gritted her teeth.

"Very well, Mr. Abbott."

Reaching past him, she gathered the reins into her right hand, since he had not seen fit to hand them to her, and reached up to the pommel. Thus equipped, she met his gaze with her eyebrows slightly raised.

She could see only the glint of his eyes under the brim of his ever-present hat, and his mouth was a straight, unrevealing line. Yet she had some sense from the rise and fall of his chest that he was not best pleased. That improved her spirits.

"Mr. Abbott?" she prodded.

He grunted and bent once more, relacing his fingers.

Here she came to an impasse. She would ordinarily rest her hand on his shoulder …

She firmed her mouth and did just that.

His head started to come up, then stopped, for which she was grateful.

"One, two, three."

On the final number, he lifted up, higher and faster than she was accustomed to. With no effort of her own, she remained there, seeming suspended.

"Are you –?"

His first syllable brought her back to herself. She pivoted, and seated herself in the saddle, both knees to the left.

He grunted and straightened, then turned away. And moved toward his horse.

"Mr. Abbott."

"What?"

With the greater elevation of his lift she had placed her right knee correctly over the second fork of the saddle, so she did not require any assistance with holding her right boot. Her left foot, however, swung free.

"The stirrup."

"You can't even get a foot in the stirrup in that fool contraption?"

She maintained a coolly dignified silence, since any fool could answer that question without any further explanation from her.

He grumbled something more, which she chose not to hear, and returned to her side. He batted the hem of her riding skirt aside, sending it swinging.

"Mr. Abbott!"

"Don't go getting your bristles up, it's not like I ain't seen petticoats before."

He grasped her booted foot – not by the heel of the boot as he should have, but by cupping his large hand around the back of her heel – and slid it into the stirrup with more force than finesse.

She could not possibly feel his hand through the leather of her boot. Certainly not more than a slight pressure. Definitely not heat. So the heat she felt, rushing from her heel, through her body to her cheeks, had to be outrage.

"Well?"

He'd asked her a question, and she hadn't responded, because she hadn't heard. "I beg your pardon?" she managed.

"Is the length right?" His surly demand came from under the brim of his hat as he appeared to stare at her boot. Without releasing his hold on her heel, he tugged at the stirrup, and she realized he'd shortened it. "No telling with this thing."

"Yes." She swallowed against dryness in her throat. "That is a good length."

At last he removed his hand from her heel, quickly tightening the strap to hold the stirrup in place.

"Lot of good this'd do you if you really had to get somewhere on this piece of broken-down –"

Rather than finish his deprecation of her mount, he tugged one last time as a check on the strap, then he patted it, the stirrup where it arched over her foot, and then her ankle.

Heat followed the path through her that it had already blazed with a speed she could not fathom, setting off sparks in side paths not previously visited.

She tried to swallow. This time her throat would not work.

He had crossed to his horse and mounted before she could gather any words.

She opened her mouth to express outrage at the liberties he had taken.

What came out instead was: "I – I did not bring my whip in my baggage. May I borrow one?"

"No." He turned his horse and tossed the rest of his answer over his shoulder without looking at her. "Jester wouldn't know what to make of it, and you can't borrow what we don't have. We use spurs. You'll just have to go at Jester's pace."

ↁↂↁ

Jester's pace matched a tortoise's. A tired tortoise's.

Whatever frustration she must have felt at that seemed to evaporate quickly, though Nate couldn't imagine why. Because his frustration kept growing.

Sure as heck, when he stopped his horse once again and turned in the saddle to wait for Jester to plod his way forward, Sophie presented an expression of bland pleasure.

The fourth time this occurred, she remarked in that schoolmarm-being-patient-with-the-dunce voice she only used at him, "If you would please proceed before Jester catches up with your mount, I believe we will get on at a better rate, Mr. Abbott. When Jester does catch up with your mount, he stops, having achieved his goal, and I can assure you that it is more difficult to restart him than it is to urge him to continue walking."

Nate grumbled a great deal under his breath – and he

didn't miss that it appeared to brighten her mood considerably – but followed her suggestion.

Determined to give her no further satisfaction, he clamped down on his dissatisfaction with the pace.

But he felt it – oh, yes, he felt it. They weren't just burning precious daylight, they had a bonfire lit under it. And he had the added irritant of having been responsible because he'd picked Jester for her.

Served him right.

The words weren't spoken, but he heard her voice saying them well enough, like a cloud of sound at his back all the way along the track.

In this manner, they arrived at the crest of a ridge that was the last main obstacle to their destination.

Before them lay a rough bowl of land. It could have been the work of a very inexperienced potter, with the far side tilted higher than this ridge. That western edge was part of the climbing land reaching toward the snow-capped Big Horn Mountains. A creek of good water came down from the mountains, ran east for a while at the northern rim of their bowl, then turned near due south below this eastern rim where they were and it gave rise to a line of cottonwoods whose tops were nearly at their feet.

The potter hadn't been any better at forming the bottom of the bowl – it dipped and rose with no sense or pattern the human eye could divine. Some of those dips and crannies, though, gave rise to good grass, even if they did make driving a herd through a cause for constant vigilance so you didn't end up with a solitary animal in every last dip and cranny.

Naturally, the first thing his eyes went to was the herd being trailed across the creek at the northern edge of the bowl. They were holding together for now, but he was glad to see String and some of the other boys were nearly to the herd to help keep it tight through this section and on to a more open valley to the south.

"It's not the least bit pretty, is it?" Sophie said from

beside him.

The words belonged to a complaint, but the way she said them made it far more than any compliment. She had that solemn note in her voice, like she had the first evening watching the sunset on the porch.

Harsh beauty she'd said.

It had been strange hearing her quote his words back to him. He'd written them never thinking to meet the person who read them, much less to hear her voice giving them a power he'd never expected. She'd said them in such a way it could remind someone of being in a church. Only it was bigger and deeper and wider than any church he'd ever been in. Except this one. This one right here, under the open sky.

All that she'd said in those few words.

Made a man edgy.

"Ain't the place for ruffles and bows and such, so, no, it ain't pretty."

"I did not mean–" She turned her head and shoulders toward him, having to look up from Jester's low back, just the way she did when they were standing side by side. Then she said with all the impatience gone. "Oh. I see."

He held on long as a man could. "What's that mean?"

"It means precisely what I said: I see."

"See what?"

"Far more than you would like, I'm sure."

And then, just as he looked at her, the infernal woman turned away so he couldn't see what in thunderation she meant by that.

"Shall we ride on?" she asked.

What choice did he have?

⚬⚬⚬

Sophie wrinkled her nose as a shift in the ever-present wind brought a swell of odor and dust, then was relieved to find that Nate had not caught the gesture. She needn't have concerned herself; he had seldom looked at her since they'd left the home ranch.

Except, perhaps, when they crossed the creek at the bottom of the ridge where they had paused.

Then he'd issued warnings about the swiftness of the flow, the depth of the water if she didn't precisely follow his directions, and the danger if she should be unseated among the rocks that marked the creek.

The last point was laughable. She was far more likely to have been stranded on the spot until Jester drew his last breath than to have the horse bolt enough to unseat her.

There was one moment when a rock slid out from under Jester's hoof and his hindquarters started to drop as if he intended to sit down. She had quickly shifted her weight forward while commanding him to go forward. Jester had resumed before Nate reached her side, his outstretched arm falling back to his side.

"Good." That's all he'd said. Yet she'd had to resist a giddy inclination to laugh.

Now he rested one forearm on the large pommel of his saddle, which the men called a horn, and crossed the other forearm atop it, leaning forward in an attitude of complete ease.

More than ease, though, was the sense of belonging, of ownership she'd seen in him as he'd first looked out across this low land toward a distant, moving black dot.

His tone held complacency as he said, "There they are."

The herd. Moving from north to south.

For the first time, it occurred to her to wonder why.

"Is this the roundup Edith has been talking about?"

He snorted. "Not hardly. This is a mixed herd from a roundup a ways north. We're trailing 'em home, then we'll sort them when our roundup happens."

"Sort them. That's by the brand?"

"Yep." He glanced toward her, then settled more in his saddle. "Cows don't stay where they're put and they don't care which outfit they're with. Plus, they wander, specially in bad weather. So we sort them by brand at roundups around the territory. Each outfit sends a rep to the other roundups to claim his home brand's cows, then gets up with some reps heading the same way and trails 'em back together so there's enough riders. That's where some of the boys have been this past week. They'll head out again for other roundups just before we have ours."

He tipped his head toward the land before them. "This valley can be near as bad as a bog hole for losing cattle if you don't keep 'em tight. You could take a week to gather 'em all up again if they break, so we got extra hands riding 'em through to the south."

She considered that.

The moving black dot slowly had resolved itself into a herd of cattle. A churning dark mass obscured by the constant cloud of dust hovering around it.

"How do you keep the brands apart?"

"Don't. Not for trailing 'em back. We'll do that at the roundup. Divide this herd up, plus a herd coming up from the south and everything we gather in between."

Here and there she recognized a taller form as a horse and rider along either side of the mass, harassing the cows to keep the herd narrowing toward its front.

"They only need to persuade that ol' mossy which way to go," Nate explained. "The rest of the critters mostly follow along."

"The old mossy is the lead bull?"

"A steer, not a bull. Bull's too easily distracted by a cow twitching her tail to take lead."

Sophie felt her cheeks heat at his language, though he had been almost absent-minded as he'd said it.

"Tinhorn should be tighter on flank," he muttered.

Just then, a bulge of cattle pushed out on the far side of the herd, and Sophie saw two more riders join the figure she believed was Jasper Tinton in urging the truants back into the main group.

That first figure swept his hat off his head and waved it

toward them.

"Darned fool," Nate muttered. "He'll get 'em all riled up."

Her first thought had been to ignore the gesture, but now she raised her hand in an answering salute. "It's very gallant."

"Won't think it's so da—dashed gallant if he starts a stampede."

Considering that he settled deeper into his saddle and tugged his hat lower over her eyes, she concluded that he had no such fear.

Now, she could make out a few of the individual animals that were swinging wider than the main mass and thus were not lost in the haze of dust.

"They are not very –" She searched for a description. "—attractive or dignified creatures."

"Attractive? Dignified?" He twisted in the saddle to glare at her. "They're cows, not some foolish romantic creature out of a picture book. What are you expecting? Some fantasy creature from some myth?"

"I said nothing about romance or fantasy. I merely commented on their less than presupposing appearance."

"You remind me of my sisters," he grumbled, by way of not acknowledging that he'd been unfair.

She raised one eyebrow. "They are clearly, then, women of great forbearance."

"Forbearance? They never had anything to forbear in their lives. Spoiled silly, that's what they are."

"I have had quite enough of your surly disposition today, Mr. Abbott. I shall spare myself any more of it and spare you my *silly* presence and ride back–"

He grabbed the reins, preventing her from turning Jester's reluctant head. "I didn't say you were silly. I said they were spoiled silly," he said, goaded.

"And since you are reminded of them while talking to me, you are saying that I am spoiled silly." She pronounced the phrase as if it were sour on her tongue.

He looked out toward the horizon, then let out a long breath through his teeth. "No, you're not spoiled or silly. I beg your pardon, Ma'am."

Her eyes stung. Though why they should when he'd offered a formal apology rather then while he'd been unfairly berating her she couldn't imagine.

"I accept your apology," she said. "Under the circumstances, however, I think we would both be better served if we part and I return to the home ranch. So, if you'll release the reins—"

"No."

"Do not treat me like a child." She'd flared up like tinder, and it took her a pair of quick breaths to regain herself. "You accord young Edith a freedom that you would deny to me —"

"Edith was born here. Knows it as well as any hand in the outfit. Better than her father. And she knows what'll happen if she doesn't heed me — no questions asked, no conversation."

"I am neither a child nor one of your underlings to be ordered about. Release the reins —"

"No," he repeated.

In fact, instead of releasing the reins he shifted his grip on them in his gloved hands at the same time he maneuvered his horse around so the beasts were headed opposite directions, yet side by side and almost touching. The result was that she and Nate faced each other across only the distance of her side-slung legs.

He tipped his head slightly and the blaze of his blue eyes reached out from under his hat's brim shadow.

"You listen to me hard, Sophie Vandercook. It seems like whenever I open my mouth something comes out that has you flapping your wings like a hawk on the attack, but this time, you just listen. You are a newcomer in a country you know nothing about. There are dangers here — dangers from men and animals and too little water or too much of it. And dangers from things you might never think about, like sun and wind and dust. This is not a place for you to be ridin' on your own. Not back to the home ranch now, not out from the home ranch to look around a bit on your own any time, not visiting another ranch. Not anywhere, not anytime. I know this country, and you don't, and I want your word on this, Sophie."

She swallowed, but she didn't look away. "Yes, I give you my word."

A flutter of dismay set up in her throat, not unlike the hawk wings he'd mentioned. What had passed between them just then? It was more than her agreeing to bide by his strictures for her safety, but what was it?

Nate did not appear to experience any such reaction.

"Good." He released Jester's reins, calmly turned his horse again so they were headed the same direction and said, "Well, then. Let's take that rise over there, so we can get a better view."

They dropped into a gully before the rise to the south he'd mentioned.

"What's that?"

His face darkened. "Carcass."

What she had taken at first for a scattered pile of branches, she now recognized as bleached bones. Many bleached bones.

"Cattle? But this must be –"

"Hundred head, maybe more."

"Why? What happened?"

He didn't respond until they were at the crest of the rise, their backs to the remains below.

"You want just what happened at the end, or the whole thing?"

She considered that. "Tell me what happened at the end. Then I'll decide on the other."

His forearm hid his face as he adjusted his hat, but she'd already seen the twitch of his mouth, though why he might find her prudent caution amusing she could not imagine.

CHAPTER FOURTEEN

"The winter before last is what happened at the end," Nate said, his voice without emotion. "It started before '86 was near done and come January it hit harder than anything anybody'd ever seen. I hope to never again see the sights that spring thaw revealed. Bones and hides of animals frozen in their tracks, and even more starved before they froze.

"And not just cattle. Most every outfit around lost a man or two. There was a fella here, took me in hand when I first came to Wyoming territory. Abel Duckworth. Old Ducker tried to make it to the barn to see after a sick horse. Fell and broke his leg. Snow was coming so fast, tracks filled in as soon as they were made. We found him, but fever set in, and that was that."

His profile as grim as his voice, he shifted in the saddle, staring out toward sunlight chasing cloud shadows across the heat-shimmering ground. Yet Sophie would swear the shiver that ran through her was from cold.

"I don't recall hearing about such a horrible winter for the cattle business. Though, I must add in fairness, that previous to this, when given opportunities to read articles about the business, I gladly passed them by."

His grunt held soured amusement. "Wouldn't have mattered if you'd read everything you could get your hands on during that winter. Most of the reports were saying five, six, maybe fifteen percent losses. But that's what the big outfits wanted their investors back East and overseas to think."

"It was far worse than that?"

"More like fifty percent."

She sucked in a breath. "But can a business survive fifty percent losses?"

"A lot didn't. Especially when last summer was drier than most."

"But the OS ...?"

"Mr. Bracken didn't stretch himself anywhere near what the big outfits did before '86. He knew the way the cattle business started here wasn't going to be the way it went on forever. So we started out some better. We fed hay some of that winter, and that helped, too. And we were just plain lucky that some head found shelter. We lost maybe twenty percent.

"Since last spring Mr. Bracken's been buying up head from some of the outfits breaking up. Careful like. Not a lot at once. Mixing some from one herd and another. Crossing the ones too tough to die with those that'll be worth the eating. So now ... "

She prodded. "So now?"

He glanced at her. "So now we see if it's going to pay off, or if the OS is just slower going down than those other outfits."

She considered what he'd said, mixing it with comments made since she'd arrived as well as phrases from Jer– no, from Nate Abbott's letters.

"And this roundup that will be held shortly will deliver that verdict?"

"It'll go a long way toward it. The real test'll be the fall roundup. Then trailing the herd to market. Deciding which railhead to take 'em to and which route to take. Choosing to go straight across water that's running deeper than usual or go Powder River where it's an inch deep and a mile wide. Any way you chose, you lose time, animals and men. There're more ways to go out of the cattle business than there are kinds of cows."

His gaze cut to something beyond her right shoulder. She twisted further around in the sidesaddle to see what.

Who, not what, she corrected herself – her host. If not for the sound of the nearby cattle, she would have heard the approach of his horse at a rapid trot.

"How was your ride out, Miss Vandercook?"

"I could not have asked for a more sedate mount," she said solemnly.

A slight frown quickly turned to surprise as he looked toward his foreman. "Jester? But you said –"

"Didn't want to take any chances with Miss Vandercook's safety, just like you said," Nate interposed swiftly. "And Jester's solid as they come."

Sophie nodded. "As solid as a rock, which he strongly resembles."

Mr. Bracken chuckled. "I did say not to take chances, but if she pleases and if your assessment is that she would be safe, surely another horse could be found for Miss Vandercook."

"Thank you, Mr. Bracken," she said with feeling.

"Yes, sir. Now that you're here, you can accompany Miss Vandercook and judge for yourself which –"

"Sorry, Nate. I've got to ride out toward Far Hills. Ezrah Shrieve said the other night that the creek's out of its banks at the Susland crossing. I want to see where else we can ford."

"I could go and –"

"No, no. You're needed here far more than I am. I can check the creek, but you can get the herd through if there's any trouble."

"Miss Vandercook might like seeing –"

"No, no. You two stay here, let her get a taste of what working cattle's all about." Facing her, he added, "You could not ask for a better instructor in the subject than Nate here, Miss Vandercook."

He raised his hat to her, wished them a pleasant time, and was off.

His parting words reminded her of comments Edith had made about Nate being the final word when it came to cattle and horses on the OS Ranch.

She resettled herself in the saddle. "I should like to hear the whole thing now, Mr. Abbott."

He did her the courtesy of not asking if she was sure, nor of making his comments simple.

He told her how cattle had come to Wyoming from Texas, how early success had led to the range being overstocked, which – combined with the weather – left sparse grass. He told her how the days of the wide-open range were over for sure. That fence was coming no matter how hard some fought it. But that with that end were also coming opportunities for cattlemen who used their heads.

She had previously not found any fascination in the matter of breeding, raising, tending and selling livestock. Now she discovered it was a far more compelling enterprise than she ever would have thought.

Although the animals were still far from handsome.

✦

They moved south along a series of ridges, parallel to the herd and ahead of it.

At some distance from the main body of the herd she noticed another grouping, this time of horses, and driven by only two cowboys.

"Horses also wander during the winter?" she asked.

"They do, but they're rounded up first thing when

winter breaks. Can't do a lick without the horses. That –"
Nate tipped head toward it. "–is the remuda."

"Remuda."

"The hands' working horses. Sort of like a moving corral."

"All those horses for so few men?"

"Horses work hard on the OS – except for Jester." Before he turned away she caught the twitch of his lips. "Need to let 'em rest or they're not much good. Besides, the boys need different horses for different work. So each hand has six or seven in his string."

He shifted in the saddle, directing his attention fully on her for no reason she could fathom.

She gazed at him, recognizing that she was at a distinct disadvantage. The wide brim of his hat cast shadow that allowed only glints of light from his eyes to escape, while her countenance no doubt was fully visible to him.

A disadvantage, however, did not spell defeat. She held the look until his shifted away, sweeping over the activity before him.

"You know that's how your future husband got his name," he said.

Ah. He apparently expected her to forfeit her composure at the reference to String. She followed the direction of his gaze, and there, not far away was String, riding a small cowpony that should have looked ridiculous mounted by his long frame, but did not.

"I should like to hear that account."

Nate stood in his stirrups and hollered so loud that even Jester shifted his feet.

String trotted over. Before he'd finished tipping his hat to her, Nate was saying, "I was just about to tell how you got your name. Why don't you sit out a bit, spend some time with Miss Vandercook, tell her the details and –"

"Can't. Working a new horse."

"But –"

"Need to work him tired. So he's not thinkin' too

much."

"I could–"

"Can't let him rest up. Gotta go." He tipped his hat again and made good on his words.

Into the silence left by his departure, Sophie said, "Since he is otherwise occupied, I shall impose on you to hear the tale of how String came by that name."

"We'll move on first."

This shift brought them to a knoll that stood sentry at a narrow opening to flatter, open ground to the south. From here, they would see the herd approach, funnel through the gap and find its way into the open meadow's high grass.

"It was his first outfit after coming over from Nebraska where he'd been a boy," Nate said, unprompted. A man of his word. "He was the greenest, so they gave him the sorriest bags of bones for his string, along with one unbroke devil of a horse. And then they waited for the fun. If he complained or got thrown, there'd be chaffing from here to San Francisco."

He paused, surveying the herd as it neared the narrow opening, then gave a slight nod of satisfaction.

"But there was nothing. Not a word out of String – if you can believe that."

She smiled at that dry aside.

"And no sign he'd come near to being thrown. Now it could've happened when he was off on his own, but they were watching, and there was nothing – no scuffs on his rig or him or clothes torn or nothing. The fella telling me this had been with the outfit, too. New enough himself to be glad of seeing someone greener. And he said the regulars were fit to be tied, wondering what was happening. Finally, the ramrod ordered String to ride each of his ponies in front of the whole outfit. And each one acted better than the others, minding their manners and working like they never had before. And then it came time for the unbroke one, and all the hands thought finally –

finally – they'd have some fun.

"String put a few cows in the ring, and then he got up on the unbroke colt, and before anybody could hardly draw a breath, he reached over that colt's head and took the halter right off it, and that colt cut those cows like he'd been doing it a decade.

"Well, right then and there, the ramrod demanded to trade strings. String held out, but the ramrod insisted. It wasn't a day before the ramrod realized his new string wasn't half of what his old one was. He couldn't force String to trade back, not without losing the respect of every hand in the outfit, but he did order the strings get all shuffled around to be more *fair*. Tried that a couple times – with nobody able to ride that colt at all – before they realized any string of ponies String had was the best, so they started calling him String.

"Was a year maybe more after I heard that before I asked String about it. He shrugged and said the tale was near enough to the truth to do. I asked him how he got that colt nobody could ride to cut cows that way, no halter and all. And he said he'd discovered first off that the colt went loco with both a halter and a rider. So taking the halter off was the only way to keep from chewing dirt. As for the cutting, he watched the colt, and saw it following the movements of a cow outside the corral fence, and he got a hunch. And sure enough, with a halter that colt was plumb loco, but without it he was a natural born cutter, and String just left him to do what he was born to do."

For a moment, Sophie was so caught up in listening – especially listening to a voice that seemed to come right out of the letters she'd been reading this past year – that she didn't react to the story's end.

She blinked, and found Nate looking at her with a guarded expression. He turned away, once more looking over the herd.

Nate's attention sharpened, and she followed it to see Edith, Gunner and Tinhorn in discussion on the near side of the herd.

The sound of hundreds of hoofbeats and the intermittent lows and bellows of the cattle, along with the shouts and calls of the cowhands, allowed no chance of hearing what was said. Still, it was clear to Sophie that Edith was not happy.

So she was unsurprised when the girl abruptly wheeled her horse and started it up the slope toward where they sat their mounts.

"Nate!" Edith yelled as soon as she reached the level area.

"Rein in," he ordered.

She did. Immediately. And she appeared more contrite than Sophie had ever seen her.

"Sorry, Nate. I shouldn'ta pushed Smoke up the rise like that."

"You know better. Specially with the herd about to go through the eye of the needle. You could've spooked 'em, undone all the good of this day's careful drive, all in an instant. Not to mention the waste of Smoke's hindquarters."

"Up's not so hard on 'im as down—"

"*Not so hard* is nothing to brag on, Edith."

"I know. I won't ever again. I swear. But Nate, you said I could rope some when they're in the flats, and Tinhorn says no I can't. And he and Gunner got me so angry – You gotta tell them."

A cunning look came into his eyes. "Sorry, Edith. I can't leave Miss Vandercook. Course, if you stayed here with her and I went and told the boys I'd said it was okay, a little later on, maybe –"

"*Na-aaa-ate.* I don't want to just sit and watch like some –"

"Lady?" He cut in with meaning. "Like Miss Vandercook."

Edith frowned, clearly confused at this new emphasis on ladylike behavior from Nate Abbott.

"Sorry, Sophie." That perfunctory obligation dealt with, the girl turned to Nate with pleading eyes. "But I don't want to just watch, and you promised. A real promise with none of that *later on* or *maybe* mixed in."

"Miss Vandercook —"

"For heaven's sake," Sophie interrupted. "Miss Vandercook is perfectly capable of sitting here on this plodder and watching by herself."

"Sure she is, Nate. So, I'll just ..." And Edith was gone.

Nate stared at her back for a long moment, then his mouth twitched. "If Miss Vandercook is sure she'll be okay —"

"She is."

"— and she'll stay right here unless a stampede starts heading her way. And otherwise keep her word."

"She will. Miss Vandercook keeps her promises."

He looked at her then, an unreadable expression in his eyes. "We'll see, won't we?"

She knew he was goading her about String, and yet there was something else in his tone.

His face did not look at all as it had in the mirror the night of the dance, yet she had the same odd sense of the earth beneath her feet rumbling.

"Okay then." He lifted his hat slightly, gave her a slow nod, then added, "Ma'am" before he resettled it and rode away at an easy pace.

She felt oddly warmed by the approval in his tone.

CHAPTER FIFTEEN

That evening, pleading the exertions of the day, Sophie excused herself to her room in order to write an account to Louisa and Alice.

She had rubbed out two attempts at a sketch in the margin of the letter, blotting it irredeemably. Paper was not so easily available here in Wyoming Territory that she could count on having an endless supply at hand. She pulled out a piece of the brown parcel paper she and Edith had accumulated for rough drawings, and began again.

Then another.

Man and horse and sky and distant mountains. Each element was there, and yet it entirely lacked the alchemy of the original. There was no sense of the heart-pounding grandeur when these elements combined in the perfect proportions. It lacked the push of the wind, the tang of the sage, the almost frightening openness.

She began another sketch, of a horse sleeked long in a full-out run, its rider low against its neck, yet fully in command.

Two-thirds of the herd had cleared the narrow gap that

Nate called the eye of the needle when a cow among those yet to pass through wheeled around and ran at an angle, against the grain. A handful of its fellows began to follow. More stopped their forward progress, seeming to weigh whether to join the revolt or not.

From out of the dust at the back of the herd, a horse and rider came flying at that first cow.

Nate Abbott.

Sophie had seen good horsemen before. Riders adept at smoothly negotiating the maze and noise of St. Louis streets.

This was something else entirely. The horse and the man stretched out, arrowing through the air. The light itself seemed to part for them.

She had read of horse and rider becoming one. It seemed a silly notion, though less so now.

And yet, that wasn't right, either, for Nate clearly was in control. Every muscle and bone of the horse's body strained in the pursuit, the legs stretching then gathering, the nostrils wide to aid breathing. But the ears twitched back toward the man atop him as much as they did forward.

There was also communication in the twist of Nate's shoulders, instruction in the shift of his weight to the outside of the saddle.

Horse and rider came wide at that cow, almost at the foot of the knoll where she sat on Jester. When the cow stopped dead at the sight bearing down on him, Nate slowed his mount, gentling the move as they turned the cow.

In a moment, the cow had returned to the herd, quickly lost from sight, while Nate subtly urged a few others in tighter to the flow toward the gap.

It had lasted not more than a handful of moments. Yet Sophie's heart continued battering at her for twice as long.

And now ... she ignored the accelerated cadence her heartbeat had adopted, and considered the drawing before her, of a rider and a horse, bearing down on a recalcitrant cow.

She crumpled the sorry effort to capture what could not be captured.

She uncrumpled the paper to preserve what remained of it for other efforts at other subjects. Perhaps this one should not be captured. Perhaps it could exist only here, in this raw, open place with air and light that defied her paltry skill.

It was so different from what she was accustomed to.

There was, of course, the geographic difference from St. Louis to Wyoming Territory. But nearly as foreign as the landscape was this male world she had ventured into. Never before had she recognized how thoroughly female her life at Mrs. Forestell's Academy was ... and had been most of her life.

I know this country, and you don't, and I want your word on this, Sophie.

As dearly as she held Mrs. Forestell, Louisa and Alice, she could not imagine any circumstance in which one of those ladies would demand she pledge her word in such a way. Their confidence in each other was built layer upon layer of sheer, subtle connections over long periods of time.

Yes, I give you my word.

She could not recall having ever pledged her word before.

She put a hand to her throat. Oh ... Only this moment did she recognize that perhaps even more disconcerting than Nate Abbott asking for her word, and her giving it, was his having accepted it as an absolute bond that she would adhere to his cautions.

"Sophie?" The voice was as faint as the tap on her door.

"Come in, Edith." She scooped up the sketches, straightening the crumpled pages and tucking them inside her sketchbook, out of sight.

Edith entered in her nightdress, topped by an old jacket of her father's. "I saw your light. Under the door." She nodded to that gap as she closed the door behind her.

"I'm glad you came. I had wanted to talk to you about our idea of remaking some of your clothes."

"But you said there's not enough good fabric."

"I did. However, I mentioned our difficulty in a letter to two of my fellow instructors at the Academy, and they have written back in a letter that arrived today while we were out riding."

"Mail arrived again? Don't usually get mail but once a month or so."

Nate Abbott had grumbled something about the place being overrun with volunteers from town delivering the mail every time he looked up. His attitude seemed to indicate this was something he laid at her door. To her mind it was a pleasant state of affairs to have the mail arrive more frequently, and his air of complaint was entirely inexplicable.

"Well, it's fortunate that we received this correspondence, because they had a mostly timely suggestion – they advise that we consider turning the fabric inside out."

"Oh." Edith's eyes went as wide and round as her mouth. "Do you think that will work?"

"We can't know until we look at your clothing and – Edith!"

But the girl was gone, off the bed, out the door and down the hall before Sophie could draw a breath. And practically before her next breath, Edith was back, with her arms teeming with apparel. Not only her skirts and bodices but also petticoats and chemises.

After closing the door behind her with one foot, she dumped everything on the center of the bed, and immediately set to turning items inside out.

"Not the petticoats." Sophie laughed, taking one from the girl. It was worn nearly through in places and surely had to be far too short for her.

But it gave her an idea. She segregated the petticoats to one side, while watching Edith's progress with the other items.

They found that if they took apart two skirts that showed wear on the outer side, turned them inside out then seamed them into stripes that hid worn areas, they provided sufficient material for a new skirt. A third skirt – inside out – could be turned into a short, gathered overskirt, with enough left to add a matching flounce to her good blue skirt.

Edith bit her lip. "But my petticoats are so short, there won't be anything to keep the flounce from knocking back against my shoes."

"I have an idea about that." Sophie shook out the petticoats. "If you sacrifice this one, we can add to the bottom of this other petticoat and to the top of your best petticoat, and have two that are long enough to suit."

"That ... that is the smartest thing I ever heard, Sophie."

She laughed. "You shall turn my head with such praise." Though she couldn't help but take pleasure in the girl's shining eyes. "As for these two petticoats and this – was this a chemise at some time? – I have no idea what use they might be. Now, let us examine these bodices."

A sadly worn bodice still promised enough fabric to create at least one new collar and possibly a pieced-together sash. With judicious seaming, two others might be remade into a brand new bodice.

"But we won't know for sure until we can take them apart and see – No, not tonight. If you start taking apart all your wardrobe tonight, Edith Bracken, you will have nothing to wear tomorrow."

The girl giggled, and subsided back against the headboard.

"This is far better than what I hoped for when I knocked on your door."

"What had you hoped for when you knocked on my door?"

"I was thinking there's probably more about being a lady that you ain– aren't – haven't told me yet. Sort of easing me into it, the way Nate does with a young horse."

Sophie bit the inside of her cheeks to keep from smiling. She nodded. "You are correct, Edith, there is a great deal more."

"Figured. It seemed kind of easy with it just being the hat and gloves and washing up better. So, I was thinking ... I need a bustle."

Sophie took her time answering, summoning up the same level of seriousness the girl had shown. "A bustle is an encumbrance when one rides. I wear the very smallest style when I ride."

"But that's sidesaddle."

Sophie envisioned the logistics. "I believe it would be worse astride. With the bustle, um, protruding behind, it would either have to go above the back of the saddle or you would sit quite far forward."

Edith considered that. "I don't ride all the time."

She conceded that point. "Another obstacle would be in acquiring one for you. The mercantile –"

"I won't get there before fall, and even if one of the boys goes to town it's ..." She trailed off as red mounted her throat and into her cheeks as they both contemplated entrusting any of the OS hands with that commission.

"No, indeed. That would not do."

So, how on earth did one go about creating a bustle? Sophie had absolutely no experience with such a thing.

"Can I see one?"

Edith's question cut across Sophie's thoughts. It had never occurred to her in all their drawing of and talking about fashion that the girl had never seen the underpinnings of fashionable dress.

"An excellent idea. It will give us a far better idea of how to fashion one ourselves than dealing with mere theory."

She pulled out both the bustles she had brought, as well as her combination – "less fabric than separate chemise and drawers, so you have less bunching at the waistline," she explained – petticoats and corsets.

Edith eyed the corsets with something close to alarm, displayed mild interest in the other pieces, before reverently picking up the smaller bustle.

"Try it on," Sophie urged.

The girl tied it around her waist, over her skirt, yet under her father's jacket, then twisted around to try to see the effect.

It was far from ideal.

"I fear any of mine are entirely too short on you. If not today, certainly tomorrow, at the rate you're growing. With it stopping well above the ground, the outer skirt cups in, and that give an appearance less appealing than no bustle at all."

"Pa says if the grass grew as fast as I do –" She pushed aside the discarded petticoats, and experimented with sitting on the side of the bed. "– we'd have the fattest cattle in Wyoming Territory."

Not satisfied with her perch, she bounced slightly, and the petticoats slipped to the floor. Sophie scooped them up, then stopped before returning them to the bed, gathering them into a tighter bundle.

"The top part's hard as a rock." Edith jiggled experimentally. "But the part where you sit gives some, don't – doesn't it?"

"Uh-huh."

Edith looked around at the distracted response. "What're you looking at?"

"Your bustle."

"What? Those old – Oh."

"We shall quilt together layers of extra fabric to stiffen the top, then take these – " Sophie twisted the petticoats and chemise into one tight roll. "And attach this to the top. It would allow you to be seated, while the stiffer top would hold its form."

She held the coil up to compare its length against the bustle Edith wore. "An excellent length. Thank heavens the style now is for a narrow line from the front so we don't need as much material. And there's no need for a shelf bustle for a girl like you. Yes, I think this will do. You shall have your bustle, Edith."

"That ... that would be ... I'll be a real lady." The last came in an awed whisper.

"Edith."

The girl cut her eyes at her, perhaps warned by the tone of what was coming.

"You know a bustle will not make you a young lady."

"I'm wearing my hat. Gloves, too. Near all the time. And using that lotion we made." She held out her hands. "I scrubbed them real good tonight. And then I used that special one with the orange scent."

Sophie caught the girl's hands. "That's excellent, Edith. I can see quite a change."

She smiled shyly. When she would have withdrawn her hands, Sophie held them a moment longer to secure her attention.

"There is more than that to being a young lady, too." Releasing Edith's hands, she stood, but forced herself to remain still when she would have preferred to pace to dispel her nerves. "Living here with only men, you have an easy, natural way about you. A lady must also have an ability to call on her restraint. There are elements of being a woman – having a woman's ... nature, that puts that requirement of restraint on us, while leaving males free of it."

Edith became very busy untying the strings of Sophie's bustle, and setting it carefully aside. "You're talking about getting babies and such?"

Sophie chose not to query into and such. "Yes. "

"I seen – I've seen cattle and horses and such – I mean,

I know how they get babies."

"A woman is different," Sophie said gently.

Edith sat on the bed again. "I know."

With halting words and flaming cheeks, the girl explained that she had begun her courses six months before, and that her father had done his best to explain about them. But she'd been so desperately embarrassed, she'd hardly heard anything he said.

Sympathy so strong it hurt washed through Sophie.

She, too, had not had a mother to explain the ways of a woman's body. But she had had Mrs. Forestell, as well as the older girls at the academy. Yes, they had teased, but they had also disseminated volumes of information. Not all of it accurate, as she had come to discover.

Yet, when she had begun her courses, she had been advised and assisted by those familiar with the process and with what was required.

Sophie came and sat beside Edith on the bed, covering the girl's hand with her own.

"It must have been difficult for you being here with no other female at all." Carefully, she added, "Without your mother."

A tear dripped down.

"I am not your mother, Edith, but there are things you should know."

She talked not only of a woman's body, but also of how a gentleman should treat a lady, of how a lady could convey how she expected to be treated, and of how to be on the alert for men who had no regard for ladies.

"So there must be respect as well as love and – and desire." Desire – was that what she had felt with Nate Abbott's image beside hers in the mirror that night of the dance? She hurried on after the slight stumble. "And that comes together to bring a man to propose marriage when he truly loves a woman."

"Like my pa and ma."

"Yes."

Shyly, Edith pulled a framed likeness from the pocket of her father's old jacket. Had the daughter or the widower put it there? It was of a couple on their wedding day, a younger, far less worried version of Mr. Bracken, and a young lady with an air of lightness about her.

"He looks at her the way String looks at you."

"No." Sophie objected. "No, surely –"

Edith's head popped up, her eyes wide. "Of course he does. Just like you said. That feeling leads to a man offering marriage to a lady. So String loves you, just like Pa still loves my Ma. Still pines for her. It's romantic, I suppose. Though sometimes I wish ... but he loves her. Just like String loves you."

Sophie stood, assuming her best instructor's pose – back straight, hands folded in front of her, voice calm.

"Edith Bracken, it is far too late at night for you to still be awake, much less talking any more of romance. Now, take your things, and return them to your room and get right to sleep. We are going to have a great deal of work to fulfill all the plans made tonight."

Once in bed herself, Sophie wished her thoughts were as easy to shoo off as the girl had been, as easy to douse as the lamp.

But they would not shoo, and they would not douse.

He looks at her the way String looks at you. ... Still pines ... Just like String loves you.

String wouldn't pine for her. Surely.

Yet, shouldn't a man pine for his wife?

Oh, but she wouldn't be a true wife to him.

A hiss of pain escaped her. String was a gentle man, a man who let his music express his heart. Didn't he deserve a true wife?

He certainly didn't deserve a false one.

Nate rode in just after breakfast, having found himself duties that kept him out on the range through the night. Sleeping under the stars on his own was a welcome change from the jawboning in the bunkhouse.

Cooked himself a meal out in the open that was well below Doughy's efforts, but kept his ribs from sticking out his backbone. Worked his muscles and his horse hard. Thought about cattle, horses, land and weather, and refused to entertain a single thought about females – at least not of the human variety.

He'd timed his arrival to be late enough for the boys to have scattered to their tasks but not so late as to find nothing on Doughy's stove.

Except the boys hadn't scattered. They were clotted up around the porch of the bunkhouse, jawing like nobody's business.

"Nate! It's Nate!"

"Where've you been?"

"You shoulda been here."

"Something awful –"

Nate glanced at the house, which gave no outward sign of a tragedy. In fact, Moosehead was plodding peacefully toward the chicken pen with a bucket of scraps.

"–Gotta do something–"

"She don't realize –"

"You gotta make her see –"

Still mounted, he raised one hand, and they quieted. "What's happened?"

And that started them off again.

"Sophie said –"

"– said it right then in the middle of breakfast –"

"– she just don't realize –"

"– said it like nothing would change –"

He raised the hand again. It took longer this time. But he'd spotted the calm at the middle of this storm.

"String. What's this about? No – nobody else says a

word."

"It's simple. Sophie and I had a talk, and decided we're not gettin' married after all."

For an instant, it felt like one of those geysers he'd seen farther west had magically gotten under Nate and was tossing him up into the sky, weightless and giddy and disoriented.

Sophie wasn't going to marry String.

And just that fast, the geyser collapsed, and he came hard back to earth.

Sophie wasn't going to marry String.

"But ..." He couldn't say it. Not the first thing that had come to his mind. And not the second thing – *Why?* – either.

"Nate, you gotta talk to her," Gunner said.

"Nothing to say," String countered calmly.

Nate concentrated attention on his friend. "You mind if I have a word with her?"

String hitched his shoulders in a lazy shrug. "Do as you like." And Nate saw that the older man wasn't just calm, he was relieved.

But as he looked at the other hands, he saw something else entirely. He saw in their faces the words none of them would say. The words he was hearing in his own head.

She'll leave now.

What was she thinking? Didn't she realize – ? Maybe she did. Maybe that's what she wanted, what she intended. To be gone from here and never return.

He had to know.

And he knew exactly where to find her.

CHAPTER SIXTEEN

"What the hell do you think you're doing?"

"Do not curse."

He shouldn't have, but he was worked up. And why was that? It wasn't like he'd wanted her to marry String. And it sure wasn't like he wanted her to stay. The female just got under his skin.

"You got him to ask you to marry him, and now you throw him over? Or was it that he came to his senses?"

She peered down her nose at him, despite having to look up. "String has displayed admirable sense all along. In a mature and reasoned discussion of our future, we came to the realization – the mutual realization – that we did not suit."

"Naturally, your realization didn't have nothing to do with the fact that you weren't going to be able to lead him around by the nose the way you'd thought at the start."

"I'm surprised at you. I thought you had a better opinion of String."

"You aren't going to find a better man in Wyoming Territory," he retorted.

She flicked him with a glance that seemed to sting like the bite of a buffalo fly on his face, yet it was too quick for him to read its import.

"I am fully aware of String's excellent qualities."

"He'd be a good and faithful and protective husband."

"I know he would."

"He'd take care of you."

She twitched her skirt as she walked four paces away from him. "I'm certain of that."

He watched her as she headed back toward him. "But you aren't going to marry him."

"No."

"Because you decided you don't want a husband?"

"No." But there wasn't quite as much snap in that negative.

Again, he waited until she was almost back to him. "Because you wouldn't be a good wife to him."

"I have no idea —"

She started to spin away to continue her rotation, but he latched onto her arm, holding her in place. "Yes, you do."

She looked down at his arm on her hand. He released her slowly. She pivoted and resumed her pacing.

With her back to him, her voice was almost as cool and smooth as the custard his Ma used to make. "Oh, yes, and you're such an expert on husbands and wives and the married state."

"Enough to know what I want in a wife, which is a sight more than you seem to know about what you want in a husband!"

She stopped her pacing at the halfway point and faced him, hands on hips. "Oh, yes, and exactly what do you want in a wife?"

There was something lurking in her tone that he didn't hope to understand. With a cooler head he might have hesitated, but then if he'd had a cooler head, he wouldn't have been in this conversation at all.

"A sweet, biddable woman, who—."

She threw up her hands and resumed pacing. "Hah! That's what every man wants in a wife. No imagination at all."

Stung, he snapped back at her, "So what do you want in a husband?"

"Not a man who wants a sweet, biddable woman!" she threw over her shoulder.

"It's a good thing, because no man would be getting sweet and biddable in you!"

She'd started back toward him. But now she pivoted away sharply. Had he seen pain in her expression? The glint of tears?

"Sophie –"

Still with her back to him she held up a hand, ordering him not to take a second step toward her before he was even aware of taking the first.

"I was just saying –"

"Oh, I know what you're saying. You've returned to calling me twisty."

"It fits. Can't say it don't."

"Then it fits two ways, Nate."

"What's that mean?"

"It means you have proven yourself quite twisty yourself."

"If you mean trying to talk sense into String. Not that he'd listen up till now –"

"You? You had not the slightest role in the termination of our plans to marry. None. Not in any way." She turned away from him before resuming with her usual calm. "No, what I refer to is your twisty behavior in luring me to Wyoming Territory."

"Luring! There wasn't any luring in those letters. They were proper letters from a brother to a sister, nothing more."

"They were considerably more than that. Certainly considerably more than I had previously received from my brother. After that first letter, I thought for sure it was an aberration. Perhaps he'd had a fever, and was in a period of reflection. I've seen girls and teachers respond so after a serious illness. Only rarely does it become permanent. I was fully prepared for a return to his old style. But then the next letter came ... You painted such a picture of this place—." She swung her arm in an all-encompassing arc. "– of this world, that no female of spirit could resist them."

"It wasn't just me," he grumbled. "Most everyone contributed to those letters."

"So I have heard. However, I have also been told that they were mostly your words, your phrases that brought the other hands' thoughts to life. Was I told incorrectly?"

"No." He rallied then. "But there wasn't any word in those letters about you coming out here. About me – any of us – wanting to have you show up here living and breathing. Not a single word."

"It wasn't in a single word. It was in every word." Her head tipped back, her gaze locked with his.

He found he could say nothing.

She spoke very softly. "You deceived me. Maybe all of you did, but you most of all, Nate Abbott. You deceived me."

There were no tears, no pain in her tone. Her back was straight and her head tall.

She surely didn't need his consoling.

He turned and left.

"I know you were displeased with the sketch you did of your father, but don't be disheartened. The foundation for catching the individuality of a person's face is to have a good grasp of his or her head."

Edith wrinkled her nose. "I'd rather draw horses."

"You're becoming quite adept at that. It is time to

expand your repertoire."

They were in the parlor, spending this first hour after dinner on what had become regular drawing lessons. Sophie also had established regular sessions of Edith reading from her father's library and doing sums. The later she attached to their sewing efforts, so the girl barely noticed the practice.

"You mean it?"

"Yes. The human figure —"

"I mean about adept. You think Pa would know Beauregard now from my drawing?"

"Indeed, I do. Now find some paper, and we will begin with a sampling of the basic head shapes. Many people think all heads are round. In fact, round is quite rare. Far more — No, not that paper. It's already used. Here, use this."

But the girl continued to examine the loosely crumpled sheet she'd drawn from Sophie's sketch book.

"Edith. Use this paper."

Even the offer of fresh new paper in exchange for the wrinkled brown sheets did not dent the girl's concentration on Sophie's sketches.

"These are all of Nate. Oh, I like this one."

Sophie fought an urge to snatch it from the girl. No doubt, that stemmed from the natural inclination of one who was far more accustomed to having her pupil's creations considered than her own. However, snatching it back might be misinterpreted, and thus give the matter far more weight than it deserved.

"You've got him for sure," Edith said.

"Thank you. Now, for drawing heads —"

"He's not handsome 'xactly. Sure not the way Tinhorn is, though it near ruins it because he thinks he's even more handsome than he is. But there's something about him — Nate, I mean." She tipped her head, contemplating the sketch of Nate as Sophie had first seen him.

She reached for another sheet and Sophie fisted her

hands under the edge of the table.

"And you got that way he sits a horse," the girl continued, looking at her efforts from the day of riding. "I'm thinking it's more in the way he rides, though, that makes you want to watch him. And ropes. And brands."

Edith's sigh almost drew a smile from Sophie. She was not unaccustomed to observing the phenomenon of a young girl smitten with a man considerably older than her, though never before had she heard the smitten girl extol the male's ability to press hot iron into cowhide.

"Maybe how he talks, too," Edith added in the same distracted tone.

She dropped the sketch back into its place in the book and let the pages fall onto it, obscuring all but one corner.

Sophie deliberately removed her gaze from it, and brought her attention to the girl, who was regarding her own sketch of Mr. Bracken with deeper dissatisfaction.

"Those kind of things can't be in a sketch, can they? Not even for someone good as you, I mean. I can't even get the look of somebody, and when it comes to truly getting a real life person – like you did with Nate on Sago – there's so much more."

"Yes, there is."

"Is that why you said no to Hodges and Royal? Well, Hodges I understand, but Royal's okay – there's a girl from town sighing over him."

"That is a private matter," Sophie said in some agitation. Those proposals had come shortly after the end of her engagement to String. Since then, she had been able to head off proposals that a number of hands had indicated they might make. "How did you even know –"

Edith waved a hand. "Oh, everybody knows." She tipped her head in contemplation. "I suppose deciding yes or no about a man's real intentions, like you were telling me last week – that's got to do with those things you can't get in a sketch."

Sophie nodded slowly. "I suppose that's true."

"So that's what you're considerin' when you're deciding who'll be your husband."

"That, and other elements, such as integrity and kindness. That's if I marry at all."

Confiding that addition to Edith surprised Sophie nearly as much as it appeared to surprise the girl.

Her eyes wide, she demanded, "Don't you want a husband, Sophie?"

"I was quite sure I did."

"But not now?"

"There remain some advantages to having a husband." A sudden memory of some of Louisa's whispered confidences about the pleasures of the marriage bed came into her mind. Far more disconcerting was that they were accompanied by an image of Nate Abbott's face in the mirror, the night of the dance, and a sensation in her palm as if it once more rested on his shoulder as she mounted Jester – "Companionship," she said hurriedly. "That is an advantage of having a husband. As is a certain standing, and freedom in the world."

"You mean there are disadvantages?" Edith clearly had not considered that possibility.

"With an unfortunate choice in husbands, indeed, there can be."

The girl's head tipped once more. "There was a group of homesteaders who traveled through year before last, and they asked permission to camp on Elk Creek. We rode out – Pa and Nate and me and some of the other boys, just to be neighborly you know, and to make sure none of our herd wandered into their cookpots."

Sophie smiled, but she didn't think Edith saw it. The girl was too caught up in her memory.

"There was this one man whaling on a woman with a stick. Pa yelled, like I never heard before, and Nate roped the man. Pa said he wouldn't kick them off the OS that night because the rest of the party needed rest, though they'd shamed themselves by not coming to the woman's aid, but the man was never to set foot on OS land again. Oh, he was that mad, trussed up like that by the rope, but still spitting and fuming about she was his wife and it was his right. But he shut up when Nate said if he ever heard of the man treating his wife that way again, he'd track him down and shoot him."

Edith looked at her now, her eyes large with questions. "Pa said the woman could come stay with us, but she said no." She shook her head. "Even with what Nate said, I wouldn't've trusted that man'd never start whaling on me again. Not with him talking about rights up one side and down the other."

"That is a testament to your good sense," Sophie said firmly. "Yet, even well short of corporal injury, a husband has rights in regard to his wife that make the choice of a husband a vital decision for a woman's future peace of mind."

"Like when I'm getting' married I want to look for a man who'd be good at running the OS?"

"Perhaps. Certainly you would want to ensure that a man you would marry would hold your best interests as paramount when your property becomes his."

"My property beco— you mean if Pa had died the ranch would belong to my husband instead of me?"

"In the normal course of things, yes."

"But ... but women can vote here in Wyoming Territory. There've been women justices of the peace and even a mayor or something – Pa made me read all about it. And when he makes me read all that about government, he always says it's because I'll be voting someday. So it's not like in the States where women don't have rights."

"Even in Wyoming Territory, a husband can decide where you live, what you will wear, what your day shall be devoted to. A husband can take whatever you possess and dispose of it as he wants – unless you take great care."

Edith's eyes had gone so wide that Sophie wondered if she would ever be able to close them again. "That sounds like another father."

"Indeed."

The girl shook her head. "That's not at all like what I've heard about in stories and such. Not even like that fella who proposed to you back in St. Louis."

Sophie propped her hands on her hips. "Edith Bracken, how do you come to know that?"

Edith colored, but assumed a breezy air. "Oh, those boys in the bunkhouse were forever reading your letters and talking all about it. I'd've had to have been deaf not to hear all about it."

"A lady does not listen in on others' conversations." A prickling memory of hearing String and Nate talking outside the bunkhouse arose. ... *Those who listen in on other people's conversations don't hear any good of themselves* ... "Even when it is entirely accidental, a lady does her utmost to refuse to recollect the substance of what she might have heard."

"Like that you thought you would not suit because Harry Jenkins was of a romantic and tragic nature?"

"Edith–" she started in a tone of reprimand that lost much of its edge because of a laugh tickling her throat.

The girl clasped her hands to her chest. "Romantic and tragic – that sounds so ... so thrilling!"

Sophie fought down her laughter to say firmly, "There are any number of events that are thrilling that one avoids if one possibly can."

"Like what?"

She searched her experiences. "Such as lightning or a runaway carriage or ... oh, or like a stampede."

"Oh."

For all its brevity, that response assured Sophie that Edith recognized her point. She made one final statement:

"If one were to have a husband, one of a romantic and tragic nature would make for a very uncomfortable home."

Nate eased back from the open door.

He'd been on his way to leave a count sheet on Mr. Bracken's desk when the murmur of Sophie and Edith's voices from the parlor had condensed into an item of strong interest – his name

These are all of Nate. Oh, I like this one.

So Sophie had sketched him.

Then they'd started talking about husbands.

And Nate had needed to rearrange some of his thinking about Sophie Vandercook.

Truth be told – to himself, anyway – he'd come to admire her sense from the years of letters.

But she was a sight less confusing in a letter than she was swirling around the OS like a pretty little windstorm.

He'd bet his saddle that she was plotting something. And he'd been so sure she was angling for a husband when she got String to propose.

Until she broke it off.

Then she turned down Hodges and Royal King. Ever since, she'd been side-stepping being alone with any of them. So how could she be angling for a husband?

She sure wasn't preaching grabbing a husband to young Edith. In fact, she sounded downright reluctant to have one.

Why was that?

He carefully retreated to the front door, opening and closing it behind him without the occupants of the parlor ever being aware of their listener.

Nate waited.

But there was no mention of Sophie Vandercook leaving the OS Ranch.

None.

The other hands, tiptoed around a couple days like they

were holding their breaths. They consumed meals at a rate that should have set world records, skedaddling out like their presence might suddenly remind Sophie that she had no cause to stay on. They hardly made eye contact, as if they feared that seeing the question in someone else's eyes would make it come true. At night, they laid in their bunks in a quiet that tore at Nate's nerves as much as the gabbing had, broken only by a sigh from this one, then that one.

Only String was immune. In fact, he damned near blossomed into a society type. He chatted away with Sophie at meals like he'd been a talker from birth. And they continued their evenings on the porch, with even more laughing and singing than before, if that was possible.

A dozen times or more came the thought, saying aloud that there was no reason for her to stay now, just to relieve the tension.

But then Nate realized the tension was gone – at least for everybody else. A handful of days, and they all settled back like things had always been this way.

No brother, no fiance. What was to keep her here?

As far as he could tell, no one else was asking themselves that very reasonable question any longer, because she appeared to be digging in deeper and deeper into the life of the OS.

And that irked him nearly as much as the knowledge of how he'd felt when he'd thought she might leave any hour.

CHAPTER SEVENTEEN

The day after overhearing the conversation in the parlor, Nate returned to that hallway, and once more paused at the sound of feminine voices.

This time, he realized. They were talking about nothing more interesting than stitches. He stepped into the parlor.

"Nate!" screamed Edith in the closest thing to Charlotte Shrieve's screech he'd ever heard her use. "Get out! You can't come in here."

"What in da– Why not?" He'd seen enough to know both she and Sophie were properly covered so it wasn't that.

He got tangled up in a thought of Sophie not properly covered, and it stopped him dead.

That gave Edith plenty of time to hop up and spread her arms across the table, as if to protect the jumble of cloth and paper covering it from a marauder.

Sophie came around the table to stand between it and him. As if he couldn't see right over and around her trim figure. Which would look just as trim in nothing more than –

"It's a surprise," she informed him.

He looked past her, trying to shake the images in his head.

"You'll see soon enough," the girl said with great emphasis.

"You're making something for me, Edith?" he teased.

Now that he thought of it, with the exception of the other day's ride, they'd been spending most of their time, just the pair of them, in here.

"No. Now go away. And don't you be blabbering all over the bunkhouse about this."

"About what?"

Sophie clapped her hands twice, as if he were a wayward student, and advanced on him. "Just leave us now, Mr. Abbot."

He didn't move, curious to see what she'd do.

She put her hands on his left arm, and with a surprising strength, drew it across his chest and gave it a push that had him turning toward the door. But only because he hadn't resisted.

He liked the warmth spreading from where she touched him.

Looking at her over his shoulder, he grinned down at her and said, "You don't really want me to go."

"Oh, but I do."

"No you don't."

And then it wasn't teasing any more and he wasn't grinning any more. And the air in his lungs went still and hot, and they were back to that moment looking in the mirror in the dark hall when all he'd wanted to do –

"Why don't we?" Edith demanded.

Sophie made a little sound, and dropped her hands from his arm, and he felt like a man who'd been thrown by a bronc, struggling to get his bones lined up right again while he wondered where the earth had gone from under his feet.

"Are you gonna tell us or not, Nate?" Edith added.

He cleared his throat, trying to find the gratitude he

should have been feeling for the girl's curiosity and how it had stopped ... something.

And because he knew an inclination to not look at Sophie, he made himself do just that and to address her. "Mr. Bracken's ordered you have a new mount. Asked String to pick you out one."

There'd been something odd about that, though. Mr. Bracken and String with their heads together, talking long after they'd finished discussing horseflesh. Nate had asked a question to String, but the hand had been uncharacteristically evasive.

He forgot that now as Sophie smiled, though she didn't meet his gaze. "How thoughtful of him – both for my enjoyment and so Jester will not be bothered by being urged to move."

"Which horse?" Without waiting for an answer, Edith told Sophie, "String's about the best judge of horseflesh in the Territory. Nate's not bad, but nowhere near as good as String. Ai–Isn't that right, Nate?"

"Yup. So, do you want to see or not?"

"Now?"

Edith didn't await his answer to Sophie's question. Apparently forgetting about whatever surprise lurked among the piles of cloth, she brushed past him and was out the door.

"Yup," he told Sophie. "Waiting on you in the yard."

When she showed no inclination to imitate Edith's move, he stepped back, clearing her path.

She murmured a thank you, then went past as calm and sure as if she'd felt nothing when her hands were on him. Though, if that were true she wouldn't have to be so careful about not meeting his gaze, would she?

He pretended not to see her select an apple from the pile Doughy was using for supper.

Sophie paused at the top of the outdoor steps at the sight before her. String held the halter of a compact bay mare. But that was just the start. A foal and a yearling hung back slightly, watching the humans with skittish interest. And a two-year-old colt stayed even farther back, as if not wanting to admit he was still hanging around his mama's skirts.

The mare stood at ease, but with her intelligent eyes and ears taking in all around her.

"Oh. Oh."

Sophie went right to the horse's head. Give her credit, she didn't rush or make a lot of noise with her skirts. She went at a good steady pace, with her usual calm economy, letting the horse hear and see her. And then she stood still, while the mare pulled in her scent.

Slowly, she extended her hand. It was empty. The mare snuffled at it gently.

"I have an apple. May I give it to her?"

"In a minute," String said. "She's smelled it already. And waitin'll make her like it all the more."

Slowly, she lifted her hand and stroked the dark mane.

"What a darling. What's her name?"

"Milly. After my mama."

"Well, I'll be da-." Nate bit it off.

Edith cast him a glance, but neither Sophie nor String blinked. All the years this mare had been called Milly, and he'd never known it was for String's ma. All the longer years he'd known String and had no idea of his ma's name at all.

ᕬ✵ᕫ

Smiling in anticipation, Sophie twitched her skirt, swinging it wide as she came around the corner to see into the office.

"You are in for a surprise that I am confident will delight you and –"

She broke off at the sight of Nate – the solitary occupant of the room – standing at the desk, holding a bundle of papers.

"Oh, I heard someone – I thought it was Mr. Bracken."

He placed the bundle, which she now saw appeared to be a periodical and other mail, on the corner of the desk, and advanced on her. "So I see."

She retreated well back into the hallway. "I don't take your meaning at all, Mr. Abbott."

"Sure you do – that skirt-swishing. Wasn't for me, that's for sure."

"I did no such –" She broke off her remonstrations, because he was looking up the stairs.

She moved to the opposite side of the stairway and both of them looking up at Edith, hesitating at the top step.

She gripped the railing so tight her still-roughened knuckles stood out like red knobs. Despite that attachment, she swayed slightly as she descended the first step. She released a bit of breath, then drew in another with a fierce frown as she took each step.

Sophie had urged Edith to wear her own boots for this first venture down the stairs in her new attire, but Edith had insisted that wouldn't be right. One look at Sophie's footwear, and they hadn't even tried to get them on the girl. Even Mrs. Bracken's old shoes found in a trunk were far too snug for comfort. Or stability. Yet Edith had insisted.

Only when the girl had two steps remaining did she look up and see who stood at the bottom.

"Sophie let me take a try at some lady clothes," she informed Nate.

"So I see," he said, but in an entirely different tone. The corner of his mouth twitched.

"Nate," Sophie said under her breath in warning.

But he was already sweeping his hat off and holding it at his side.

"Good day to you, Miss Bracken."

At that moment Gunner swung in from the kitchen with half a biscuit in his hand and what appeared to be another whole one in his cheek.

He skidded to a halt and gawked up at Edith, then swallowed audibly. "What's that get-up you're wearing?"

"Get-up!"

"You're all–" He circled the hand with the biscuit like a tornado. "Bound-up like. Don't know how you could ride, much less rope."

"It's not for riding. Or roping. I'll have you know, it's right fashionable, Gunner."

Edith's voice sounded strained. Was it tears? Or the unfamiliar tightness of a corset affecting her breathing? Sophie took a half-step toward her.

Gunner's eyes narrowed. "It's a corset under there, ain't it? Well, you must have it on wrong or something. Because you look like a heifer being yanked by ropes going every which way."

Other than bringing his hand and the hat it held up so it covered enough of his face that Edith might believe the sound he made truly was a cough, Nate also made no motion.

Sophie froze in her progress toward Edith, unable for that instant to imagine how the girl might react to such a comment.

Edith, however, was at no such loss.

All uncertainty forgotten, she stormed down the final two steps, and pushed hard at the center of Gunner's shirt. He stumbled back, Edith followed and gave him another push. This time his backward motion connected with a corner of the low bench that sat under the hooks by the front door. The bench skidded into the doorway to the office. Trying to avoid it, Gunner lost what was left of his balance and went over backward, the motion popping free the biscuit he held.

Edith snatched it out of the air, clamped her teeth around a bite of it, spun around, hiked the skirt up to an alarming level and pounded up the stairs at a pace totally unlike her descent.

Only the sound of a door slamming upstairs broke Sophie from her frozen state.

"Gunner – are you all right?" She hurried to where he was disentangling his long legs from the shattered elements of the bench's structure along with a tufted cushion.

The slamming door apparently also unfroze Nate Abbott, although with an entirely different result. He sat on the second step from the bottom and laughed. Laughed so hard that Sophie – when she could spare a glance from Gunner – saw tears sliding down from the corners of his eyes.

"You could help," she snapped. "He could be hurt!"

"He's not," Nate declared, after sucking in a deep breath. He laughed some more before adding, "Are you."

"No, I ain't hurt." Gunner brushed off the seat of his pants – as if his encounter with the bench, cushion and floor might have deposited more dust there than his days on the range had – then bent to retrieve his hat. "Look what she done."

"Can't blame that on Edith," Nate said, still chuckling. "You're the one who sat on it. Never seen you get throwed by a bench before."

He glowered. "What in da–"

"Gunner." Nate's warning had no laughter in it.

"Tarnation," the younger man amended, "got into her – that's what I want to know. She went pure crazy."

He lovingly re-shaped the hat.

"Let it be a lesson to you." Nate stood, putting his own hat on.

"A lesson? To stay away from crazy females – begging your pardon, Miss," he added, his usual shyness beginning to resurface as his ire ebbed.

"Not to pass comments on a female's undergarments," Nate said baldly.

Sophie felt her cheeks heat and saw a similar reaction spur color into Gunner's face.

"Wouldn't you agree, Miss Vandercook?"

She straightened, then pointedly turned her back on Nate, addressing only Gunner.

"A gentleman comments on a lady's attire – her outer attire – only when he has a favorable observation to make."

Her tone to him might have been more astringent than she had meant, judging by the young man's crestfallen expression.

"As you have always done so kindly to me, Gunner," she reminded him.

He revived instantly. "That's cause you always look pretty as can be."

"You are very kind."

"Just telling the truth. You're the most beautiful lady I ever seen." He sucked in air and added, "Or hope to see. Ever."

"Enough of this palaver, Gunner. Let's go."

At the tip of Nate's head toward the kitchen, Gunner was on his way, though not before he cast a quick, shy smile back at Sophie.

Nate, too, sent a look back at her. But it was neither shy nor smiling.

"Another conquest? This one's going to stir a mess of trouble. And that's on your head, Miss Vandercook."

Then he was gone.

She hadn't liked the way he'd said her name –that drawl with an edge to it. And she hadn't liked what he'd said.

Gunner a conquest? Absurd.

CHAPTER EIGHTEEN

They had eaten cold meat and bread for supper the night before, just Edith, Mr. Bracken and herself in the kitchen.

Hands had been departing at an increasing rate, always with the explanation that they were heading out for some task associated with the roundup.

Nate Abbott had left several days ago, to organize the drives — the men's finding of widely dispersed cattle and sending them toward the roundup grounds.

Now the time for her own much-anticipated trip to the roundup had arrived.

Yesterday, the rest of the hands left early and Doughy had departed at mid-day, taking a wagon he'd stocked to feed the OS hands during roundup.

This morning, their little band of three was to follow.

Just as Doughy had made his preparations — which to Sophie's eye had included packing up nearly every edible item on the ranch and more than half of the pots and pans — so had she.

Starting with the day she had been introduced to Milly,

she had ridden daily, sometimes twice, both to become acquainted with the mare and her entourage, and to accustom herself to longer periods in the sidesaddle.

Under Edith's tutelage she had packed only absolute necessities in tight bundles. Only in one area had she allowed herself more. Doughy had agreed to take her drawing materials wrapped in a slicker and stowed away with the dry firewood in a hidden sling under the wagon.

This morning she was dressed for travel, using only the traveling corset and no bustle at all.

"You look lovely, Miss Vandercook," Mr. Bracken said gallantly.

"The best that can be said for my attire, sir, is that I am prepared for what comes." With that she gestured to the cowboy hat Edith had given her and the long scarf she now used to assist the pins in holding it to her head.

Edith could barely contain herself. And Sophie acknowledged a persistent flutter of excitement in her stomach that made breakfast far less important that an early departure.

"Though this isn't a big roundup," Edith said with would-be calm.

Mr. Bracken chuckled slightly. If Nate had not told her all that rested on this roundup, she might have missed that despite the chuckle, there was a tension in the man's usually pleasant expression.

"Edith is right. In years past, when the big cattle companies dominated the territory, the roundups were huge indeed. With so many of the big companies broken up in the past few years and the losses ..." Memories seemed to merge with worries.

"Whatever its size, I am delighted to see a roundup," Sophie said.

"Hope we're all delighted when it's over," he said in a low tone.

S ophie's education on cattle ranching, the history of the OS ranch, the vagaries of Wyoming Territory weather, the life cycle of prairie dogs, the varieties of sagebrush, the most advantageous grasses for livestock, as well as the vast inferiority to the OS of every other outfit that would participate in or be represented at the roundup, was delivered in spurts by Edith from the time they left until their arrival well past midday.

Where they arrived was to a sight Sophie could never have imagined.

From the top of a ridge that would have qualified as a mountain in St. Louis, they looked into a valley with smaller ridges starting and stopping around three sides, while the fourth side consisted of cliffs rising to what were mountains even in Wyoming Territory.

It was fully six times larger than the bowl of land through which she had watched OS hands trail cattle weeks back. And yet in that first moment, the expanse of land seemed to shrink under the population of cattle streaming into it through two creek-bed gaps to the north. The sun beat down on it all so bright and strong it seemed almost a mirage.

"Oh."

"It's a sight, isn't it?" Mr. Bracken sounded nearly as awed as she felt.

"Pa? Pa? Can I —"

"Yes. But don't get in the way."

Edith, attired in the serviceable split skirt that allowed her to ride astride, had transferred from the wagon to Beauregard a mile back, and now was on her way with the first syllable.

"There, that's the OS camp."

Bracken pointed to where nearly a dozen well-spaced wagons dotted along a crooked creek at the northwest corner. She picked out Doughy in his red-banded hat.

Mr. Bracken identified the camps of other outfits,

adding the names and brands, until her head spun.

She spotted another figure, this one mounted. Nate looked up at them, then started toward their position at an easy lope.

"What are the men in the wagons doing, over by that small bluff?"

"Bringing in wood for the branding fires. Cattle don't like going uphill much, so that rise will help hold the branding herd. Then they'll position the wagons to close it off more, and brand in the center."

She squinted against the brightness. "I don't recognize them. Are they OS hands?"

He shook his head. "What crew we have here has all been out on the drives."

"What crew – but I thought all the OS hands had left the home ranch?"

"That's true. But some are at other roundups. Repping for us."

"Oh, yes. Because the cattle wander during the winter."

He nodded. "That's right. But when I said all the OS hands are out gathering, I should have said except for Nate. He's mostly been here directing everything. He's roundup boss, since it's on OS land. And with him occupied, I'm in charge of the OS outfit."

He grinned deprecatingly. "Not that it takes much, because the boys know their business – that's why I draw that duty. They don't need me being here to tell them how to drive in the rest of the cattle."

She felt her eyes widen, then immediately narrowed them against the sun. "There will be more cattle than this?"

He chuckled again, that faint, not entirely humorous sound. "I hope a considerable number more, and may every calf require the OS brand!"

"Truly, this is a smaller roundup? I would not have believed that there could be so many cows in the entire territory."

"Two years ago the herd of just one of the large cattle companies wouldn't have fit in this valley."

She glanced at him, and saw the worry again.

"The cattle business has changed so much, then?"

"Yes," he said simply. "And it'll keep changing. Wyoming Territory can't keep fences out forever, and with fences you won't have the herds mixing like this, and that'll be end of roundups like these."

He sounded both intrigued by what fences would mean and saddened.

"Then I am all the more grateful to you for this opportunity to see this one, Mr. Bracken."

"It is my pleasure, Miss Vandercook." He swept his hat off and they smiled at each other.

Nate appeared abruptly, his horse coming around a knob that must have hidden him from view.

That instant of man and horse appearing tripped her heartbeat to a stuttering cadence, suddenly making her traveling corset feel as if it had been tied tighter than was prudent.

After the exchange of greetings, Sophie turned determinedly back to her host.

"You mentioned, sir, that you hoped every calf would require the OS brand — how do you determine which brand a calf should carry?"

"Nate, you explain these things best of anyone I know, you tell Miss Vandercook."

She waited, but the foreman said nothing until she cut her eyes toward him. Even under the brim of his hat, she could tell he had both brows raised, faintly taunting her.

With cool courtesy, she said, "I should appreciate the explanation, Mr. Abbott."

"What it comes down to is the calves are branded with the mother's brand. No telling which brand the bull wore, but with calves trailing along after the cow's milk, there's no doubt there."

She felt heat rise in her at the mention of the bull, the

implication of its role in the process, the mother cow and its nourishment for its offspring, but she refused to allow that to affect her composure.

"That is very clear. Thank you."

"Oh, that's just the start. Because sometimes you can't hardly tell what brand's on the mama's hip. And sometimes there's two, three, even four brands there, what with selling and less straightforward methods of transfer. So it's a matter of interpretation and negotiation, one outfit's rep with another. And then there's mavericks."

"I have heard the term. It means–?"

"Yearlings and up that haven't had a brand put on them at all. Even the best outfit has some slip through ever year. So, then there's dividing those up best we can. And they're ornery cusses, or they wouldn't have got to be mavericks in the first place. Ropin' and throwin' and brandin' them takes some doing."

He slid a look toward her, and she braced for his next poke at her.

"And then there's turning bulls into steers."

She was not completely naive. She was aware of the process. Though to have it mentioned in polite company – well, not polite company, with Nate Abbott doing his best to make her blush and run.

"I should like to see all aspects you have described," she said very firmly, though she wasn't entirely sure she would. But now – now she would see it no matter what.

"You won't like it. It's noisy and dusty and smelly."

She gritted her teeth. "Nevertheless, Mr. Abbott, I shall see –"

"Branding won't start for another day."

"Then, for now, I should like to see how these preparations are made."

"Not much to see. And what there is to see, you can see better from up here – without swallowing dust. Plus, Milly won't have to carry you back up this steep before you start back to the home ranch." He squinted at the sun.

"And the way the daylight's going, you'll need to start soon to get back to the home ranch by dark."

"I will bear that in mind on the day I am leaving," she said.

His head whipped around in an entirely satisfactory manner. "What do you mean the day you're leaving."

She felt no obligation to explain other than to add, "Which is not today."

"The plan was for you to come out for a day –"

"The plan has changed." She fought back a triumphant smile.

"You are not staying in a roundup camp."

"Edith is, and I shall chaperone her."

"Edith sleeps out in the open like the rest of us. You gonna roll yourself up in a blanket and use a rock for a pillow?"

Mr. Bracken cleared his throat. "I had a tent packed in the wagon for Miss Vandercook. Edith will share it with her this year."

Nate's brows crashed down as he turned to his employer. "I thought –"

Mr. Bracken spoke hurriedly. "We discussed it further after you left, and I agreed with Miss Vandercook that it would be a shame for her to miss seeing more of the roundup."

"She should go back to the home ranch tonight. Stay in the house."

Sophie did not care to be discussed as if she weren't there, or capable of making decisions herself. "Go back? When I have only just arrived, whyever should I?"

"When you're not accustomed to it, the sun and the heat can do things to a person you wouldn't expect. Days of it –"

"You needn't worry about me. I have a sturdy constitution."

"It's not suita–"

"Oh, for mercy sakes, please don't start on that note

again. You are the most ..."

Her words withered under the recognition that Mr. Bracken was looking from her to Nate and back again with a peculiar expression on his face.

He spoke under his breath, as if only to himself. So perhaps she misunderstood, because she could make no sense of his comment that sounded like, "Ol' String is right. He's absolutely right."

When the OS owner met her gaze, he coughed into his glove, then cleared his throat before speaking.

"Nate," he said calmly, "I didn't like to have Miss Vandercook alone on the place with only Mulehead left behind. She'll sleep out in the tent for the two nights, then I'll return with her. By then, Hodges should have returned from repping down by the Platte and the day after, assuming Royal is back from the Basin, I'll return here to help wrap up."

"Thank you, Mr. Bracken." She paused only long enough to give Nate a dagger look. "For explaining to your foreman the thoughtful arrangements you have made for my comfort and for making this experience possible."

"Fine. Just – just don't tie that personal remuda of yours to the wagon."

With that Nate pivoted his horse and rode away.

"Of all the ..." She let that die as her host began coughing again. "Are you quite well, sir?"

"Yes, yes. Just dust. In my throat, I fear. But you must heed Nate about not tying up to the wagon. Doughy will refuse to serve you. It's the dust, you see. The horses stir up the dust, it gets in the food, and then he'll be in a fury. He gets a mite touchier about cooking out here."

Sophie found it hard to believe that the cook could be stirred to a fury, but had no intention of adding dust to the ingredients of what he was cooking.

She soon acknowledged to herself that Nate and Mr. Bracken had accurately predicted Doughy's mood.

He emitted a consistent low grumble of muttering of

words Sophie decided she could not quite make out, punctuated by exclamations of irritation. He already had a Dutch oven over a fire and was setting out other pots and pans.

"Eat as much as they want! Sure, when it's me's gotta fix it! Enough to make a man miss even that no-good Mulehead!"

He subsided a bit then erupted again. "And drinkin' enough coffee to fill every ocean there is!"

"Doughy?" she ventured, "could I place a pot on the fire for you?"

His head jerked up with a growl. Then he blinked, as if seeing her for the first time.

"Miss Vandercook ... What – ? Oh. No. You're not to do any such a thing. You just shoo on out of here, and leave me to tending fires and such."

"But –"

"Shoo."

She bowed before the authority in that command, retrieved her sketching materials, and found a perch on the seat of the wagon.

Her first view of the roundup camps dotted along the creek had indicated a rough order. But at this level, all seemed chaos – groups of horses being trailed this way and that, wagons drawing in and camps being set up, riders grouping together for a quick exchange before dispersing again, and cattle shifted here and there with no pattern she could discern.

She sketched until her hand ached, then she sat and watched.

"Sophie!"

Edith, astride Beauregard, drew up next to the wagon. Excitement sparkled her eyes and reddened her cheeks in a way most ladies would deplore, but Sophie could not fault.

"Isn't it – Isn't it just the most magnificent thing ever?" the girl demanded.

Sophie laughed. "It is certainly an amazing event, with

all this activity."

"Oh, this ain't nothin'. Most of the hands are out to round up the herds, they'll start bringing them in closer tomorrow for branding and such. Why, with Nate running things, they'll have three, four branding crews going easy. Then you'll see something. It's –"

A call from a neighboring camp rose up, accompanied by a resounding clatter, the bellowing of a cow, and irate shouts.

Edith twisted in her saddle to look behind her. "Land sakes – there's a cow loose in the Bar G camp."

Sophie stood, trying to look over the front corner of the wagon's canvas cover. She was too short to see.

"Oh! Went right through the cookfire."

Stepping first on the side of the wagon, Sophie swung herself up to stand on the seat, now with a clear view to the besieged camp. Three cowhands afoot flapped hats and kerchiefs at the animal. Rather than directing the cow in a particular direction, it had the effect of sending it plunging madly back through the camp, which already had pots tumbled about, leaking their contents into the ground.

A rider came in swinging a rope. "Stand clear!" he ordered.

Sophie held her breath to see if the rope would find the constantly moving animal.

But the rope fell flat to the ground, and stayed there.

"Of all the ..." Edith started in disgust.

At that instant, Sophie realized two things. The rider who had yet to reel in his rope to try another throw was staring at her, along with all the hands afoot, now frozen in place. And the cow was on the move again.

"It's headed this way," she said. "Oh, dear – right toward Doughy!"

"Oh, no!" Edith spurted forward on Beauregard, then wheeled him around to backtrack toward the impending collision of cow and cook.

But with the wagon between where the girl was and

where she needed to be, Sophie had no hope that Edith would be in time.

She opened her mouth to shout a warning to Doughy, but then realized he saw his peril.

Instead of getting out of the way, however, he stood in front of his cookfire, hands on his hips, feet spread and a scowl on his face as he faced the cow.

The animal appeared unintimidated, never slackening its speed.

"Oh –!" Sophie looked around quickly for something to throw, hoping to distract the animal at least, and saw only a coil of rope. With both hands she heaved it.

It fell well short of the line that connected cow and cook. The cow's gaze did flicker in that direction, but then it resumed its charge.

"Doughy!" she called, a plea rather than a warning.

A horse appeared so suddenly from beyond Doughy that Sophie could have believed it was dropped from the sky. A horse and its rider – Nate.

Directly between the cow and Doughy, the horse stopped so abruptly that it went well back on its powerful haunches.

Then it was up immediately in a deft pivot that set its mane to flopping as it met the cow's feint in an attempt to circle around to resume its stalking of Doughy.

Horse and cow were nearly nose to nose – both started one way, then the other, then back to the first. Like two people blocking each other accidentally on a city sidewalk. Though this wasn't accidental at all.

It was so near to simultaneous that Sophie marveled that the horse could anticipate the cow's moves. To her they seemed random and unpredictable. Yet the horse – and its rider – were right with him. The horse's legs splayed awkwardly wide sometimes, other times mincing sideways, others still with pivots both powerful and delicate.

The animal turned at last, the horse paralleling his

movement. It gave one last half-hearted lunge toward Doughy, easily thwarted by Nate's horse, then loped off.

Nate called out something, and Sophie saw that String had arrived and was already swinging a rope. She watched it settle around the cow's neck before String began to patiently shorten the animal's freedom. Edith and Royal reached Doughy near the fire, with exclamations peppering the conversation she could not separate any into individual words.

And then Nate was there, beside the wagon, blocking her view. "Get down from there."

Her mind still whirled with images of the action she'd just witnessed. If she could sketch that scene... "That was – that was like a dance with only one willing partner. The most amazing –"

"Get down from there now. You're making a spectacle of yourself."

This time Nate's low words penetrated.

A glance over his shoulder showed that the staring cowhands had multiplied. She'd entirely forgotten about them. Only now did she piece together the cause and effect of their staring at her and the cow going free to threaten Doughy and the OS camp.

But that gave Nate Abbott no right to say such things. She stood her tallest on the narrow seat, and began in her frostiest tone, "I am not making a–"

Her only warning was a low growl from Nate's throat. The next thing she knew his arm was clamped around her waist. He curled her so tight against his side that for an instant her face was also under the brim of his hat, his grim mouth only a breath from hers. Was he —-?

No.

He swung her back out, depositing her with far less gentleness than she would have liked into a seated position.

For a breath, his gaze bored into hers. She saw such depth and complexity there that it robbed her of thought, yet she could not name it.

Then he turned in the saddle and growled a single order to the still-staring cowhands.

"Git!"

CHAPTER NINETEEN

S ophie Vandercook was a walking, talking, wagon-seat-standing female mistake.

He'd warned Bracken. Told him every way he knew how that having her at the roundup was like begging lightning to strike. And he'd told him again after those slack-jawed idiots from the Bar G ogled her like she was one of the sporting girls kicking their legs on a Cheyenne stage.

"Nearly got Doughy killed," he'd concluded.

But the owner had chuckled in a way Nate couldn't remember him doing much of, and clapped him on the back and said it would all turn out fine.

And now, there she sat with Bracken and Edith and String and a couple other hands by the small fire in front of the ladies' tent, chatting away, never once noticing this pair of two-footed coyotes approaching fast.

Three times since supper, Nate had already pushed invaders from other camps back from the invisible border he'd set up in his mind. It didn't help his temper one bit that half of this fourth go-round was an OS hand.

Tinhorn skirted Doughy, going straight for the cook fire, but with his eyes on the gathering at the smaller fire beyond it.

"How 'bout a little in the dish for a hungry cowpoke," the other coyote was asking Doughy.

"Not even if you were riding for the OS," Doughy said, clamping down a lid on Tinhorn's reach into his pot, drawing an exaggerated yowl.

"What in thunderation –?" started Tinhorn, then cut it off as he saw Nate emerge from the shadows.

"Aw, c'mon, just a biscuit or two," the other hand was saying to Doughy, "like you're famous for, and then we'll just say howdy to your owner and –"

"Lost?" Nate asked the talker. He didn't recall the name, but he knew he was from one of the formerly big outfits to the south.

"Naw. Tinhorn here suggested I stop by to be sociable like, experience some of that hospitality we're always hearing the OS offers and take in the sights, so to speak." He added a leer for good measure.

"I never invited him –"

Nate stopped Tinhorn's protest with the flick of a look, then concentrated on the interloper. "No time for hospitality at roundup. We got too much work ahead of us, what with all the OS head to handle these next few days, and we don't want anyone to think we're not doing our share."

Since the word was that the interloper's outfit was dwindling fast and that this particular hand would run Vandercook a close second for a lazy cuss, it was a well-aimed thrust.

"Nothin' wrong with getting a look," the cowhand said, abandoning pretense, with a man-to-man tone. "Tinhorn tells me she's a stunner."

He tried to peer over Nate's shoulder toward Sophie. Nate stepped and turned, blocking his view and edging the cowhand back two steps.

"What is your –?" He broke off as he met Nate's gaze. And then he smirked. "Oh. Hoping to put your brand on her yourself, are you? Thinking you can beat out Tinhorn? Never heard tell you were much of a favorite with the ladies. Now that she's shaken off ol' String, Tinhorn's all set to step in – and he ain't talkin' about marrying her. He'll snap her up before you can say boo."

Nate felt his hands fist, but he said nothing.

"Quit your yapping and get on outta here now," Tinhorn said. His voice held some uneasiness, as if not sure how much trouble he was in with his ramrod.

"Yeah, yeah, I'm going." The other hand smirked one last time at Nate, then turned and went.

"And don't be coming back," Doughy grumbled toward the departing back. "Bad enough with the OS lot having empty gullies for stomachs – I ain't cookin' for the whole blamed Wyoming Territory."

"Nate, I never –"

"Never what? Never bragged? Never talked to hands you don't know any better than a tree about Miss Vandercook? How'd you think she'd like that? You never invited him – might as well have with your mouth flapping like that."

"I –"

"Get your bedroll and get what shut-eye you can. You're on last night herd."

"And don't be thinking you can get anything from my cookpot til I call for breakfast," Doughy added. "Not even coffee."

If the cook had meant the ban on coffee, that would have been a far harsher punishment than what Nate had just handed out by putting Tinhorn on last night herd.

But it wasn't the grub and it wasn't the coffee that had Tinhorn bragging even more than usual and other outfits' cowhands circling around.

It was her.

She was trouble. From the top curl on her head to her

stubborn little feet.

And he should have cut off his arm before he'd pulled her in against him like that, smelling the woman of her, feeling the soft warm curves against his chest, seeing questions in her eyes that were about to go up in smoke at the heat from the answers flashing between them.

It didn't even matter that she didn't understand the questions, much less the answers.

He did.

She was trouble all right.

And the worst of it was, he wasn't even asleep yet and he was already dreaming of every way there was of being in trouble.

The OS cowhands just rolled up in a blanket they called a bedroll and went sound asleep.

Sophie had witnessed several of them do that before she and Edith retired to the tent for the night.

Then Edith did nearly the same as soon as they were in the tent, falling asleep even as Sophie was asking a question about what the next day would hold.

Sophie performed her abbreviated toilette and prepared for slumber.

But the images of a day filled with new sights and experiences tumbled through her mind, leading to the near-disaster with the marauding cow. The scene played out in her memory, each detail claiming her attention, right up to the cow's retreat and roping. Then Nate Abbott was before her in memory as suddenly as he had been in reality.

Their words exchanged, his arm reaching out –

Her eyes popped open and she sat up.

If she wasn't going to sleep, she might as well get up.

She tied her wrapper at her waist, then added a blanket around her shoulders against the nighttime chill that never seemed to leave this high country.

Outside the tent, the sounds of the cattle were more pronounced, and the breeze brought snatches of a song one of the nightriders must have been singing to his charges.

The moon slid behind a large cloud, and the stars sparkled their pleasure at holding all the stage. To her right, the western mountains propped up the stars. But looking left, to the relatively flat ground to the east, the stars seemed to cascade right down to the horizon. If she reached far enough, it seemed certain she could scoop some up where they met the ground.

"Get back in your tent."

She jumped at the voice from the shadows. Nate Abbott.

"Mr. Abbott. You are the single most unobliging male I have ever had the –"

"Get back in your tent. Now."

"There is no reason –"

"There is every reason, and if you don't know that, then I've been sorely mistaken about your good sense."

She sucked in a breath.

Did he mean – ?

She gave him no further answer, but turned and stooped to reenter the tent with all the dignity she could muster.

It didn't matter what he meant. His meaning – indeed Nate Abbott himself – was not worth her thinking about. Not a single one of her thoughts.

She drew up the blanket, closed her eyes and worked so hard at not thinking about Nate that she barely slept at all.

⚜

The call to rise came with not a hint of gray in the sky. But Edith was up and out of the tent immediately, having clearly slept as fully dressed as the cowhands did. Requiring some additional time to ensure she was properly attired, Sophie emerged from the tent to a scene of constant motion.

Despite the oddity of the hour and her lack of sleep, she discovered herself famished for breakfast.

Some hours later, with the arriving sun still streaking the sky with gold, she regretted eating quite so hardy a repast. Her mouth tightened against the roiling in her stomach.

Branding was not appealing.

Burning cowhide and panicked bellows of animals mixed with thick dust in an uncomfortable stew. The process of turning male calves into steers added even less pleasant sights and sounds to the mix ... as Nate had said.

Carefully, she stepped back from the end of one of the wagons blocking in what they called the branding herd. In usual circumstances, retreat did not sit well with her. In these circumstances, however, retreat appeared the wiser alternative.

Just before the corner of the wagon would cut off her view, she saw Nate's head come up, and their gazes met for a moment.

His seemed to say *Told you so.*

She was nearly back to the OS camp when String trotted up on a spotted horse.

"There you are, Miss Sophie. You shouldn't oughta be on foot 'round here. If one of those critters breaks loose – well, you saw what near happened to Doughy."

"I was just returning to the camp wagon. I thought I'd get my things, and climb up the ridge to sketch."

He cocked his head at her. "Can't get up in the sidesaddle contraption on your own?"

She chuckled, even as she recognized that if someone else had said that she would have bristled. But she and String had become quite comfortable with each other since the end of their engagement.

"You are very astute, String."

"Don't know about that, seeing's I don't know what it means, but I got some sense. Don't you worry none about getting into that sidesaddle. We'll figure it out. Then I can show you the roundup proper, the way Mr. Bracken said to."

He was as good as his word.

And she felt none of the awkwardness accepting his help that she had with Nate Abbott. Which only proved that String was an innate gentleman.

In a series of switchbacks that lessened the abruptness of the climb, String led them up to a ridge.

From that spot, he pointed out the dayriders holding a herd to one side. "Hands hate that duty," he said. "Driving's dusty, thirsty business, but at least you're moving. Dayriding's just setting. Everybody wants to be down there."

He tipped his head toward the branding area.

From this vantage point, she could see the organization of the event with Nate Abbott at the center of it.

A number of cowhands kept the herd bunched together against the incline of the bluff, nor far from the branding fires. Nate, astride the same horse as yesterday, smoothly swung his rope over the head of one, and led it to crew around one of the fires.

"He'll call out the brand, so they know which iron to use," String said.

Having delivered the animal to the men on the ground to brand and ... *handle* ... Nate returned for the next one, leading it to another fire.

After a dozen such, one cow balked.

"See that," String said as the horse below pivoted from its haunches, though not nearly as dramatically as yesterday. "Strength comes from the rear – er, back legs. But what's steering that strength comes from up front – between a horse's ears, between a rider's ears, and then the reins connecting 'em."

The horse seemed to do no more than shift its weight

to one side, and the cow meekly turned and trotted directly to where the branding crew needed it.

"There!" String shook his head. "He's a rare one."

Nate's mount wheeled and maneuvered into place for him to throw his rope again.

Sophie tsked. "The horse is doing all the work." No wonder each hand required six or more ponies as they called them.

"Not hardly. Some horses get spooked by the herd being at their back, and that's one right there Nate's on. Got to keep their minds occupied all the time. Not give 'em a chance to think of anything else. Watch Nate. You'll see."

She clamped her jaw on a sharp answer about not wanting to watch Nate Abbott, Instead, saying mildly, "Now, String. Even Edith says that you're a better judge of horseflesh than anyone else, including Mr. Abbott."

His slow nod acknowledged the truth of the words. "I can pick 'em. But he gets most out of 'em."

"Of course. That's Nate Abbott to all of you, isn't it? Ever the paragon of OS Ranch."

Immediately she regretted snapping at String. Even more so when he calmly replied, "Couldn't say. Don't know what a paragon is."

"It's someone who's the best example of something," she said matter-of-factly.

String nodded. "Then that's Nate. Best I've ever seen for cow sense, and he wasn't even born to it. If it weren't for him, the OS would've been bust by now."

"But he said —" She caught up her surprise and selected her words more carefully. "Mr. Abbott indicated that Mr. Bracken's management and steadiness in these past difficult years have kept the OS on course for a great opportunity if this roundup and the one in the fall ..."

"Told you that, did he?" He snorted and gave his head a shake, as if at the vagaries of his foreman. "Here, watch him close like."

Once more, Nate was bringing an animal to the closest crew to their vantage point.

"Watch his hands," String instructed. "And his legs. There – see him press. With his leg. Guiding that horse just right. And ... his shift. Way he sits the horse."

That cow expeditiously delivered, Nate was after the next.

"His posture is not good at all."

"Ain't s'pose to be. Don't want to be perched up, all straight and stiff." He cut her a look. "No offense, Miss Sophie."

She inclined her head, fully aware she was perched on Milly, all straight and stiff.

"Sittin' like that you're a rock on a log, easy to get knocked off any time. Nate's moss growing on the log. Part of it. Never slowing it down when it's thinking right, but thinking for it when it gets stupid."

Sophie might have smiled at the thought of all the abilities String attributed to moss and a log. Except she saw exactly what he meant.

"Sometimes, less you see, the more's going on," he said. "Oh, here's a dodgy one, a herd-quitter if I ever seen one."

"Isn't that what you want? A cow that you can remove from the herd to take to the branding fire."

"Under a rope, sure. But not if they get it into their head to do it themselves. Cattle is followers. They see one leaving the herd, they think they can go, too. Get all upset. And pretty soon you don't have a herd at all. It's easier to rope when they're in a bunch."

Nate had come up to the animal in question. It tried to angle around horse and rider. In the background, the movements of the herd had become sharper, more agitated.

"How odd," she murmured. "The hands keeping the herd contained seem more active suddenly, yet their movements are quite slow."

"That's right, Miss Sophie. Got to stay on top of those critters without givin' 'em any excuse to raise a ruckus. They'll settle once Nate gets this a one wrapped up."

Time after time, the animal tried to evade horse and rider. Each move it made toward the herd was countered by Nate and his mount. Yet the cow kept trying, sometimes – as now – seeming to take a moment to consider its next move.

From an instant of utter stillness with horse and cow nearly touching noses, the cow started to dart past. The horse wheeled, stirring dust with his haunches.

It was a feint.

The cow immediately changed course, jumping to the opposite side of the horse.

In a move so sharp that its mane flew one way and tail the other, the horse reacted. It was as if the horse had left its hoofs in the dirt while its body blocked the cow's new move.

And all the while, the man atop sat almost perfectly still, except for the small motions and adjustments String had called to her attention.

He seemed to be in a state of complete concentration. And yet ... Was he smiling?

The cow made another lunge, this one easily countered. It ducked its head with almost the same air as a man might assume who was throwing up his hands in surrender, and stood still, letting the roper throw his loop over its head and lead it on to the proceedings.

String cleared his throat, and she looked around to find him pensively watching his foreman rope the next animal.

"What Nate told you. It's true. Mr. Bracken knows the numbers. He's a good owner. He bought good land. He makes good bargains. He keeps clean books. He treats his hands right. But without Nate he wouldn't have a ranch. Nate runs the outfit. The hands, the horses, the cattle – that's what Nate knows."

"Why doesn't he have his own ranch?"

"Money. Takes a stack of it to get started." He tipped his head. "With the way things are changing there might be room for smaller outfits, but up to now you had to be big just to elbow your way up to the bar. Little ones'd die of thirst at the back."

As if satisfied that she had no response to that, he nodded before adding, "Best get you back to camp for dinner now or there'll be none left with the hands come in."

They rode in silence for several minutes.

"I might've told you a lie, Sophie."

She looked around at him in surprise. "A lie?"

"Not intentional like, but a lie all the same. It's not just money keeps Nate from having his own place. An outfit needs a Nate and it needs a Mr. Bracken. It's not often one man'll combine both. The OS is mighty fortunate to have one as the owner and the other as ramrod."

"You are very wise, String."

"Nah. Just some horse sense."

"You are," she insisted, though her thoughts had moved on. "But will a foreman be satisfied to go on in that capacity forever?"

"Now that's a question, Sophie. That is a question."

CHAPTER TWENTY

The two days Bracken had said she'd stay at the roundup had stretched right through to this last day.

Nate couldn't say if it was from her asking to stay or from Edith begging not to leave or from both, because he'd done his best to steer clear of her.

Even when he'd been called on to run off boys from other outfits who prowled around the OS camp so much like coyotes that he'd expected them to break out in a howl any moment, he'd skirted well wide of her.

At first stirring today – already clear it was going to be a second scorcher in a row after having cool weather luck most of the roundup – Bracken had said that he'd head back to the home ranch come mid-morning, leaving Nate to wrap up. The owner – not one to stand on dignity – would drive the wagon carrying Edith and her, and they'd travel along with Doughy.

The slower-moving wagons would arrive at the home ranch about the same time as those hands who'd be returning there for a rest.

Other hands would move sections of the herd to new grass, not yet grazed. Those who'd rested would go out and take the others' place until every boy had had a breather from the roundup.

Then in another week, maybe two, most of the hands would drive the herd up to higher land for the fresh grass there.

And there'd be any manner of reasons for the ramrod to stay well clear of the OS home ranch for weeks on end.

Sophie saw that for the first time of what seemed the entire roundup, Nate was both alone and unoccupied.

She trotted Milly up beside his much taller mount as man and horse looked down into a shallow gully stretching toward the east.

"Mr. Abbott?"

He stiffened slightly, but turned politely enough. "Morning, Miss Vandercook."

"Good morning. I shall not waste your time with further pleasantries. I have a question." Perhaps she rushed it because she entertained a niggling concern that he'd simply ride away. He had shown a marked tendency to depart her vicinity precipitously these past days.

And if her approach were merely caused by an interest in general conversation, she would not have approached at all. Indeed, she wondered at herself for seeking him out even with this purpose in mind. Perhaps the heat that had risen up in fierce waves yesterday had affected her somewhat. Especially since she had spent nearly two hours sketching, unaware that the shade of the tent had moved on while she had been so occupied. Certainly she had slept very little last night, shifting uncomfortably against a heat that seemed to reside both under and atop her skin.

But he did not ride away. He raised his eyebrows.

"You look mighty flushed, Miss Vandercook. You feeling all right?"

Deeper heat surged into her cheeks. She sat straighter. "Quite well, thank you, Mr. Abbott. I hope you will tell me how the roundup has gone. I cannot ask Mr. Bracken, for it would seem impertinent to inquire into what are, after all, his private affairs. I wasn't certain Edith would have a grasp on the situation. Nor do I want to concern her over the issue."

There was also the matter of trying to catch the girl with any opportunity to talk. She seemed to spend as many hours in the saddle as any cowhand. She had been low-spirited after a day of dayriding, then high-flying when Nate let her rope.

"But you think I'll have a grasp on the situation –"

"I would hope so."

"And you don't mind concerning me or possibly being – what was that? – impertinent to me."

She debated pointing out that he had told her the importance of this roundup to start, so he was the natural source of information. Instead, she said simply. "No."

He laughed.

Another surge moved through her. One she did not examine.

"Fair enough, Miss Vandercook. It's not the best we could have hoped for, but it's on the good side of where we needed to be."

She expelled a long, relieved breath.

For the first time it occurred to her to wonder what he was doing in this spot, so she asked.

He tipped his head to the west.

She realized then that the ever-present background sound of cattle had become progressively louder as they'd talked.

To her right, Sophie saw a line of cattle heading east within the confines of the gully, with Gunner and Lester at its head. The procession would pass directly past their position, with the depression of the gully giving them – if not a bird's eye view – certainly an improved prospect.

"I thought the herd was being taken north and west over gradual stages."

"The main herd," he confirmed

"Then where are these cows –?"

"Steers," he corrected with emphasis, reminding her of her retreat from the branding fires the first day. "These are just a few culls. Going to be sold or used at the home ranch. You do like to eat, don't you?"

She ignored that, and shot him a glance. "Sold? Is cash needed to –"

"Cash is always needed." She suspected he had not meant any grimness to come through, but it did. "Heard about some good stock for sale down toward Casper. If we get enough for these to cover most of that purchase, the OS'll come out ahead in the end. Bracken's always open to improving the herd."

She'd learned enough during the roundup's close quarters to know that was true – the OS owner was open to improving the herd, and to trying new methods. She had also learned that most of the ideas for those improvements and new methods were brought to him by Nate Abbott.

Just before the leaders drew even with where she and Nate sat their mounts, Gunner, on the side farther away from them, looped his rope lightly over the wide-flung horns of the first cow – steer.

"Well done," she called out.

She could see his grin under the shadow of his hat, though her attention was already shifting, because from the near side of the dry creek bed, Lester had swung his rope, too, lassoing the second steer in the row.

Nate grumbled something about showing off.

For a moment, they formed an orderly tableau as they continued along the narrow creek bed.

Afterward, she was certain that the next thing that

happened was that Nate muttered a curse, and before she had made full sense of it, was easing his horse down the embankment.

Beyond that, everything seemed to happen simultaneously.

The first steer twisted and arched. Gunner held on with a triumphant shout.

The second steer reared back with a bellow, then turned and ran to the side — only it did not run toward Lester, but in the opposite direction.

It went behind Gunner's horse, trying to scramble up the side of the far embankment. When it could not accomplish that, it turned to run ahead again. Still with Lester's rope around its head, the rope now stretched all the way across the file.

Gunner's horse had stopped in place, bracing its legs to give Gunner leverage to control his plunging steer.

"Let go! Let the rope go, Lester!" Nate shouted, still descending.

"I can't! It's hung up."

With Lester's steer running past, the rope tightened sharply against the hindquarters of Gunner's horse. It screamed and bucked hard against the rope.

"Go ahead, Gunner. Ride him forward!"

"I'm tryin!"

Gunner, who had dropped his rope, was holding on and spurring his horse to do just what Nate had said — move forward, away from the pressure of the rope. But his steer, now freed, appeared to decide to settle a score, twisting around, trying to hook horse and rider with his horns.

"Slow up easy, Lester!"

Nate urged his horse down the last bit of embankment and across the dry creek bed, shouting and shaking his coiled rope at the oncoming steers that were charging forward toward the scene in their own frenzy.

The sound and motion seemed to check them. At least

enough to let Nate and his horse come up behind the steer Lester had roped.

Nate pressed his horse harder, going up on the angled surface of the embankment. Sophie gasped, certain both would topple.

And then Nate leaned out so wide that it seemed the upper part of his body must separate from the lower portion still gripping the saddle and horse below it.

He spun his rope, with a quick, tight motion.

Masked by Gunner's wild gyrations as he tried to maintain a hold on his panicked horse, Sophie was sure Nate had missed, for there was no abrupt slowing in the steer's wild race.

"Easy now," Nate shouted.

At last, Sophie saw they were slowing. Gradually, slowing. Easing the pressure of the rope rubbing against Gunner's maddened horse.

The creek bed widened, and that allowed String, coming up the side, to go around Lester and add his rope around the first steer, pulling it away so his horns no longer threatened Gunner or his horse.

With the pressure of the cattle coming behind them, they all kept moving forward, but, finally, with both steers contained, Gunner's mount responded to his urging, and shot forward, away from the danger and confusion. After a short time, he brought the horse up the now shallowing embankment, and horse and rider gasped for air.

Only as she neared him did Sophie realize that she had unconsciously guided her own horse in a parallel path along the embankment as the drama had unfolded below.

She slowed her approach to a walk, and spoke quietly to avoid spooking the horse, still inclined to show the whites of its eyes. "Are you all right, Gunner?"

He said nothing, but gave her a white-faced look that so resembled his horse's that she had to stifle an urge to laugh – nerves, she knew.

At that moment, Nate joined them. He gave Gunner a

shrewd look, then mundanely ordered him to ride flank.

Sophie opened her mouth to protest that the boy was in no condition to continue working. Then she closed it. He would not have thanked him for making a fuss. Already, Nate's prosaic order appeared to have steadied him.

He nodded, and turned his horse to walk toward the still-moving line of cattle.

"Damned idiot," Nate said when he was out of earshot. "Showing off for you, you know. Both of them. Good way to get trampled or leastwise lose a thumb."

She should call him to account for cursing. She did not feel up to it. "I don't quite ... I feel foolish to be – rather shaken."

"You're not foolish. If Gunner's horse had gone over, he'd have gone with it," he said flatly. "If that hadn't killed him, those steers, spooked as they were, would've trampled him. Oh, hell – don't you go and faint on me now."

"I won't –"

"You're swaying like a feather in a wind storm. Here. Drink this. "

She took the leather-encased flask he held out, and swallowed.

It was not water.

"Lord Almighty, woman – a swallow, not a gulp. And a gulp the size of a lake. Are you going to spit it out?"

She shook her head. It was already down.

But she couldn't speak.

Or see.

"Ah, there you are, Miss Vandercook" came Mr. Bracken's voice from somewhere beyond the burning haze that both filled her head and surrounded it. She thought the other sound she heard might be the rumble of the wagon. "How fortunate to find you here. We are departing this very moment. If you'll just climb up in the wagon, Nate can tether Milly to the back, and we'll be started."

"Yes, of course," she managed in a voice that did not sound the least like herself.

"Sir, I don't think Miss Vander–"

"If you wouldn't mind helping me dismount, Mr. Abbott." It was the only thing she could think of to stop him from telling Mr. Bracken of what had occurred. Though it was murky in her own mind whether it was her imbibing of whatever had been in the flask, Gunner's near disastrous effort, her apparent unwitting instigation of that behavior, or some combination that she did not wish for him to share with the OS owner.

Nate was beside her knee in what seemed the next moment, though he must have dismounted himself and secured his horse's reins. When she looked down at him, his face had the disturbing tendency to shimmer and swirl, like a reflection in the pond at Lafayette Park on a windy day.

His voice came clearly, however. "Dismount and then what?"

"Ascend to the wagon, of course."

He grunted.

Before she could translate it, she felt a compression around her waist and a dizzying weightlessness as the earth and its rules evaporated beneath her feet.

She was flying.

Floating.

No, far more improbably, she was being lifted from the saddle by Nate Abbott and gently conveyed to the ground. Impressions, moments and sensations jumbled together. His solid shoulder under her hand as she had mounted Jester. Soaring as he boosted her so high into the saddle. Heat and more when he patted her ankle.

All that coming together now in one instant, multiplied as many times over as she had seen cattle at this roundup.

Air would not, could not find purchase in her lungs.

She was falling.

Fainting.

No ...

No, even more improbably, the hold on her waist now raised her. Seemingly straight up. And she allowed it. Trusted it. Knew he would bring her to where she needed to be.

And that, beyond anything else, brought a lowering stinging to her eyes.

What was this? What –?

"Here you go, Sophie."

Edith's strong, long-fingered grasp took hold of her arm and tugged her into position.

Sophie opened her eyes. Despite an odd blurriness spread across her eyes, she recognized that she now sat on the wagon bench beside Edith, with Mr. Bracken beyond the girl.

Her vision cleared sufficiently to make out Nate's face peering up at her with – What? The thought came that deciphering the meaning behind his intent gaze would answer many questions.

But she couldn't decipher it, even with not one bit of his face obscured by his hat because of the way his head was tipped back.

She had never seen this expression on his face before. What could it –? Oh. Oh, dear.

The expression was shifting, escaping her as it reformed ... into something entirely different. Something ... Yes. There. ... Now, this expression she did know.

Disapproval.

"Get out of the sun," came his brusque order. "Even if you have to sit in back."

"No room in back," Edith said cheerfully.

"Don't you have one of those –" he made a circular motion with one hand that forced Sophie to close her eyes against a sudden dizziness. "– parasol things to keep the sun off her?"

Edith laughed. "A parasol? At a roundup?"

"I'm quite all right," she managed to get out.

"You do look rather flushed, Miss Vandercook," Mr. Bracken said. From the sound of his voice, he'd leaned around Edith to look at her.

"Momentary, I assure you. We had best get on our way. Good day, Mr. Abbott," she added in clear dismissal.

She straightened her back and looked straight ahead.

He made a disgusted sound and wheeled away.

CHAPTER TWENTY-ONE

The sound Nate Abbott made at not having his order instantly obeyed had stiffened her posture for only a minor portion of the trip to the home ranch.

Jolting, swaying, hot.

They'd been traveling this way forever, and they would continue forever. The home ranch was a mirage she'd thought she'd seen half a dozen times.

Even the traveling corset felt horridly restrictive. She longed to unloose it and to slide between unwarmed sheets in the frigid attic of Mrs. Forestell's Academy for Young Ladies on the coldest day of a St. Louis winter. Yet there were moments when only the corset seemed to hold her upright.

Jolting, swaying, hot.

Forever.

The wagon heaved over what must have been a mountain, then the wheels settled into what felt to be a track. She looked around, and saw – yes, surely that was the main house.

Yet, Sophie could not muster any enthusiasm for the

reality now that it was here. She felt as drained of energy as the wood of the house was drained of moisture. As desiccated as the bones of those poor animals that had died in the storms of '86.

The wagon stopped, but not even that stirred her. Though her sense told her the wagon was still, she reached out a hand to steady herself.

Edith hopped down from the other side and dashed off, the movement tipping the seat so that Sophie had to close her eyes against a sudden dizziness.

"Miss Vandercook?"

She opened her eyes to find Mr. Bracken extending a polite hand to assist her. Summoning a smile, she accepted it, as he solicitously aided her to the ground. "You must be tired beyond measure, Miss Vandercook. You must rest now."

She murmured a thank you, but he had already turned away, his attention caught by the hallo call of Royal, who had been at a distant roundup. Their heads already together over papers Royal handed over, they immediately stepped into the house, just as Doughy emerged with a bucket dangling from one hand.

"Mulehead!"

An involuntary step backward at the noise brought Sophie back against the wagon bed.

"That danged Mulehead. Wagon to unload, stove not lit, and not a drop of fresh water in the kitchen. How'm I supposed to get dinner for those hands that'll be coming in any time now? Where is that no-good —"

"I'll get it," she said hurriedly, sensing the windup to another shout. "The water."

Water. Yes, that's what she needed. A cool drink. She'd go to the creek, and get a reviving drink, and then she'd fill the bucket for Doughy.

"Nice of you," he grumbled, thrusting the bucket at her. "One'll get me started. Though I'll need a sight more before the cookin's done."

Before she could muster a response, he'd thumped back inside.

She must have followed the path automatically, because the next thing she was fully aware of was sitting on the log by the creek with the empty bucket beside her, and hearing a voice calling her name.

"Miss Vandercook! Oh, here you are. Doughy's hoppin' mad. Said you came for water an age ago, and haven't bothered to come back."

It was young Gunner.

She licked her lips. "Water?"

"Yeah, for cookin'. Here, I'll get it."

He grabbed the bucket and was back in a flash, sloshing some of the water over the bucket's side, onto her shoe and the hem of her skirt.

"Sorry. Sorry, Ma'am." He yanked off his bandana, and knelt beside her daubing at the moisture. Red flashed up his neck as his touch encountered her ankle beneath the layers of cloth. "Sorry – I didn't mean no–"

"Drink," she got out. Proprieties seemed very distant at the moment.

"What? Oh? You want some water? There's no ladle. I'll just –"

He scooped his cupped hands into the water, then hesitated as the precious liquid dripped back into the bucket. She cupped her hands under his, drawing them up at the same time she bent her head, drinking as much as she could before it drained away to mere moisture on his skin.

"Again," she demanded, dropping both their hands into the water and bending to the impromptu cup once more.

Four times they repeated the motion, until she began to feel that her body might not turn to dust in the next instant.

Still, her senses must have remained dulled, for she was aware of young Gunner talking most earnestly, as now he held her hands between both of hers.

With a man, she would surely have withdrawn her hands from his clasp. But it would require such an effort at this moment, and surely with Gunner, it was not so very improper.

"... and come next year's roundup, why, I might be at point. You'll see – I'll make you proud."

She smiled – at least she thought she smiled. "I'm sure I would be proud. But I won't be here." She feared she garbled some words, but finished strongly, with "... return to St. Louis."

He rocked back on his heels, and she realized he'd still been kneeling before her.

"Go back to St. Louis?" he repeated with a frown. "But I'm staying here."

She tried the smile again. "Of course. Because you so love Wyoming Territory."

His frown disappeared into a blinding smile that made her blink. "See? See! I knew you would understand – that rare woman who truly understands her man. That's perfect."

"Is it?" She felt as if she were back in the wagon, jolted and swaying, and not at all sure what was her imagination.

"Sure is. After fall roundup, I'll come visit winters in St. Louis, then be back here for spring."

His enthusiastic hug wrapped her in arms that didn't yet know their strength. He squeezed the air out of her lungs, at the same time she was denied access to a new supply by having her nose and mouth pressed firmly into his shoulder.

She was positively lightheaded when he finally released her. She sat back, breathless and dizzy.

"You've made me the happiest man ever. You –"

"Wait. I don't –"

"– won't regret saying yes, Ma'am –"

Had she said yes? To what? He seemed so sure. But with her head swirling ... "I–"

"I mean ... Sophie! *Dear*! I swear you won't. I'll take care of you, like you deserve. I'm not one of those waddies who's got no more to his name than his saddle. I've been saving up my wages right along. And after a few more years I'll have a real stake. Enough to take care of a wife like a man ought."

A *wife* ...?

But that would mean –

"That's, uh, admirable, Gunner," she murmured, trying to piece together their conversation, but her head simply would not stop swirling.

He shifted. "Yeah. But there is something I should tell you, Miss Va – Sophie. Darling."

Indeed, there *was* something she needed him to tell her: Had she said yes to a proposal?

But she didn't recall a proposal. She'd said no so clearly to the other proposals, surely she had done so to this one, too.

Of course, she had said yes to String. But that was before she had recognized a flaw in her plan.

She thought she heard a familiar voice, and turned toward it. "Nate?"

But it was not Nate Abbott who sat beside her, it was young Gunner.

What had he been saying? Something odd. Something about –

"It's just that Colt isn't really my name."

That caught her attention. "Gunner?"

"No, that's just what they call me here, after I told them my name's Virgil Colt. But like I said, Colt's not really my name, Neither's Virgil. It's what you might call an alias. Like Billy the Kid."

Like Billy the Kid? "The outlaw?"

He nodded. "Here in the west a man can be whoever he wants to be, can leave behind what he did in the States. That's what I did when I came out here."

Her thoughts swirled erratically. This fresh-faced young

man had done things back in the States that he'd felt a need to leave behind? Surely not ... but then wasn't it said that the outlaw gained the sobriquet The Kid because of his own boyish, seemingly fresh-faced appearance?

And the nickname. Gunner. Oh...

"More than a year ago," Virgil – no, not Virgil – said.

She touched a hand to her forehead. It was dry, and quite hot. "What?"

"When I came west more than a year ago, that's when I took the name Virgil Colt. After the gun, see? That's why they call me Gunner."

She let out a breath. A much more benign explanation than the swirls in her head. "I'm afraid I don't see, Gun – no, uh, Vir – what do I call you?"

"My real name's Warrington Webster Scott." She blinked at him.

"But I'd prefer if you didn't tell anybody here that, and just kept calling me Gunner. Course I'll put the right name on the marriage certificate – my father's a lawyer back in Chicago, and I know everything has to be done right for it to be legal. It's just, I wouldn't want the other boys to know. So if you could keep it to yourself. They get after me something fierce already about the way I talk and the book-learning. I can just hear them if they knew the truth of it about Warrington Webster Scott and my family and all. I'd never hear the end of it about servants and society and such. But we can trust Nate to take care of getting the right name on the certificate without it getting around."

"Nate?"

"Sure. Nate's up to all the tricks."

"Yes. So, he knows you are, uh ..." She knew the word. She was sure she knew the word. "Incognito."

"Sure. And I don't plan on staying Virgil Colt forever. It's a hard life out here on the older hands. Nate's holding up okay, but he's got a lot going for him, being foreman and all." He leaned back and laced his hands behind his head. "Yeah, when I get old, I'll give up the cowboy life.

I'll go back to the States – St. Louis would do fine. Don't want to go crawling back to Chicago like I'm a kid. But I'd put my stake to work. Maybe even decide to be a lawyer. Once it's clear it's my decision, and nobody else's."

"I ..." She could think of nothing to follow that syllable. Her mind was an absolute void.

"It'll be grand, you'll see."

"What'll be grand?"

She didn't need to turn her head to know that question came in the voice of Nate Abbott. That was fortunate, because if she had needed to verify it and thus needed to turn, she feared her head might fall off her neck. In addition, she wasn't entirely certain she wouldn't cry if he were another mirage.

"When I get old and leave cow work, and settle down with Sophie back in St. Louis and –"

"What's this nonsense? You were sent to see what was keeping Miss Vandercook and the water and you're yammering about –" As she sensed his presence coming around in front of her, Nate broke off what he'd been saying with what she thought might be another oath. She should object to such language. Except at the moment she couldn't recall what he'd said. "Sophie, can you hear me?"

She tried to say that of course she could hear him. It came out as *Ummbleh*.

Nate clicked his tongue, and said under his breath, "Fool woman. You're swaying sitting down."

"You're not listening, Nate." Gunner's voice sounded tinny and distant. "You're the first to know – Sophie's going to marry me."

Nate's face swam into view before her eyes, and she realized he'd crouched in front of her.

"Is she now?" His voice was so low, so close, so soothing. He brought his hand up, and brushed the back of his fingers across her cheek, then caught a curl and tucked it behind her ear.

It felt ... It *felt* ...

Was this the romantic sensation Louisa had alluded to in whispered confidences in the dark of night about the mysteries of the marriage bed?

"Yes," Gunner said from that ever increasing distance. She was aware that he said a great deal more, but none of the meaning of the words penetrated.

If one were to have a husband, one of a romantic and tragic nature would make for a very uncomfortable home.

Perhaps not so uncomfortable if this were romantic ...

Certainly it was nothing like her response to Harry Jenkins' impassioned petition for her hand in March in St. Louis.

Romantic and tragic nature.

She wasn't entirely sure, since she had only a child's remembered observations to form a judgment now, but it occurred to her that her mother might have been of that nature.

Though if these sensations were romantic, then ...

"Not romantic at all," she mumbled.

"What was that, Sophie?" Nate asked from so close that it was a whisper.

She turned to his voice and her lips brushed across something stubbled and warm. Was that his chin? She moved her head again to repeat the sensation, and gladly paid the price of dizziness.

"Caused a stir," she acknowledged. "Sorry."

"Wasn't your fault. You did fine," he murmured, shifting more to her side. She felt his arm across her back. It felt solid. Strong.

"– and further discussing our plans for the future," came Gunner's voice.

"Well, that's fine," Nate said. "But I can tell you that Miss Sophie's immediate future is going to consist of getting in out of the sun and heat, and getting plenty to drink."

Nate picked her up – a very peculiar sensation. But as he set off with her, any other considerations perforce gave way to the manner in which the motion accelerated the swirls in her head.

"Put your head on my shoulder, Sophie, and close your eyes before you pass out for sure. And you get that water, Gunner, before Doughy pops all his buttons from pure irritation."

So it was that she was carried into the main house of the OS Ranch and up the stairs to her bedroom by Nate Abbott, while her second betrothed followed behind, carrying the water bucket, and detailing his plans for their future.

CHAPTER TWENTY-TWO

Sophie slept straight through to the next morning, when Edith appeared in her room with a tray for breakfast.

"Nate and Pa say to stay tucked up this morning, and to drink your fill. And when you think you've had your fill, drink some more."

Sophie was heartily glad of the rest, for she felt as if she had forfeited every vestige of energy to yesterday's sun and exertion. She had also acquired an ache between her brows, as well as an odd heaviness above her ribs.

She gladly closed her eyes and slept again.

It was not until Edith returned to gather the tray and to bring her more lemonade that the girl's unusually subdued manner captured her attention.

"Were you also affected by the sun yesterday, Edith?"

"Me?" Her voice skidded up, and Sophie added two more observations: Edith's surprise was genuine and it was the first time she had looked Sophie in the face during these two missions of mercy. The latter observation was brought home when the girl quickly looked away again.

"I'm fine."

"I'm glad to hear of it. Although ... is something amiss, Edith?"

"No. No. Nothing's amiss." She produced a sickly smile. "I suppose any soul around could appear long-faced compared to what you're feeling right now, that's all."

"What I'm feeling."

Billy the Kid.

Now, where did that thought come from? And why did it drop a cloud of foreboding around her?

"It's just comparing your joy to us ordinary mortals that has you thinking there might be something amiss with me."

"My joy."

You won't regret saying yes.

"Yeah. You and Gunner. You should have seen him at breakfast – he was over the moon."

"Gunner." *No ... no ... Oh, no.* Foreboding blossomed to full-blown dismay. "Gunner."

"Yeah. Your husband-to-be."

❧

Dinner was a jocular affair among most of the OS outfit.

Sophie arrived at table braced for an awkward encounter with Gunner, but from the moment they exchanged hellos, the joshing and chaffing of the other hands kept him fully occupied. Right up until Nate ordered them all to eat and get back to work, or go back to work right then and be hungry the rest of the day.

Mr. Bracken appeared puzzled. Edith was silent even as she ate her usual hearty meal. Nate was unreadable.

Like the rest of them, Gunner ate, and headed for the door as soon as he'd finished. Only he paused at the door, turning back to tip his hat to her, saying, "I'll come by to see you later ... dear."

Shortly after that, Mr. Bracken, noting that Sophie had only picked at her food, recommended that she return to her room for further rest.

She enjoyed no repose, however. After a half hour, she searched for Edith, to see how her studies progressed. The girl was not in the house, and her papers remained in the same neat stack as when they had left for the roundup.

Sophie took a bit of mending with her and went to sit on the porch.

She would need to see Gunner at some point. Better to do it soon. She certainly was not going to hide in her room. Even though she had no plan.

Everyone considered them betrothed. Except herself. Though, if she had said yes – which was not at all clear in her memory – she was committed.

No, she amended, she was committed regardless. How could she possibly say that she believed it had all been a misunderstanding – though she wasn't entirely certain.

She could not.

Gunner would be humiliated before every soul in the OS outfit, and from what she'd learned of the communication among cowhands, across all of Wyoming Territory.

She let her eyes close, phrases and fragments running through her mind, reforming into a patchy, yet recognizable memory.

A familiar cadence of boot heels rapping across the front hall, heading for the door to the porch, jolted her upright, her heart tripping.

The door swung open to reveal Nate.

"Are you all right, Miss Vandercook? You still look rather peaked."

"I'm fine, Mr. Abbott."

"Perhaps that frown, then, is from disappointment not to see your betrothed."

She kept her gaze on her mending to avoid glaring at him.

"Sorry, I needed to send him out a ways on some work this afternoon. Won't be back till supper. Maybe later."

"As you have said previously, he's a hard worker. I am not surprised you relied on him."

There. If he thought to goad her about Gunner, let him make of that what he would.

He crossed to beside the bench where she sat, poured a glass of lemonade from the items on the tray she'd brought out, and offered it to her.

"No thank you."

"Drink it. What happened yesterday was nothing to fool with."

She flicked a look at his face to see if the double meaning she thought she'd caught in his tone was clearer there. It was not.

She took the glass. "Thank you. And thank you for your –" She faltered, then picked it up again. "– assistance yesterday."

"My pleasure."

She chose to disregard any semblance of additional meaning in that beyond the usual courtesy.

"I suppose I might owe you some apology, too," he added

She looked up quickly. "Apology?"

"In addition to a fine case of sunstroke, I might have contributed – accidentally – to your, uh, not being entirely yourself yesterday."

Heat rose up her chest, heading for her cheeks. She refused to hide by bending over her mending. She lowered it to her lap, and looked directly at him. "Not at all, Mr. Abbott."

His eyes glinted at her from under the brim of his hat, but his voice was serious. "Yes at all, Miss Vandercook. That was quite a volume of whisky you swallowed yesterday morning."

"*Whisky!*"

"Yep. What did you think it was?"

"When I drank it, I believed it to be water. Afterward ... I did not speculate."

"Well, it was whisky."

"I was under the impression that imbibing was not allowed on the OS Ranch."

"It's not – not for recreation. But times come it's needed medicinally. That's why the ramrod carries a healthy amount. Leastwise it was a healthy amount before you got hold of it. You took in an amount that could fell some men twice your size who'd been drinking whisky since they were weaned."

For a moment their eyes met, and she understood perfectly what he was saying between and behind his words.

She could claim she hadn't known what she was saying when she accepted Gunner's proposal. Which was true.

Yet, it came back to the same matter as before – he would be humiliated. And for no fault of his own.

She picked up her mending, setting a single careful stitch as she considered. Then another, and a third.

She looked up before the fifth.

"I would appreciate it if you did not share with others that I drank whisky – however inadvertently."

Their eyes still met, but now she had no idea what thoughts were behind his eyes, and he gave her no words to consider except, "Ma'am."

She expected him to leave then. Instead, he took the second glass she'd brought out in expectation of Edith joining her at some point, filled it, then leaned back against the railing, facing her.

Not prepared to wait meekly for whatever else he chose to say to her, she set her mending in her lap once again, and looked up at him. "At what point were you going to tell me the truth about Gunner, Mr. Abbott?"

"What truth?"

"About his real name, about his home in Chicago."

"Ah, he's told you, then, has he? I expected he would.

Not one to try to fool people or keep secrets."

Her brows rose. "You don't consider not using his real name and hiding his background as keeping secrets."

"It wasn't any of your business. Not until you agreed to marry him. He's not doing it to push nor pull somebody into doing something for him." After a brief pause, he added. "There's no real harm in the boy. So I figured he'd tell you – at least some of it."

She eyed him narrowly. "What do you mean, at least some of it?"

"His family's one of the wealthiest in Chicago. So you're coming out of this mighty fine."

"I do not need his money. I–" She closed her eyes. She must still be lightheaded to come so near to ignoring her grandfather's advice. And to this near-stranger, when she had not told *anyone* of her inheritance. "I do not have an avaricious nature, Mr. Abbott."

His sideways tip of the head could have been dismissing the topic. Or disbelieving her. "Hear the family's real important in those fancy society doings and all, too. And I never yet heard of a female who didn't enjoy parties and such."

Perhaps her head was clearing, because now she fully recognized the probe behind his words. And recognizing it, she determined to return the favor.

"You must have a very narrow acquaintance among those of my gender to have experienced such a limited range of character."

"Wide enough acquaintance."

"As you said of Powder River, a mile wide and an inch deep."

"That's plenty deep for me. So you'll have everything you could ever want back in the States."

"He informs me that he's staying here, on the OS Ranch. Until he's old." She shot him a look. "Like you."

His mouth twitched – with a grin.

"No he won't. He probably wouldn't be here at all if

his father hadn't tried to keep him on too short a rein back in Chicago. Ordered him to become a lawyer, never giving him a chance to breathe or think on his own. Only way Gunner could show him he was becoming a man was to leave."

"You sound as if you might have had a similar experience."

Now that made him shift his feet. "Me? No. Nothing like that. My father's no fancy lawyer in Chicago. No secret of a wealthy family here. But don't worry. Gunner'll go back soon enough. You'll have your perfect married life. Though you're in the same situation as with String – have to wait to autumn when the preacher comes back."

His eyes were on her again, watching her closely.

This time she did avoid the examination by concentrating on her mending.

The beginning of an idea had taken hold.

"Why do you think Gunner will go back soon? You haven't – gone back to the States, I mean. You came out here when you were about the same age he is now, and you've stayed."

"I didn't come out here for adventure. I came for a life. Now Gunner's had his adventure, he'll be ready to head back to the States with you and start married life."

CHAPTER TWENTY-THREE

Nate didn't slow his pace when he caught Sophie's voice. Nor when he recognized the male responses came from Gunner.

He didn't give a fig that they were betrothed. He wasn't going to have one of his hands whiling away the afternoon spooning with his sweetheart by the creek.

He was near enough to catch words now, though still out of sight.

"... so unfortunate we haven't been allowed an opportunity to talk before this."

"Darling!" declared Gunner.

A rustling sound of fabric came as if Sophie had moved quickly. "To talk about our future, I mean."

"We did. That day I proposed."

If they thought they could steal away any time they chose, he'd have Gunner back out on the range fast as a —

"Ah, but not in detail," she said so smoothly that Nate would almost believe she remembered details of that interlude if he hadn't been there himself and knew for a fact she hadn't been in her right head.

Just look at the way she'd leaned into his touch on her cheek like a flower reaching for the sun. Or the way she'd curled against his chest when he'd picked her up. Sophie in his arms, her sweet weight against him, her head tucked under his chin, so that wild hair of hers tickled at him until his heart felt as big and soft as another part of him felt big and –

He shied away from that memory just as Sophie's words rose up to grab his attention.

"–a lawyer just like your father."

"But, Sophie," Gunner protested.

"Oh, I know not right away. You'll have to study first. And it will take time to work your way up in your father's firm."

Now what in tarnation was that female up to, when he'd told her the boy had run away – ?

"My father's firm? No," Gunner said. "You're going back to St. Louis, and I'll visit you there winters."

"Oh, I know that was the original plan." She sounded breathless. Like one of those females whose head was empty enough that the wind would whistle passing through it. Yet devious. "But you must agree it makes far more sense for us to be in Chicago. Why start at the beginning as a lawyer in St. Louis when your father's already made a name for the family in Chicago."

"But I don't want –"

"Of course!" she interrupted. "We'll live with your parents while you are establishing yourself in the firm. That will allow me to learn from your mother all the ways to take our place in the top ranks of Chicago society. The opera –"

Nate began to back away from his listening post, though he did catch a low groan from Gunner.

He couldn't help but feel sorry for the boy, though it was a necessary dose of medicine.

He was as near certain as a man could be that it would do the trick. And do it in a way that wouldn't leave the boy's pride smarting over being turned down by his first love.

That thought caught at his insides like a stitch in his ribs from being kicked by a horse. He ignored it, as he would a physical pain.

Yeah, Sophie's way would do.

He'd wondered what she'd intended when she turned aside his offer to let it be known she hadn't been herself that day. Wondered, even as he'd respected her for not having her way out be paid off at the expense of Gunner's pride.

And he'd do his part, by making sure Gunner was near enough to the home ranch for a while so she could work on him good.

As for him, he could keep one eye on the home ranch, but from a distance. He didn't need to be seeing Sophie day in and day out while she was betrothed to be married. Even if she was doing her best to get out of it.

❧

It was done.

Sophie could not remember ever being quite so weary.

Day after day of pressing Gunner to live a life that neither he nor she wanted, always with cheerful, unyielding blindness to his growing misery had been the hardest work she had ever endured.

Edith's distance had added another layer to her own unhappiness.

Then there had been the frowns from Mr. Bracken.

And an uneasy discomfort among those hands who had passed through the home ranch on their way to or from assignments on the range.

String had been the only exception, even patting her on the shoulder one evening as he bid her goodnight after everyone else retired early from a morose gathering on the porch.

The only person who might have understood what she was doing and why she was doing it had absented himself completely from the home ranch.

Not that she wanted Nate Abbott as a witness to slowly persuading Gunner that she was a mercenary, ambitious, gold-digger. Not at all. He was the last person she wanted around.

Or perhaps the last person she wanted around was herself.

How had this all gone so —

"So you decided not to have him."

Nate's voice came from behind her. She looked steadily toward the stream. "I prefer solitude at this moment," she informed him.

"You look worn out. You'd think this engagement-breaking would be getting easier for you with practice."

"As I said," she enunciated with deadly calm, "I prefer solitude, Mr. Abbott."

"That's what they said you'd said when they told me you'd broken off your engagement from Gunner."

"I did not break —"

"The hell you didn't. But don't get yourself in a twist. They all think it was a mutual recognition that you would not suit." He minced those words, before resuming in his normal tone. "Just so you know I'm not addlebrained enough not to know that whatever words were spoken, whoever said them, you did the breaking."

He sat beside her on the log, his legs stretched out before him, almost close enough to touch.

She turned her head to fix his face with a glare that even he could not misunderstand or withstand.

"I am astonished, sir. You say you knew that I had expressed a preference for solitude, yet you came here. I confirmed that wish, and yet you impose yourself on me."

"Don't see why you'd be astonished. You told me I was the most unobliging man you've met, so I'd think you'd be expecting this."

With a quick jerk, she twitched the fabric of her skirt away from him, as if fearing contagion from potential contact.

The motion had the unintended consequence of sending the bottom of the skirt in a larger sweep, which fully exposed her boots and several inches of leg above them. She flung the fabric back to remedy that, and now it cascaded over his lower legs.

She felt the flick of his gaze on her face, but she forced herself to neither return it nor to jump up and run away. With cold resolve, she gathered her skirt back, so that it fell in proper folds in the space between them.

The recognition that it was now where it had been at the start stoked the fire under her emotions to such an extent that she could not stop herself from demanding, "How can any one individual be so ... so rude?"

He said nothing for a moment, then asked in a tone entirely devoid of emotion, "Why'd you come here, Sophie?"

"What right do you have to quiz me on such matters? And you may address me as Miss Vandercook."

The corner of his mouth quirked. "That's more like it. Get some color in those cheeks. I'll tell you what right I have to ask about such matters, Sophie. You seem to be getting engaged to my crew one by one, but never quite coming to marry any of them, and it's as unsettling to them as lightning cracking all around a herd. If I'm not careful, I'll have a stampede on my hands, not knowing which direction they'll take off or if they'll just mill around and around until they trample each other to death."

Her mouth dropped open. She closed it with a snap. "Are you – are you accusing me of inciting the ranch hands here to ... to violence?"

"I'm saying you're like lightning. And I'm asking why'd you come here?"

"Surely even your understanding is sufficient to recall

that I came to visit my brother."

"Lay your bristles, woman. I'm asking a simple question. And if it was to see Vandercook, why didn't you leave when you discovered he was dead?"

She turned away once more. She would vouchsafe no answer.

"You knew he was no good, didn't you?"

The question so astonished her that she twisted back around and met his gaze before considering it.

Proper words of denial were stillborn. Truth emerged. "I could not be certain, but the family history predicted it. Our father was certainly not of good character."

He gazed at her. She saw neither condemnation nor pity, but solely acceptance.

The sting of tears ambushed her. She started to drop her chin, but his hand came under it, holding it steady.

His lips brushed her brow, her eyes drifting closed under the warmth of that touch.

Then her check.

The corner of her mouth.

Her lips.

His mouth was against hers – harder than hers, yet not harsh.

Her own lips parted, and for a moment the brush became more than that, a pressure that teetered toward something more.

Then he drew back.

Her eyelids rose, slowly, heavily.

He was looking at her again. Now with a very different expression. It seemed to promise and demand far beyond her experience or expectations.

Don't see why you'd be astonished. You said I was the most unobliging man you've met, so I'd think you'd be expecting this.

But she had not expected *this*.

She'd had no time to prepare. To establish a plan.

And she did not know how to respond. To the kiss, or to the openness of his gaze.

She dropped her own gaze to her hands, woven together in her lap. Words spilled out unconsidered.

"I suppose Jerry was a spendthrift, as our father was. My grandfather absolutely distrusted my father. He went to great lengths to preserve the money he gave to my mother from my father's control." She did not mention that those efforts – and the funds – extended an additional generation, to her.

He shrugged. A glimpse from the corner of her eye showed him apparently entirely at ease once more, though his eyes were shadowed by his hat.

"My Grandpa Tompkins never liked my Pa above half," he said. "He'd say Ma could have done better for herself. And Pa said the same about each of my sisters' beaus when they were courtin'. Ma used to laugh and say it was always the way of fathers and their daughters, right back to the first one."

"I don't doubt that such was true for your family. However, I remember from earliest childhood my father's continuous complaints to my mother about not having the funds to defray household accounts, and how her money should have been available to him. That proves my grandfather's view of him."

"Maybe he needed the money to keep the household going," he said prosaically. "From what you've said – and the bits Vandercook said – your mama wasn't much for minding accounts."

"Indeed?" she inquired coldly. His words swept away any misty uncertainty she had felt with brusque efficiency. First, he backed her father, then he insulted her mother and now he tried to make it out that it was her own words that led him to these calumnies? "If I have led you to believe that my mother was improvident I beg your pardon," she said in a tone meant to let him know that he should be the one begging pardon. Seeing he was about to speak, she continued quickly, "And my mother's ability to keep close household or not is beyond the point."

"Well, what is that point then?"

"To put it baldly, what does it say of a man that he had two wives who declined and went to an early grave?"

"Are you saying your father killed his wives?" he asked with mild interest.

"No!" she snapped, irritated at his turning a delicate matter into a blunt instrument. Alice and Louisa had understood immediately, sighing with her over her father's failures as a husband. Why couldn't he understand? "But there is another kind of behavior which can lead to some woman declining."

"So now you're saying he ignored them to death?"

Because he chose to condense her nuances into blocks of ice did not mean that she must do the same. She would persevere in her explanation, even if he failed to take it in. Sometimes with students, an explanation did not penetrate immediately, but lay fallow until it erupted in understanding at a later point. She could hope it would be so with him.

"When a woman is surrounded by a complete lack of sensitivity–"

"Thought you said you turned down one of those suitors back in St. Louis because he was too sensitive."

She ignored that as well. "—and is forced to live in an atmosphere where no word of sympathy, of understanding is ever spoken, such an existence can choke off the will to live."

He narrowed his eyes and studied her. "I don't see you losing your will to live under a stampede of cattle, much less because of what a man might say or not say to you."

She didn't know whether to be insulted or oddly flattered. "I sincerely hope to never be under a stampede of cattle, so the matter does not arise," she said tartly.

"Well, it just seems to me that if you'd wanted one of those mooning, poetry-reciting dandies, you had a chance at one back in St. Louis. But it doesn't seem to me that it would be real comfortable. And from how you and

Vandercook talked about her, I've got my suspicions that your mother was just such a one—only female."

She forgot that similar thoughts about her mother had bobbed into her thoughts. She forgot her own comments to Edith about marriage to someone of a romantic and tragic nature being uncomfortable.

She had the right to consider such matters. He did not.

"The suitor you so dismiss is an intelligent young man of a fine family and upstanding character. His prospects are excellent in life. And he adores me. As for my mo–"

"Sounds like you should have snapped up that feller when he came calling. Would've saved you a trip out here." His brows had dropped, creating slits of his eyes. "And it sure would've kept this outfit a more peaceable place to be."

"Yes, though my sentiments are not expressed in such colorful language, I am coming to realize that I would have been far better off to have accepted his offer than to ever have conceived that there might be a match one might call equal for me in Wyoming."

He opened his mouth, snapped it closed, then rose and walked off, thus proving that not only had she bested him in that argument, but also that he was rude.

It was that discourtesy that caused her eyes to sting as she watched his long strides head away from her. That or, perhaps, the dust.

CHAPTER TWENTY-FOUR

Through the open window of the parlor Sophie heard a shout of "Nate! Come quick!"

Her gaze met Edith's as they both stilled with their needles poised. The girl's avoidance of her had ebbed with the end of her engagement to Gunner a week ago, though their former closeness had not fully returned.

Sophie had only another instant to contemplate that she had not been aware that the OS foreman was within shouting distance of the main house – a rare occurrence of late – before contemplation fled.

A sharp, echoing sound, followed by the roar of men's voices, had both of the room's occupants on their feet and rushing out the door, through the hall, out the front door, across the porch and down the steps.

Sophie might have expected that her training as an instructor at Mrs. Forestell's Young Ladies' Academy would have honed her reactions to a razor's edge, but Edith had the offsetting advantage of having been raised on the frontier.

They were in a dead heat as they crossed the bare earth

toward the bunkhouse, skirts held up for speed.

A knot of men formed rough semicircles around the door, all apparently craning to get a view inside.

They were only halfway to their destination when Nate emerged from the ranks of the men, which re-formed behind him as he strode toward her and Edith.

"What happened?" Sophie demanded.

"Somebody get shot?" Edith added.

Sophie stopped where she was. "*Shot?*"

Of course. That was the sound. Now that the word had been spoken, she knew it. "Oh, no. Oh — was anyone hurt?"

"No." Nate snapped the word, then took one last, long stride and snagged Sophie's arm in a most ungentlemanly manner. "You're coming with me."

She was turned and started toward the creek before she knew it.

Over his shoulder he ordered Edith, who'd started to come after them. "You stay put. All of you," he added, apparently to the hands.

Sophie gave him another half dozen paces, nearly to the line of trees, but he still had not slowed or released her.

"Really, Mr. Abbott, this is uncalled for."

"Really, Miss Vandercook, it's entirely called for." He did, however, adjust his hold and his pace. Not quite to her comfort, but to an acceptable level.

At the creek's edge, he halted for the space of two breaths. Not looking at her. Yet, she felt somehow that he was entirely aware of her. As aware as she of the way his large hand still encircled her arm.

He huffed out a breath and he released his hold at last.

Her arm dropped as if it were unconnected to her shoulder — or her will. She refrained from rubbing it, rather concentrating on maintaining her calm and her dignity.

"I am relieved no one came to harm in —"

"*Harm!*" He spun around to her on the repetition. "That is the third fight in the bunkhouse this week — in the bunkhouse alone. No way of knowing how many others there've been that I don't get called Nate-come-quick's about. There're as many bruises and split lips around this outfit as we'd get in a month of bronc-busting. All because of a bit of thing that should have stayed in St. Louis where you belonged."

"Are you –?"

"And this time one of those goldarned idiots pulled a gun. It's no fault of theirs we don't have two dead boys lying in that bunkhouse instead of a hunk of the roof missing."

"Am I to understand that you are faulting me for the behavior of the men under your supervision? Is that what you're trying to convey?"

"Da– Yes. That's exactly what I'm saying. You're to blame."

Having made his pronouncement, he crossed his arms over his chest, tipped his head back and glared down from his greater height at her.

"I have not done a solitary thing to stir those whom you call boys – though most are anything but – to misconduct. You can not point to a single action of mine –"

"You're here. That's plenty."

"I can hardly –"

"And you go around all the time. Looking like ... like *that* –" He swept one hand down to indicate her simple attire. "And with your hair all – all tumbled like, even when it's up. And ... and *smelling*."

"Smelling? I do not –"

"Like those damned flowers – danged. Those danged flowers. Those – oh, hell."

He gripped her arm and swung her around so sharply that she lost her footing and was certain she would crash into him. But before she could, he had wrapped his other hand around her other arm, and secured her with her toes just touching the dirt.

And he kissed her.

Kissed her as she had never been kissed before.

That – the remaining practical portion of her brain acknowledged – was not difficult since she had only been kissed once before on the lips by a man. One week ago by Nate.

A gentle pressing of his lips to hers ... except for that instant when it had not been quite so gentle, and she had wanted that to continue, but it had not.

This ... this was entirely different. It was not gentle, and it did continue.

Was this what Harry Jenkins had sought to do when he dove at her on the settee and she had needed to arise abruptly to elude him?

But it wouldn't have been the same, instinct informed her.

She would not have pressed her lips back to his. She would not have let the force of his mouth part her lips. She would not have held on to his arms as strongly as he held on to her. She would not have slid her arms up to clasp her hands on his shoulders when he wrapped his arms across her back.

She wanted ...

She didn't know what.

His tongue followed the line of her lips and it shocked her, forcing a gasp, which opened her mouth wider to him. And then she felt his tongue touch hers, and knew she wanted to mirror his explorations.

Under her arms, raised to encircle his neck, he brought one hand.

He cupped her breast in that large, capable hand of his. A touch through the layers of cloth, yet the warmth and gentle pressure so beyond her experience ... and then he brushed his thumb across the point.

Heat bolted through her, buckling her knees. As if he knew to prepare for that reaction, Nate clasped his other arm across her back, holding her so tight to him that she could not breathe. And she was glad of it.

Her body ... was not her own. These sensations ... This ... *this* was the heat behind Louisa's whispered confidences. The emotion that she had heard in the woman's oblique words but never understood.

Until now. Until Nate.

She shifted, only vaguely realizing that she had given him greater access, but reaping the benefits in waves of heated pleasure. Her hands explored the prickling, tough contours of his face, then one circled around to the soft, fine hair at the nape of his neck, tightening there to do her part to draw them closer, ever closer.

His hands gripped her hips, bunching up the material there and drawing her as flush against him as the clothing separating them allowed, and there was no mistaking –

He wrenched away, turning his shoulder to her.

The shock of the release, of her body bereft of his, held her immobile, gasping for air and sense.

"I don't want you thinking –" His voice was raw. "I never should have-" He bit that sentence off with an oath under his breath.

He didn't want her thinking he felt that way about her?

He never should have let her think he might feel that way?

Humiliation began to well up in her....

And just as quick it was gone.

All it took was one view of his face.

She'd seen him look like that once before. His words from then came back, sharp and clear.

It was a long time ago when I was a stupid boy. ... Nothing to do with you.

But it was.

Long ago or not, stupid boy or not, it was to do with her. Entirely to do with her. And with his letting go when she'd thought he never would.

"Nate–"

"Go back to the house. Go now."

She ignored that harsh command.

"Tell me, Nate. What happened?"

"Happen? Just came to my senses, is all. Because I don't care to be the next conquest of Miss Sophie Vandercook of St. Louis."

The fire in her cheeks burned inside and out, but she kept her gaze on him. "What happened back in Ohio?"

He wouldn't tell her.

How could she make him? Yet there was no way around it if she didn't know what *it* was. If he never told her –

And then his words were coming out, sharp, stony words that had been inside him far too long for him to hold back now.

"Oh, it's a story you'll enjoy. Just your kind of tale. I'd spent my whole life watching my sisters connive and come on things sideways, so I should have known, I should have seen it, but I was as big a fool as any that they twisted around their fingers. No, a bigger fool. Because at least my sisters reeled in the catch they wanted. And they're good wives to those men. But me – well, I had to do it up big. I wasn't satisfied to be pulled in like any ordinary fish. Oh, no. I fell for the prettiest girl in the region. Everybody agreed about that, just like everybody agreed Mary Carlyle ran the county the way a ramrod runs an outfit. Only child of about the richest man in the county, lived in town in a nice house, a real nice house. There was the son of an even richer man in the next county over who everybody said was courting her, but time kept going on and she still wasn't spoke for. Some started whispering that he wasn't ever going to make her an offer. A few even laughed about it a little, when she wasn't around.

"Not me, though. And then one day I was fishing on the river and she came by, and she'd hurt her ankle. It was a long way back to town. So I got our horse, and I put her up on his back …"

Sophie thought she could almost see a younger, softer

Nate looking at the girl he'd just helped up onto the horse. Looking up into her beautiful face.

A twist set up under her bodice – a pain in sympathy with his pain.

Certainly, it was pain speaking behind his anger. Just as she'd thought before when he'd reminded her of Lizzie Wendersham, so angry in her sorrow at her brother's death.

"We talked then, talked all the way back. And we laughed – best laugh you ever heard. She asked me to come see her, uncertain-like. As if I might've said no. I took to spending every evening there on her back porch. And there was a barn-raising and a dance, she gave me twice the dances of anyone else – even that rich man's son from the next county. We started making plans that night and Mary let me kiss her – let me!" he scoffed. "What am I saying, like I had anything to say about it! She kissed me."

"You loved her."

He cut her a look then away. His voice had gone gruff when he resumed. "Thought I did. Fool that I was, I was sure I did. I asked my Pa what to do. Not if I should marry her, but how to go about it. He tried to hint me away, tried to let me know what I was letting myself into. Even Nellie – my nearest sister – tried to tell me it wasn't right, but I was having none of it. Why should I listen to anyone else when Mary'd been telling me something different not only with her words but with her eyes and her smiles and her laughing? So there I went, all full of this rosy future, went right up and knocked on the front door ready to ask her Pa for her hand."

His voice shifted again, flat now. "They were having a party. The rich man's son from the next county had proposed and she'd said yes. Not that I believed that right off, even with her Pa telling me so there at the front door. I should have gone away right then, but it was … I couldn't take in what had happened." He shook his head, as if trying to clear it even now. "She loved me. I was so sure she did. I pushed right past Mr. Carlyle, and she was there in the parlor by the hall, and somehow I had her wrist and was tugging her outside, thinking if we could talk – just talk alone … Everyone followed, yelling, threatening. I just kept talking to her – fast as I could, because they were coming – saying she had to tell them the truth. And then she laughed. That beautiful, beautiful laugh. And she said she thanked me for helping her and her intended see the truth of their own hearts. But all the time she was looking at me, her back to the rest of them, so only I could see her face, and I knew – I knew. She'd done it all on purpose."

"Oh, Nate. I'm sorry." She said the words, but they came out so soft she didn't think he heard.

"I stood there a long time, long after they'd all headed back in. Seemed like near forever, with the light and the music and her laughter spilling out those open windows, and me standing. Don't remember leaving, don't remember going home, but I must have, because then I was home, and they'd already heard all about it. And there were my sisters, even Lily who'd told me daily that I was making a fool of myself over Mary Carlyle, all being nice to me. Talking to me sweet like I was a man about to die or … or … or the village idiot. So I got the hell out of there. Headed west that very night. Never looked back."

"And you came here?"

"And came here," he confirmed.

Where the women were few and many, many miles between. Where his heart was unlikely to get snagged by anything more demanding than his best horse.

"You never miss your home?" she probed gently. "Or your family?"

"No."

"I suppose the letters are a comfort to you."

He cut her a look that would have sliced a delicate skin.

"I meant your family's letters, of course," she said. Only she hadn't. Not entirely. She'd heard a yearning in his letters to her ... And she had recognized it. Empathized with it. Even as she'd known it was not for her. "Someday you'll want a wife –"

"No. Females thinking of marrying can't be trusted anymore than a rattler, and every female from the time she puts her hair up is thinking of marrying. Even Edith is starting to get loco. Give her a couple more years and she'll be near as bad as Mary Carlyle – or you."

"Because you think I'm like her, this Mary Carlyle?"

"Yes." The word sounded as if it might have hurt his throat. It certainly lodged an uncomfortable lump in hers. "It's why you came here, isn't it? Came to get yourself a husband?"

She sat on the log, composing her hands in her lap and staring straight ahead. "I see."

"Isn't it?" he demanded again.

She said nothing.

She was aware of his scowling down at her, but she didn't look up at him. And when he turned and left abruptly she did not look around.

CHAPTER TWENTY-FIVE

She was glad he had left. It was a relief. It would allow her to think. To work this out in calm, rational manner. That's what she needed.

To face the facts of a situation as she always did.

Not to be turned inside out by the heat of a mouth on hers in a way she had never expected, never imagined. And as for how his touch had made her feel, and what she had done in touching him back and wanting to touch him even more, and to have him touch her –

She dropped her hand, which somehow had gone to lips that seemed to have grown sensitive simply from a memory.

She clasped her fingers together again, more tightly now.

Think.

Because you think I'm like her?

Yes.

Ah, yes. Those remembered words wiped out the memory of his embrace. As certainly they would have done for him, as well. Believing her to be like that she-devil Mary Carlyle who had used his honest heart in such a way, he could not possibly retain any of the feelings she might otherwise have attributed to him based on that kiss.

She sat even straighter. There. That bracing reality focused her mind once more.

Although she wasn't like Mary Carlyle … Or was she? She certainly hadn't abused the heart of one of the hands to wring an offer from another. But was her plan as bad as Mary Carlyle's plot?

Or didn't *as bad as* matter? Not when it wasn't as good as it should have been. Because if her plan had been good – *right* – she would be married to String by now. Or she'd have left herself engaged to Gunner.

Instead, ending those engagements had been the right thing to do – even logical, since no part of her plan was to become the wife of a man who had not entered into marriage with her from a similar perspective.

Entered into marriage from a similar perspective …

She propped her chin on her cupped palms, which were supported in turn by her elbows propped on her knees.

She was at fault, deeply at fault, for not having considered that when she formed her plan. She had not given consideration to the feelings of the man who would be her husband, and she felt sharp regret having caused String and Gunner any pain.

What she required was a man for whom the arrangement would be, if not as advantageous as for her (since unmarried men did not suffer the restrictions that hemmed in an unmarried woman), yet beneficial and agreeable.

The image of Nate Abbott formed, and was immediately banished.

No, indeed. While there was no denying there was between them what Louisa Scroggins had told her of, he yet was quite free with his low opinion of her.

Moreover – while she doubted he would retain his

resolve to never marry – he would never be satisfied with a wife who went her own path, especially a path that led back to St. Louis.

Yes, he'd kissed her, and that had made her feel ... feel as she had not felt before.

But he had also shared kisses with Mary Carlyle, and consider how he regarded that female. *That* was whom he likened her to.

She blinked her eyes hard against a sudden stinging from a shaft of sunlight piercing the shifting leaves above her head.

She sat up, brushing her palms against each other, as if ridding them of lingering flour.

She needed to leave this place. First, she either needed to follow her plan or to leave without a husband. Then return to St. Louis where she belonged. Far away from –

Her spine straightened.

Her plan. She would think of her plan, and only that. And in fulfilling her plan it would end any foolishness in the bunkhouse, because her future would be settled ... just as it would end any foolishness in her thoughts.

To pursue her plan, she needed someone in whom she did not stir deep feelings, someone who would not expect or want a true marriage, someone who would be happy to have her return to St. Louis while he remained here, someone who she could be satisfied would benefit by such an arrangement.

An image of a handsome face bearing a broad, knowing smile came into her mind.

Someone so satisfied with himself, so selfish, so vain that there was no fear of his having deep feelings or of entering any arrangement that was not entirely to his benefit.

The very man to make her plan successful at last.

Once married to an absent husband, she could return to St. Louis and pursue her life as she saw fit, and never again think of her time in Wyoming Territory, or of a particular man forever bound in her mind and memories to this place.

⁂

ate watched her through the trees.

Now what was she up to? That head of hers was whirring and plotting for sure.

What he wouldn't give to know – no. No. He didn't care what she was plotting. Or thinking. Or feeling. None of it.

He'd been a fool to kiss her last week. Which had nothing to do with coming back and hearing she was once more unengaged. It was those waterworks of hers.

Well, not waterworks precisely, because she'd held back the tears like a demon.

Maybe it was that. That, and her being so brave about the hurt her family had laid on her. Hurt she was trying so hard not to show.

That's why he'd kissed her then. Just a little. Barely kissing at all, really.

Not like today ...

... when he'd been a damned fool to kiss her.

All het-up about those two idiots in the bunkhouse. He'd wanted to knock their heads together and tell them not to even think about her, much less say her name or think either one of them had the least hope in hell of having her be his wife.

He'd been angry. That was it. Angry with those two boys and the rest of them. Angry with her.

That's why he'd kissed her.

She'd felt like lightning he'd caught in his arms. The heat and light of her thundering through his blood for sure and near to exploding in his head. He'd wanted to kiss her and kiss her, until they both dropped to their knees with it. And then kiss her more.

To kiss her in places –

No. NO.

It's why you came here, isn't it? Came to get yourself a husband?

Why had he asked it? Had he hoped she'd say no?

He'd said it, and he'd meant it – she was every bit as dangerous as Mary Carlyle. More dangerous, though it wasn't necessary to figure out how or why.

All that was necessary was to stay away from her – far away as he could get – until he was sane once more or she went back to St. Louis, and neither one could happen fast enough for him. No, sir.

⚜

Which is how it came about that Nate spent near a week in the saddle, with brief periods out for bad meals and worse efforts at sleeping, before he returned dusty, tired, sore and hungry, only to discover the home ranch abuzz again with news about Miss Sophie Vandercook.

She was engaged to another OS hand.

Jasper Tinton.

They would wed in the fall when the preacher returned from his summer roamings. And she would stay at the OS in the meantime.

Frederick Bracken told him all this. And then had more to say.

"I was quite surprised," Bracken said. "I thought Miss Vandercook a better judge of character – not that there's real harm in Jasper. But he does not have the quality I could hope for as a husband for a lady such as Miss Vandercook."

The owner seemed to wait for some response.

Nate had none.

"Miss Vandercook's visit has made me give thought to a number of things I had considered far in my past. I concede you were wise in hinting me off when she first arrived."

He paused, but his foreman had nothing to add.

"But there's no reason I can see that a lady nearer my own years couldn't provide Edith with a mother figure and me with companionship. A man certainly benefits from the companionship of a woman who has sense and backbone. As Miss Vandercook does."

Nate ignored the significant look his boss sent his way.

"I own I thought there was a growing feeling between you and Miss Vandercook, Nate. I could not help notice, at times, a certain atmosphere that quite reminded me of ... Well ..." Bracken cleared his throat. "In short, I sensed a true attachment between you and our Sophie."

"You were mistaken, sir."

"Was I?" The owner considered him. "Was I, indeed?"

Within the hour, Nate had new supplies and was back in the saddle heading out, never once having seen the betrothed couple to offer his congratulations.

"Sophie! Sophie!"

The shout had Sophie half rising from her seat on the porch, where she and Edith were sketching.

She'd seen an unfamiliar rider coming in and going to the bunkhouse, and now here came Gunner running full speed toward them.

Nate had been gone for days and days without anyone hearing a word. Even String was getting testy about it. Could something have –

"What is it? What's wrong, Gunner?"

"Nothing's wrong – something's right. Real right! You'll be happy as all get-out when you hear."

Sophie sank back into her chair, sucking in a breath.

"Well, stop standing there like a mush-head and tell us," Edith ordered, standing at the top of the stairs, while Gunner stopped one below her.

Gunner bridled like a rooster fluffing up its feathers. "Don't go bossing me around, Edith. You're just a child!"

"I am not a child!" The girl slammed her hands on her hips, having the effect of throwing back her shoulders and thrusting out her as-yet insubstantial bosom.

"Are, too," Gunner replied.

Sophie watched his gaze drop to the portion of Edith's person now closest to him.

These children will make a match of it someday.

The thought threatened a sting of pleased tears. They would deal well together, with their generous hearts and hard-working hands. She shook her head and confined that future possibility for later consideration.

"What is it you have to tell me, Gunner?"

He blinked, as if needing to recall her presence, then turned to her with a smile that threatened to split his face. "The preacher's in Grayley."

"Oh!" Edith squealed. "That's the best news, Sophie!"

"Is it?" What did these two find in these words to produce such raptures?

"Of course! Now you and Tinhorn can get married right away – well, not right away, because we have a deal of things to do to get ready. But three, four days that should be plenty of time."

"Three or four days? Oh, no, you're mistaken. Nate said there couldn't be a wedding until autumn."

"But that's before the preacher came back to town," Gunner said.

"But Nate said –"

"Why is he back?" Edith asked.

"Broke a leg. Oh, don't worry, Sophie. It's not so bad he can't be brought out here in a wagon and stood up to say the words. Leastwise, we might have to hold him up some, but we have plenty who'll help with that."

"No," she said. Or maybe it was only in her head.

"Throwed by his horse?" Edith asked.

"No. Got it run over by a wagon. There'd been a dance

the night before up almost to Goose Creek."

Edith nodded wisely. "Rev. Osborne doesn't hold his drink well. But don't you worry about that, neither, Sophie. Pa will see to it he doesn't do much drinking until –"

"But there's no need –"

"– after you and Tinhorn are married proper. And by then we'll be having a party this whole territory will be talking about for years. First thing, we gotta talk with Doughy. Was that Fascom I saw riding in with the news?"

"Uh-huh," said Gunner. "He said –"

"So everybody between here and Grayley knows already, and he can confirm the day on his way back to town. So Gunner, you get off to the South Range where the TS hands should be starting to bring their head up and start spreading the word."

"Wait. *Wait*," Sophie pleaded. "There's no need to hurry this–"

"I don't take orders from you, Edith Bracken."

"You sure do when all I'm saying is good sense. Land sakes – what else would you be thinking? Bet you got a horse already saddled in your mind."

"We'll wait until autumn just as we planned," Sophie said.

Edith and Gunner glanced at her, but neither seemed to hear her.

"And tell Mr. Shrieve to bring his fiddle," Edith added to Gunner.

"He don't need you telling him that, and neither do it." But he started down the stairs in apparent preparation for following her orders.

"Pa!" Edith shouted as she headed inside. "Doughy! Wait'll you hear!"

The front door slapped closed behind Edith. Gunner left only a curl of dust rising from his path as he ran to the corral.

And Sophie was left alone on the porch to contemplate her impending marriage.

String and Gunner rode up to where Nate sat astride Sago, looking like the opposite sides of a coin.

String was as glum as a March mud hole. Gunner shone like a sparkling June noonday.

At least they didn't greet him with any "Nate come quicks!"

"String said we'd never find you," Gunner announced, full of proving the older hand wrong. "Especially not in time. But it only took a bit over a day. So there's plenty of time."

Nate didn't ask time for what.

"Tell him," String said, looking out to the mountains like he was talking to them.

Gunner complied. "Mr. Bracken says for you to come back and join the festivities – there's going to be a wedding! Morning after tomorrow. If we hadn't a found you now we'd've had to have headed back ourselves or miss it."

"You go on back, then. And don't waste any time about it," he said. "I'm staying here."

"But the wedding–"

"It's our Sophie," interrupted String. As if there'd been a score of females who might've been getting married at the OS home ranch. "The preacher broke his leg, so he's back to town now instead of the fall, and he's coming out to marry them up proper. And everyone's coming from all around. Doughy's working like a demon in the kitchen. Edith said there'd even be a real wedding cake."

"I'll live without eating wedding cake."

"But Nate–"

"She's going to marry Tinhorn," String interrupted.

"I figured, since they were engaged last I heard. Though I wouldn't've put it past her to have dropped him and picked up another bridegroom these past days. Either way it's best news I've heard all season. Because once she's married, she'll high-tail it back to St. Louis, and we can all get back to normal without that little bit of –"

"Stop that," Gunner commanded in a deep voice unlike his usual tone.

Surprise silenced Nate.

Shifting his horse around, the boy squared up to him, his jaw out like the prow of a ship. "You've given Sophie the rough side of your tongue right along, and I mostly figured it was between you two. But you won't talk that way about her, Nate Abbott. Not anymore. Not as long as I can say different. You hear?"

"What in damnation do you –" He swallowed the words, and a fair amount of his anger went with them, leaving bemusement. "Why're you taking me on about this now? If you had a problem with how I was talking to her you should've said it when she was your intended – that would've made sense."

Gunner shook his head with deliberation. "I would've had to plug you one then. For talkin' that way about my intended. So I didn't say anything. Now I can say it, because if I plug you now, it'll be because you deserve it for being unfair to Sophie, not just because you said something against my intended."

Nate threw up his hands. "You think a single word of that makes sense?"

"I do," String said.

Nate twisted around to him. "Oh, do you?"

Untouched by the sarcastic drawl, String said, "Not only do his words make sense, but Gunner's got the right of it, too, about you being as testy as a rattler around our Sophie from the moment she spoke to us so nice outside the Mercantile."

"You, too, with this nonsense?"

"Yup. Tell you something else."

"Don't bother, because I ain't listening."

Apparently String wasn't listening, either, because he

added evenly, "You got to come back for the wedding."

Nate emitted a low sound from his throat that had all three horses shifting uneasily.

"You don't, and you might as well turn the OS right over to Tinhorn, he'll be that full of himself." Gunner predicted.

String nodded slowly. "True enough. Worse, even, you don't come back and see her hitched, and you might as well give up on pretending you're not pining for our Sophie."

This time only Nate's mount moved. He couldn't have sworn it wasn't because he'd clamped his legs hard enough to let Sago feel a bit of the spur.

"I ain't pining for her."

"Then prove it."

CHAPTER TWENTY-SIX

Sophie watched another petal fall from her wedding bouquet to the porch floor.

It landed on the right shoe of the preacher. His left foot was clad only in a sock that stuck out beside the crutch he used.

When the day dawned clear, Edith had declared they would move the ceremony to the front porch so everyone could gather round and see. That would have been impossible inside, the girl had added because every soul on the OS Ranch and most of the county had arrived to see Sophie wed to Jasper Tinton.

Not every soul.

Not Nate Abbott.

Sophie had known that, even before she'd emerged from the front door to the violin strains of Ezrah Shrieve playing "Strolling Through the Park One Day." Even before she'd made eye contact with String and he'd given her a slight shake of his head.

That was when her hands began to shake. She'd clenched them around the ribbon-wrapped stems of the wildflowers Edith was so proud of, and that's when petals began to drop.

"Will the parties stand up, please," intoned the preacher.

At least she thought that's what he said. He had a very strong Scottish accent.

"They are standing, Reverend," hissed Edith from beside Sophie.

Edith had been everywhere and done everything these days leading up to the wedding. Sophie had tried – oh, how she'd tried – to slow the momentum, but Edith was not to be resisted.

And, if it came to that, why should Sophie not proceed with this wedding? Was there any reason? Any reason at all not to marry Jasper Tinton?

"I don't want to get shackled," he'd protested in that first discussion. "Though I wouldn't mind a wedding night …"

Side-stepping his attempt to kiss her, she had been precise with him – no wedding night, she would leave for St. Louis shortly after the wedding, and she had no expectation of visits or otherwise seeing each other ever again.

Jasper had frowned at the first restriction, but brightened up considerably over the rest.

When she'd finished, he'd said, "So, the gals looking to rope me into marrying them and staying tied to their apron won't have no look-in, but you won't be round to stop me from kicking up my heels with the other sort of female?"

"Your conduct will be ruled by your conscience," she had said sternly.

"That's fine then," he'd said with a wide smile that appeared to confirm her opinion that his conscience was a most lenient ruler.

But she would be far from here, and feel no repercussions from his behavior. She would be in St. Louis, establishing a household as a married lady, with all the freedoms that would provide her – along with the freedoms provided by her inheritance.

She would never return here. She would never see any of the people associated with the OS Ranch. Never again.

All she had to do was go through with this ceremony.

"Why, so they are standing!" the preacher exclaimed. "Now, the parties shall give their names and their places of abode."

Sophie cleared her throat twice, yet her voice still shook as fiercely as her hands as she pronounced her name and home of St. Louis.

Her bridegroom smoothed his hair, smile toothily, then boomed out, "Jasper Albert Tinton, and right here on the OS Ranch, Wyoming Territories."

That drew a brief cheer.

Through her shaking, Sophie felt a trickle of something go down her back. It wasn't moisture. More like a finger of ... of warmth.

She looked around, but the preacher was talking to her again and she had to concentrate to understand what he was asking.

"Oh, yes, sir. I am a single person."

"But not for long!" shouted a voice from the gathering, drawing laughter.

She looked around, into the faces fanned around the porch steps. Most were grinning. Gunner looked back at her with a slight frown that might have been concern, or the sun in his eyes.

"And you come here of your own free will and accord?" the preacher asked.

"Sure did," Jasper said, to more laughter.

"You, Miss?"

"Yes. I ..."

But the preacher wasn't listening. He was talking with Jasper about the ring – though making clear it wouldn't be needed until later.

That was fine, because Sophie stopped paying the

preacher any heed.

Nate was here.

She saw him standing just beyond the outside ring of guests. He was grim, his frown clear even from this distance. Slowly, he stepped forward, shouldering his way through the group.

Sophie stopped shaking. She also stopped breathing.

The preacher spoke from behind her. "Now, Jasper –"

"With my body I thee worship, with all my goods I thee endow –"

"Not yet, not yet!"

"Mighty anxious to get to that body part." Called a voice from the far side of the steps. Something like a growl emanated from Nate, and people in front of him parted, so he was halfway to the steps now.

"Don't rush your fences, young man," ordered the preacher. "First, I ask, Do you take this woman to be your lawful wedded wife, forsaking all others, and keep to her as long as you both shall live?"

Silence.

And stillness. All except for Nate, advancing at the same calm pace.

"Now you say it," the preacher said.

"With my body I thee worship, with all–"

"Not that –" The preacher interrupted Jasper. "Say, I will."

"Oh, right. Okay. I will."

From the corner of her eye, Sophie was aware of the preacher turning toward her. "Do you, Sophie Mary Vandercook take this man–?"

"No." She said it looking at Nate. Only at Nate.

"What's that, missy? Did you say something?"

"No –." She jerked her head around, breaking the connection with Nate, looking at the preacher once more. "I mean, yes, I said no. I can't do this."

Then she looked at her bridegroom.

"I can't marry you." She thrust the bouquet into

Jasper's unresisting hold. "I'm sorry, Jasper. I'm sorry, Mr. Bracken. I'm sorry, String and Gunner and Edith and –" Her gaze skittered away from Nate. "–everyone here on the OS. And all you who came all this way for today. I'm sorry. I can't do this. I can't. I – " she gulped in air, then let out a hiccup. "– can't."

She departed the porch with more speed than grace. She opened the front door no more than necessary to slip into the dim interior, then shut it quickly behind her. For good measure, she turned the key in its lock, so no one would follow.

She took one step forward, then stopped.

She had no idea of what to do next – or ever.

Her mind was entirely blank.

Sophie Vandercook had no plan.

N ate couldn't ignore his reaction this time.

He was so relieved he was almost sick with it. At the same time, he wanted to whoop and holler and wave his hat, like the rawest cowpuncher in the wildest cow town after the longest drive there'd ever been.

That wasn't normal.

Wasn't sensible, either.

And he had to do something about it.

While everyone else was just starting to stir out of shocked stillness, he turned on his heel and strode toward his destination.

"Marry me."

Sophie blinked up at Nate.

The first instant he'd appeared she'd indulged the notion that he was merely an apparition conjured from her wanting him to be there. Then sense took hold, and she realized he'd come in through the kitchen, and was as real as she was.

It relieved her greatly that her good sense was starting to seep across the frozen emptiness of her mind. But it still had a good ways to go.

"What?" she asked, to buy time.

"You heard me. Marry me, Sophie."

"But –"

"No buts. I know you. You know me. Marry me."

"I ..."

"You don't dither, Sophie Vandercook, so don't start now. Look at me, and tell me, yes or no."

She looked at him.

"Yes."

They stared at each other for a long moment.

So many thoughts, feelings and fragments flooded her mind, all moving at top speed, so they blurred together like the colors of a whirligig.

At last, Nate gave a sharp nod. "All right then. That's that. We're getting married."

He leaned forward.

Everything that had been moving inside her head dropped to her stomach.

His lips touched her cheek. Brief, proper. More like the first time he'd kissed her, though not as nice as that, now that she knew the alternative. And entirely unlike that other kiss. The one that came to her so often during the day, and always at night.

He hovered over her. Holding as still as she did.

She could feel his breath on her cheek. The faint moisture from his kiss made the skin there tingle.

"Sophie."

His breath came with her name, and the tingling spread in a crackling rush through her.

She tipped her head back to meet his gaze.

And saw in it that other kiss.

"Yes."

She knew what was to come. It pulsed through her blood, and deeper inside of her where she hadn't known she could feel –

"Wahoooo! Lookee here!" shouted a voice she thought belonged to one of the TS hands. "Nate's getting a lead on every last one of you pieces of coyote bait."

Nate spun around to face the intruder who had come from behind him, leaving her entire view taken up by the back of his vest. But she could hear thudding footsteps and protesting voices, apparently as others followed the route Nate had blazed through the kitchen.

How had she not heard the lumbering approach of all these cowhands?

Nate stretched both his arms back, as if to pen her in behind him. She stepped around his left arm so they stood side by side.

"Bout time," String said.

"Bout time what?" a voice from the back demanded.

"Nate and Sophie getting married."

"She's engaged *again*? She's just barely *not* married Tinhorn."

"What?" came a yelp. Jasper pushed his way to the second row, where he was stalemated by those not willing to give way.

"Tell 'em, Nate," String ordered. "Tell 'em you and Sophie are getting married."

"I asked, and Sophie said yes," Nate said.

"I don't believe it." Jasper declared. "You don't like her above half and she don't like you at all."

String made a sound at that, but all Nate said was, "It's the truth."

"Let's see you kiss her, then. Right here, right now." Jasper's face had gone sly. He clearly thought he had Nate dead to rights.

That thought had barely formed in Sophie's head, before Nate had a hold on her and was bending to her, leaving no time to see what was in his eyes.

Not that second kiss, that was for sure.

His lips pressed firmly against hers. That was it.

This was neither the proper kiss on her cheek of moments before, nor the nowhere-near-proper kiss she couldn't forget. Nor was it whatever it was that had hovered between them just before this interruption.

She considered that as a cheer erupted from the men. Nate released her immediately.

The OS hands came forward with varying forms of congratulations, some formally shaking her hand, a few patting her on the shoulder, one or two sharing good wishes, and a handful of the least articulate merely nodding and smiling in front of her. Each then moved on to unanimously pound Nate on the back.

All the while, she was thinking hard.

She had so little experience with kisses. However, her ability to assess situations could be applied even to kisses.

The first time Nate had kissed her had been gentle, almost sweet. It had to do with her being a lady.

The next one had to do with ... that heated fluttering she felt around Nate Abbott at the times when she wasn't wishing to strike him with something large and hard in a manner far from ladylike.

The chaste kiss on her cheek a bit ago had to do with his proposing to her. And, she supposed, her accepting. It was nearly a solemn handshake, though suited to the agreement they'd just made to marry.

But this kiss ... this was entirely different. Not unpleasant, not hesitant, yet not at all what she liked.

Because the kiss had not been for her – it had been for the men now surrounding them.

Her frowned deepened as a new cheer went up, and voices started explaining to newcomers at the back what had happened.

She looked sideways up at Nate. He was grinning back at Hodges, the current back-slapper.

"Well, guess I got to marry her – only way to keep this

outfit in one piece."

She stiffened.

"No." She projected as she would to an unruly class. "No!"

"What's that?"

"No. I won't marry you, Nate. No."

"Sophie –"

She twisted away from his reaching hand. "No."

She ran up the stairs, closed the bedroom door, and this time she locked the solitary door that gave access to her sanctuary.

Though there was no need for such a precaution, since the only knock that came was Edith's.

And that ceased after a spell of no response, allowing Sophie the quiet to resume assessing the facts before her.

CHAPTER TWENTY-SEVEN

"Nate! Nate, come quick!"

Nate clamped his jaw so tight he could feel the muscles there popping in protest.

Could only be one thing – one person – at the root of his being hailed that way.

The last person on earth he wanted to deal with this morning.

A morning that suited his mood, with boiling, grumbling clouds piling up around the mountain tops and streaming down the hills toward the home ranch.

He'd spent the rest of yesterday digging fence holes for a new corral to the west of the home ranch buildings. It wasn't something that needed doing right now, but it was hard work that a man did alone. And for reasons he had no intention of examining he hadn't wanted to ride off to some distant chore.

Supper had been silent and glum, with Sophie's chair glaringly empty and Edith prone to sniffles.

He'd started the night in the bunkhouse, equally silent and glum, until String told him to get to his own room and close the door, because looking at his face was setting up all the hands to have nightmares. Instead, he'd taken his bedroll and come down here to the creek.

He hadn't had nightmares, but then he hadn't slept at all.

"Can you not leave a man a moment of peace?" he demanded as String came into view. "You kick me out of the bunkhouse and now you come roust me –"

"She's gone."

"What do you mean, she's gone?

"Mulehead came and found me right off – Milly's gone. And so's the sidesaddle. Sophie must've left well before first light – what light there is, with this storm coming in. And you're wasting time."

He growled the same sentiment when Nate insisted on looking at the empty spot where the sidesaddle was supposed to be, checking out which halter was missing, and verifying that Milly and her posse were gone.

The growl got worse when Nate announced he was going after her alone.

"I'd a gone to Mr. Bracken if I'd known you were thinking such a thing, and now he's off escorting the Shrieves as far as the river to check for a better fording spot. It's coming on to storm, and she'll be out there on that sidesaddle. I can hitch up the wagon and –"

"No."

"If she's headin' to town, she won't get there afore the storm."

"I go alone."

"Ain't right, Nate."

He stared back at the older man while several of the other hands around them shifted their feet at String's protest.

"I go alone," he repeated.

String's final growl was a promise of retribution if any harm came to Sophie.

Nate trotted his horse until he was out of sight, then slowed up.

He let Sago plod along at a steady pace, while he did what he'd avoided doing all last night – hell, avoided doing all day every day since that morning outside the Mercantile – he considered his feelings about Miss Sophie Vandercook.

And when he was done with that, which didn't take all that long, he considered her possible feelings for him.

Then he had one more factor to add to his considering: the character of Miss Sophie Vandercook.

He gave the sky another look, calculating.

Finally, he gave his horse a nudge to pick up the pace and he chased down the trail of dust he'd been watching up ahead, rising like a peacock's tail.

Sophie only turned her head once to see who was coming up behind her.

And that was when he was far too close for her to have done anything about it if it hadn't've been him. A circumstance that made him far less obliging than he might have been otherwise.

He came up alongside, reached over and took a good hold on Milly's reins.

"Please release the reins," Sophie said, calm as you like.

"Well, it's good to know you can saddle a horse with that contraption and get in it on your own if you want to bad enough."

"I could always saddle a horse. As for mounting, I had access to a box that proved quite adequate. Now, I repeat, please release my horse's reins."

"Not your horse. She's an OS horse."

"I have every intention of leaving Milly and the others with the preacher in town."

"He's not there – he's still at the ranch. Sleeping off celebrating not marrying you to somebody yesterday."

"With his household," she corrected with a bit more of a snap. "And you needn't worry, I will provide for their upkeep."

"I wasn't accusing you of not caring right for Milly, and

I wasn't accusing you of stealing her and her brood. What I'm saying is she's an OS horse, so she's subject to the OS ramrod – that's me."

"Nate –" That wobbled a bit.

"Come to think of it, so are you."

"Wha– I am no such thing." No wobble there.

"You are. You pledged."

"I'm sorry – I know I said yes, but I realized almost immediately – I can't. I can't marry you, Nate."

"Not that pledge."

He was glad he'd thought of this ahead of time, or her bringing it up might have caught him unprepared for remembering those moments after she'd said she'd marry him and before she'd turned him back down, those moments when he'd thought he'd pulled in so much air into his chest that he'd just float right up, bust through the roof and keep going up into the skies, reminded him of all that. And he wasn't sure he'd've been able to think of a word to say feeling like that.

"The pledge you made that first time out on the range. When you promised not to go ridin' on your own, not anywhere, not anytime. You gave your word, and I'm holding you to that. And there's a powerful storm coming on. This is not the time out."

But maybe he'd said it all a little too fast, so it sounded like he'd been practicing it in his head, because her eyes narrowed at him a little.

Then she looked up at the sky. She held that way a moment, before bowing her head.

"I did give my word."

"All right then."

He turned Milly, guiding her back through the little herd that milled around her in a moment of confusion. Then, with Milly and his horse set on the path back to the OS, he dropped Milly's reins. and they rode on side by side.

Sophie spoke only once – when they turned off the

main track.

"This isn't the way to the OS home ranch."

"We won't make it back before this storm breaks." He made sure to speak slower this time, so as not to give away he'd been practicing these words, too. "We need to take shelter closer by. There's a cabin was built a while back by one of the big outfits that sold out a couple years ago. Nothing fancy, but it should keep most of the rain out."

When the cabin came in sight a few minutes later, he realized "most" might have been overly optimistic.

Part of the roof was stoved-in. He hadn't remembered that. But then he'd never noticed particular, because he hadn't ever thought about bringing Sophie here before.

At least the part that still had its roof included the door and the chimney wall.

He swung out of the saddle, looped both horses' reins, then had his hands at her waist to help her down.

She made a sound that brought his gaze up to her face. Her eyes were glazed by tears, her chin wobbled, but her back was firm, and her look at him was straight and honest.

"I do sincerely apologize, Nate, if I caused you any embarrassment before your men. I was hasty in accepting your proposal of marriage. And – We would not suit."

"Sophie, I shouldn't have said what I said about having to marry you to keep peace on the OS. I know that. Knew it as soon as the words came out. I didn't –"

"Please. This does not need to be made difficult or awkward. After the storm passes, I should like to go on to Grayley. When you return to the OS, simply tell Mr. Bracken that we made a mistake." She tried a laugh that sounded harsh and odd. "That I made yet, another mistake."

"Sophie –"

"No. There's nothing more to say. Except that I am returning to St. Louis."

Lightning struck just the other side of the ridge.

"Not now you're not," he said grimly.

He swung her down from the saddle, and tucked an arm around her to hustle her inside. He had to push the door with his shoulder, but his first view inside told him that, all things considered, it wasn't too bad.

Where the roof had come down, it had swung like an arm, creating most of a fourth wall, and the other walls appeared intact.

"I'm going to see about sheltering the horses in that other side." He tipped his head past the now vertical portion of the roof.

"I could start a fire ... if you think it's safe?"

He followed her dubious gaze to the rock fireplace. "No sign the chimney's bad. But keep it small in case critters have made themselves to home."

The other side of the building hadn't fared as well, but it offered more shelter than these horses had experienced many a time in their lives. He strung a rope from one side of the ruins to the other, and tethered them to that, so they wouldn't be having to chase them down when the storm passed.

The skies opened as he dashed back to the other side, carrying his things, and the one bag she'd had hooked to Milly's saddle. The sound and the look of the sky said this wasn't a blow-by storm. It was settling in for a good drenching.

She had a small fire going, though the rain coming in the chimney threatened to douse it. She added a piece of fallen rafter to it, then gathered up more pieces into a pile nearby.

He set out his bed roll in front of the fire, and hooked the arms of his slicker over the posts of a couple of seatless chairs to help catch the warm of the fire and protect them from mist seeping through the partial roof behind them.

"I got coffee, some tomatoes and bacon," he said. "How about you. What's in your bag?"

She colored.

"I left a note for Mr. Bracken, asking that my other things be sent on to me when the wagon next made the trip to Grayley."

"So, what's in the bag?"

"My drawing things."

He grunted. "Paper might come in handy for the fire."

"No!"

He dropped his head to hide his grin. Could be those were some of those pictures he'd heard Edith say were of him? Could be she didn't want to burn pictures of him?

Maybe this would turn out okay after all.

He got the coffee started, while she remained uncharacteristically quiet. Soon as they'd each had their first sip, he dove right in.

"You said outside that there's nothing more to say. But I'd say there's a sight more to say, Sophie."

He felt her tense, though she'd made sure that even in these tight quarters of sitting on his bedroll on the dirt floor that they weren't quite touching.

"I still want to know why you came here. I thought from the start you were plotting something, and I figured it was to get yourself a husband."

She drew herself up with dignity. "If I were plotting to get myself a husband, as you so elegantly phrase it, I would have remained in St. Louis, where I have received offers of marriage, which I turned down."

"I'm not surprised. Not at the offers – you're not a bad-looking female, even if there isn't all that much of you. Of course, if they got the rough side of your tongue a time or two, that might be enough to scare off some," he added judiciously.

She huffed, which he found encouraging, but said nothing.

"And not at you turning them down," he went on, undeterred. "Seems to be your way. And I've got to think that if it's a husband you're wanting you've got a strange way of going about it."

She didn't meet his gaze.

"If you're really sorry about jilting me in front of all the hands not five minutes after saying you'd marry me, here's what I want from you, Sophie. I want to know what you've been after this whole time."

"That smacks of blackmail."

"That's what I want," he repeated. "To know what you came here for."

"Not for a husband – not a real husband. For independence. Freedom."

He waited.

Her chin came up and the words jerked out of her. "It's to not be tied up and constrained by what a respectable young lady can do and can't do. And to not exchange all those strictures and rules for the yoke of matrimony. I want to be a woman free of a man's tyranny."

He faced her, but she stared straight ahead.

"How'd you plan on doing that?"

"Marry a husband who'd be absent. I wouldn't take his money – I don't need to be supported. I have an inheritance coming that will keep me from being a burden on a husband. I just don't want a husband to rule me."

He nodded slowly. "I heard you talkin' with Edith one day about husbands, and how her husband would likely take over the ranch when it passes to her. I can see how that would rile a girl of Edith's nature. Can't see that she'd sit still for that when the time comes – nor pick a man who'd be that kind of husband, for that matter. But it seems to me, you don't think much of husbands of any kind."

"I suppose I haven't. Didn't." She swallowed hard. "Don't. That was ... I saw –" She sucked in a breath, then let it out slowly to start again. "I was wrong to accept offers from String and Gunner, for they offered me far more than I could offer them. I realized my error, and thought that a union with Jasper would suit both my needs and his. But then I found … I could not do it."

"That sounds like the Sophie I know."

"You don't know me."

"Yes, I do." He waited until she looked at him. "From your letters."

She tipped her chin up again. "And what of your letters? Do you then say that they have revealed you?"

"I suppose so. Though I had other hands in them, telling me what they wanted in and such."

"But it was your telling of the events that made me want to come here. Your insights. Your … "

He pretended he wasn't aware of her pulling in another breath, this one edging too near a sob for his liking. "I did some thinking while I was riding after you this morning. Sophie. Thinking about your letters and what I knew of you before you even came here. A woman who's honest, smart as a whip, more tart than sweet, sometimes strong-minded and other times bull-headed, and –"

"No doubt you call me strong-minded when I agree with you and bull-headed when I don't."

He opened his mouth to fire back, but a chuckle came out instead. "See, right there – smart as a whip and more tart than sweet. Now don't go pokering up like that. I liked all that about you in your letters."

"Oh."

"Just took me a while longer to see their benefit in person. Or, maybe I was trying hard not to see what I liked about you with you here on the spot."

She poked at the fire, leaving him her profile, where he could see color rising up her throat.

"But there were other things, too. Like wanting to know your brother. No way for you to know he wasn't what you hoped he'd be. And coming out here at all for that matter – that took gumption." He took his hat off, feeling that the occasion called for it.

He'd made the decision riding after her.

He was going to marry Sophie Vandercook.

He just needed to get her used to the idea, too.

CHAPTER TWENTY-EIGHT

"Like how you are with Edith," he continued. "You took that girl right in and have given her what none of us ever knew she was needing. Oh, she's still a darned good hand, but I can see she'll be a real woman someday, too. I see her feeling more settled like with herself, now she knows some of those lady things. You being here's made Bracken easier with himself, too. Not quite so shut.

"And you've brightened up some of the boys a whole lot more than I'd've ever thought could be done. And Gunner and String have got their feet under them better."

He cleared his throat. "As for me ... My feet have been knocked right off the ground by you."

He glanced at her, then away. Then he stopped turning his hat in his hands, and slowly brought his gaze back to her.

"Happens every time I see you, Sophie. Or hear you. Or smell you. Or think about you."

She looked up at him, her eyes wide. The smallest slant of her lips giving her a smile that shone in her eyes. And then her lips parted. Just a bit.

It was more than he could take.

He gathered her in, his arms around her, drawing her to him at the same time he went to her.

Their mouths came together. The taste of her was what he remembered and far beyond memory.

He opened his mouth, to taste her beyond just lips to lips. And his Sophie opened her mouth to him. Delicate, like, a little hesitant, but not scared.

Not his Sophie.

Need swelled in him, pushing, demanding. He had to move. They shifted together, circling, to find new angles, new ways to bring their mouths together, their lips, their tongues.

Her hair tumbled over his fingers, and he reveled in it. He felt her fingertips brush at the bristle of hair at the nape of his neck, and if he'd been standing his knees would've buckled for sure.

Nate dragged his mouth away from hers. Sucking in air along with a bit of sense.

There were still things to say.

"I have feelings for you, Sophie. Strong feelings. But I'm not going back to St. Louis with you. You have to know that. This is where my life is. This is where I'm staying."

"I know, Nate. I wouldn't ever ask you to leave here."

That wasn't what he hoped to be hearing from her. But he wasn't a man who gave up easy.

He drew the pad of his thumb over her lips. "And if you're set on going back to St. Louis, we shouldn't ..."

He let it dangle there. If he could get her to admit to wanting him, too, it might be easier to lead her away from being so all-fired intent on going back to St. Louis. And then he could say the rest of what needed saying.

He knew she did want him. They couldn't feel so right together, if it wasn't as right on her side as it was his.

Trouble was ... this was Sophie.

She wasn't slowing down for the talking they needed to do. Not one bit.

Her fingers brushed at the back of his neck. That's all it took for fire to flash through him, pooling in his gut with the best kind of hurt he'd ever known.

But Sophie wasn't done. She pressed her fingertips into his neck to guide his mouth back down to hers. She opened to him, and darted her tongue against his, and he thought he went a little crazy.

"I don't know how ..." Her voice in his ear, the warm moist heat of the words and the sound of the voice he thought he'd first heard in his heart in her letters, brought him back. At least a little.

They were tugging at each other's clothes.

"... to undo these," she finally finished.

"Yours, either," he said.

But they'd made a fair amount of progress. His shirt was off, his pants open. Her bodice revealed a neat chemise and creamy skin above and beneath it that had his hands shaking, even as he stroked it.

"Sophie ... this isn't."

Her eyes went huge. "I'm not doing it right."

"No –"

Hurt flooded her eyes now.

"No, I don't mean you're not doing it right," he said. "I mean no, you're not, *not* doing it right. Oh, hell, if you do it any more right, I'm going to go up in smoke right here."

That cured the hurt. She smiled as she stretched up to resume their kisses.

He held her off. "But ..."

The word and the hold on her brought the questions back to her eyes, and he couldn't bear it. He had to think of something here.

He had to think ...

He couldn't think.

He kissed her.

He rolled her, cupping her head in his one hand – the

only pillow she had against the hard floor.

He kissed her again. And again.

Kissing and touching.

Drawing her scent and her taste so deep inside him it would never leave.

His pants were gone, his one-piecer well open. In another minute – less – he would be inside her. Where he wanted to be more than anything he had ever known.

He stopped.

Panting with the effort of not moving. Then sweating with it.

"Nate?"

He looked down at her.

A mistake.

She was ready for him. Warm and soft and welcoming. As if it were reaching to him, the darkened tip of one breast pushed against the fabric of the chemise that was all she still wore.

Another minute – less ...

If they stopped now, he might die. Worse, he could see the hurt and questions starting to edge back into his Sophie's eyes.

No.

He let his clothing fall back into place, as he slid his hand slowly up the inside of her thigh.

If she ended this ... if it was her choice ...

But she didn't.

She watched his face, until he couldn't take that any longer, or he'd be getting inside her the fastest way possible.

So he kissed her again. Kissed her and kissed her until his hand reached her opening. And with their mouths open to each other, she shifted. Just that little bit and his finger was there, sliding into the sweetest heat he'd ever known.

She made a small sound. He stilled.

But before he could do more, her hips lifted slightly

under him. Dropped, and lifted again.

He stroke his finger into her, withdrew, and again, with the rise and fall of her hips. He brought a second finger to stroke just outside ...

Her gasp broke their kiss. But he didn't mind.

He put his mouth to that dark tip of her breast. Through the fabric, first. Then he pushed that aside with his whiskered cheek, drawing a sound from Sophie that nearly ended him right there. And when he touched her flesh direct with his tongue, they both made the sound.

He drew her into his mouth, setting a rhythm that matched his fingers. Her hips still moved with it, too. More now. Stronger. Her fingers clutched at his shoulders and her voice whispered his name. Then called it out in a way that struck right to his heart.

He brought his knee up tight, unable to resist resting some of his weight on her softness.

She shook, and she shuddered in waves, her flesh pulsing around his fingers, and all the while she held onto him like he was saving her.

He held her like that until she quieted, then he rolled her to rest on his chest, drawing her discarded bodice up to cover her one shoulder not nestled against him. He thought she was full asleep until she slid her hand in his where it rested on his chest.

Then she gave a sigh, and fell asleep for sure.

He was left to contemplate that small, white hand lost in his large, sun- and work-darkened one. Yet that hand of hers was so powerful. It could bring him to his knees.

Now he just had to get married to her before she killed him with the wanting.

⁕

Sophie Vandercook did not flinch from facts.

Even when the facts were less than abundant. Consisting, as they were, of oblique comments and glances exchanged between married women, such as Mrs. Forestell and her sister. Whispered confidences of Louisa Scroggin of discomfort, possibly even pain the first time.

She had not experienced that.

Added to her store of facts was a basic understanding of human anatomy, furthered by observation of classical artistic studies.

Added to this was an internal sort of knowledge – or perhaps it was instinct – of this male form so unlike hers, of this body, of this man.

Not, perhaps, the most practical or solid of facts on which to base a conclusion.

Yet, taken together, they satisfied Sophie that she was correct in her assessment.

"Nate."

"Hmm."

"Was that ...? Was I ...?"

"You were perfect Sophie." He stroked one hand up her back, under her hair, his fingers lightly stroking at her neck. "Bright as lightning."

She raised her brows, though he could not see. "Every reference I've heard you make to lightning has been in connection with a stampede. You have not been complimentary."

"True." He smiled, still with his eyes closed. "And it fits. Just like lightning, you scare the bejabbers out of me because I never know when you're going to strike, and you can stampede cattle, or cowhands, or me in a heartbeat. But also, because when I look at you, I'm in awe."

Her heart thudded at the words, but her mind held firm. The fact was, he *wasn't* looking at her, and there remained the other matter.

"That was ... not the end, was it?"

He made a sound that blended pain and amusement. It solidified her assessment into certainty.

"Near enough for you."

"No. It's not."

That opened his eyes. It also jolted his heartbeat under her hand. As a window to Nate Abbott, she believed that heartbeat would serve far more reliable than his words or expression. She allowed herself a small smile.

"It's as much as is going to happen," he said firmly. "More than should've unless we're married. But leastwise we haven't done what a woman does with her husband. We need to talk a–"

"I won't ever have a husband."

"Sophie –"

"I know that now. But ..." She slid her hand down his chest, into the opening provided by undone buttons in his one-piecer, then back up. "I want to know, Nate."

He groaned her name. "You will have a husband. And a nice house, and a kitchen full of kids."

She shook her head slowly at each of his predictions, then a final time. "I won't." Only when she added, "And I want to know, Nate," did tears fill her eyes.

This time when he groaned, he caught her to him, his arms crossed over her back, one palm pressing her face to his chest. And she once more felt that telltale thunder in his heartbeat.

"If you can wait just a bit –"

"I want to know," she repeated, feeling the storm that sentiment set off in his chest, letting it spread into her blood and bones. The opening in the one-piecer allowed her hand to venture below his waist. Her own heartbeat thundered so hard in her throat that she thought she might not be able to breathe. But she needed to say this. "Now. With you. Only with you."

She kissed his throat, and his head fell back.

"I want to know with you, Nate."

He shifted them so he was above her, looking down.

Her heart beat so fast she thought she might faint with the waiting. It was like those moments of flying when his arms lifted her from the saddle and into the wagon out at the roundup. But with no sun, no whisky to explain it away. And now, even as she flew, she felt the weight of him above and against her that she wanted to wrap herself around and hold onto forever.

"Sophie?"

She opened her eyes to him, welcoming the dizziness of looking into those blue depths.

"Yes."

And lifted her hips to him.

⚬⚬⚬

"We'll get married right off."

It was the second time he'd awakened, and this time it was to look directly into her eyes.

The first time he'd come awake, the storm outside had finally quit, and it was full dark. The kind of dark, though, that said dawn was coming. He'd poked the fire back to life, heating the coffee, waiting for her to wake before they did something about breakfast, because they'd taken no time for supper.

Then he'd watched her sleep.

He must have drifted off again, because when he woke this second time, she was watching him.

He wasn't full sure he'd spoke the words aloud, so he said them again, stronger.

"We'll get married right off."

She sat up, poured him coffee before responding. "No."

"I know it's not what you thought, the kind of life you thought you'd have in St. Louis, but you like this country — I see it in you."

"I love this country," she said simply. The impish smile returned. "I am even coming to accept that cattle have their good points."

"Well, then. Marry me." He touched her bare shoulder. How could anything human be so soft? "Sophie —"

She quieted him with her mouth on his, her body close enough to feel its warmth and softness welcoming him. Drawing him back to her, into her.

◦◦◦

The coffee was cold, their bodies significantly warmer when either of them could speak again.

"Sophie. Sophie, be my –"

"I'll be your business partner."

"Don't want to be your business partner," he murmured idly against her flesh. "I want to be like this with you every night and every morning."

She held her discarded chemise to cover herself and she backed up enough to sit on her haunches, away from him. "I told you I have a bit of an inheritance, but that's ..."

"Mm-hmm," he murmured, reaching out far enough to stroke the skin just above her knee.

"I ... I told you ..."

He looked up. Only now that she'd spoken again did he catch that what had stopped her before was some internal storm bubbling up in her. "Uh-huh."

"I *told* you."

By her tone, he knew he was missing something, but she'd let the chemise slip and his mind was contemplating the swell of her breasts and whether he had the strength to sit up so he could put his mouth to her flesh there.

"I have never before told anyone that I will inherit on my twenty-first birthday."

"Said you wouldn't be a burden on your husband," he recalled.

"I won't." She was worrying her lower lip, looking at him from under brows drawn down. "I was not to tell anyone."

"It's good as forgotten." He sat up, leaning toward her. She shifted away, so his mouth found her shoulder, which

285

was very nice, but a bit of a let-down, considering.

"But I did tell you. And that's – well ..." With the air of one determined to reveal all, she sucked in a bushel of air that gave him an even more enticing glimpse beyond the chemise. "The point is, that I did not convey the full measure of the matter. More than not being a burden on a husband, I have a substantial sum coming to me. With it, you could be partners with Mr. Bracken. And together you could buy the breeding stock you want, expand the herd –"

"No." It came out sharp enough that she started. He tried to gentle his voice, but the words came out nearly as strong as the feeling behind them. "I won't take your belongings. That's final. You keep your money. Every bit. I want to know if you're with me that you're with me because you want to be. Not because you don't think you have a choice. And not because you think I don't have a choice."

She frowned at him. He wanted to change that.

"Tell you what, though," he said, smiling, "I'm ready and willing to be married to a partner in the OS, as long as it's you. You got some money coming to you? You buy in with Mr. Bracken. I'll go on as foreman. And we'll be married."

Slowly, she shook her head. "No."

"Okay, then, no partnership in the OS."

"No," she repeated, making it clear that wasn't what she'd been referring to, as he'd full well known. And hadn't liked one bit.

"We're getting married," he declared.

"No."

"I wouldn't have done what we done if we weren't getting married. We're getting married," he repeated in his best ramrod tone. "It'll be good. You'll see, Sophie. I know it's not what you planned. Not what I planned, either. It'll take some adjusting. But that's okay. Just some adjusting."

She straightened her back. She might have looked prim

and proper if she wasn't next thing to naked with her hair tumbling around her. "No."

"Sophie, if you're willing to give me this money you hadn't told anybody about to buy in to the OS, it only makes sense that you'd be willing to keep your money while getting me as husband besides."

He tried a grin, but it wouldn't come as he watched her breathing pick up, like a filly about to bolt.

"It's different for a woman," she said. "A husband decides what she can do from then on."

"I won't —"

"I do want to invest in the OS through you. I consider you a very sound investment. Not with me as Mr. Bracken's partner. You should be the partner. I would not consider the OS nearly as good an investment without that stipulation."

That's when he saw what she was doing. Clear as day. Pushing him away, just as she'd pushed Gunner away with talk of his being a lawyer. Only that had been for the boy's own good. And this wasn't for anybody's good. This was —

And then he knew it.

Sophie Vandercook was scared.

Well, he couldn't rightly blame her. He'd been terrified of her from the instant he heard her voice outside the Mercantile.

That's what he'd realized on the ride after her yesterday. He'd been scared because he loved her. Had come to love her somewhere in the lines of those letters, and had just been lying to himself. Flopping around like a fish that was already well and truly caught.

And now she was just the same. Only he'd had all these weeks to get past the being scared — yet only accomplished it as he rode after her yesterday morning.

He had to get her past the scared.

"I shall be returning to St. Louis immediately and —"

And fast.

He had to do something. Say something. Anything —

"You don't have to worry about a husband doing what you said before, about deciding your life – not if it was like you wanted – where you lived in St. Louis and your husband was here in Wyoming. Maybe to come back East to see you every winter, and you'd come to see me here if you wanted. If it was like that, like what you wanted, you could marry me that way, Sophie."

He hated the idea, even as he said the words, he felt the misery of being away from her for months on end. But if it was the only way he could get her to say yes now, it would give him time …

The wave of his own anticipated misery took him down so low and so fast he almost missed her nearly silent answer. "No."

"Quit saying that," he snapped. "Listen, I understood those other boys – you didn't have the feelings for them you need to marry somebody. But you can't tell me you don't have those feelings for me."

"No."

"No?" he repeated, something like panic squeezing his chest.

"No, I can't tell you that."

"Sophie–"

"No," she repeated, louder, and now he could hear in her voice all the imagined misery he was feeling. "I couldn't be married to you that way, Nate."

His spirits split apart at that, soaring and sinking all at the same time, leaving his body stuck in between. Soaring because it meant she really did love him. Sinking, because it meant Sophie was fighting not only him, but herself. And to his mind, there wasn't a tougher force to overcome than Sophie Vandercook.

CHAPTER TWENTY-NINE

"You were out all night," Bracken said.

Still holding Sophie's hand from helping her down off the sidesaddle in front of the main house, Nate looked up at the OS owner, who stood forebodingly at the top of the porch steps.

"Yup."

He tugged slightly at Sophie's reluctant hand, and they walked up the steps together.

"Ain't right, Nate. Not being out there all night with Miss Vandercook that way."

"I know it, Mr. Bracken."

The owner of the OS stood taller. "There'll be a wedding. Now. Preacher's still here."

"Ain't woke up yet. Had too much to drink," came Edith's voice from behind the partially open door. "Again."

"Edith. I told you to go to your room."

"Aw, Pa."

"Edith."

This wasn't what Nate had planned when he'd insisted

they come back to the OS Ranch. Sophie had finally agreed to return, but only to gather her belongings properly so as not to burden the Brackens with that task. And she seemed to think he'd agreed that she'd be heading back to St. Louis right after.

But now Mr. Bracken had just handed him an opportunity that was a whole lot better than buying time by hiding every OS horse miles from the home ranch for as many months as it took to make her change her mind.

"Have to be a shotgun wedding then," said Nate.

Bracken's jaw worked, but he didn't back down. "I'm disappointed in you, Nate. Never thought to say that, but I am. Deeply disappointed. But if that's what it takes … Edith, get my shotgun. And tell Doughy to get the preacher. We'll do this thing right now."

"I understand your thinking, Mr. Bracken. And I say you do what you gotta do. Just know one thing, sir. When Edith comes back with that shotgun, you'll have to point it at Sophie. Because she's the one saying no."

Bracken gaped at Nate for a long moment, with Nate looking back at him, partly to let the man see he was telling the truth, and mostly to keep from looking at Sophie. All he knew of her reaction at the moment was that she hadn't run and she wasn't saying a word.

Slowly, and with his jaw still hanging down, Bracken shifted his gaze toward Sophie.

Nate heard a sound from her that might have been meant as a word, but came out more as a croak. She cleared her throat and tried again.

"It's true, Mr. Bracken."

Nate looked at her then, and wished he hadn't. Red pushed up her throat and into her cheeks, the kind of red that felt like your skin had been rolled in prickly pear, even though the sensation came from the inside.

He might have wished he hadn't laid this at Sophie's door, except he knew – knew for certain – that he needed allies if he hoped to persuade Sophie to stop fighting herself and him.

She stood so straight and firm – despite the stare being leveled at her by Frederick Bracken, despite that painful color in her face, even despite the approaching sound of booted feet on dusty ground that said the boys were drawing near – that Nate was as proud of her as a man could be.

"Nate's done nothing wrong," she added, her voice louder, pitched to reach the approaching cowhands, though she looked only at Bracken.

"He offered to marry you?"

"Yes, sir." A faint tremble there, though it didn't show in her face.

"Other than the other time Nate asked her, you mean, don't you Pa," prodded Edith, now on the porch side of the door, no shotgun in sight.

"Yes, yes, of course. We're not speaking about that previous, uh, brief time day before yesterday when Nate asked you, and you said yes. Then no."

"After Sophie told Tinhorn no in front of the preacher, and Nate found her in the hallway," Edith further clarified.

"Yes. Indeed." Bracken cleared his throat. "But we're not talking of that. I am asking you if he offered to marry you after ... uh, after ..."

"Since she started riding toward town yesterday," Nate offered.

"Yes. Well. Very well, yes, since then – has Nate offered –"

"Asked her to marry me," Nate interrupted again.

Bracken cleared his throat again. "Asked you to marry him?"

"Yes," she said.

"And you said no?"

"Yes, sir."

Those words were nearly drowned out by the rumble of the men forming a half circle behind them.

"That's two bits you owe me, Lester," said Doughy. "I

told you she wouldn't have none of us."

"Is that it, Sophie? Ain't we good enough for you?" asked String plaintively.

She spun around to him. "Oh, no, String. That's not why at all. You're the most – the best … You're the truest gentlemen I have ever encountered."

"But then …" He scratched his head. "I don't see it, Sophie, I just don't see it at all. I understand you not marryin' me, and Gunner's a good enough boy, but he is young, and Tinhorn's a gadabout, so there's none'll fault you for those. But Nate? I seen you and Nate and the way you two look at each other, 'specially when the other one's not lookin' … Why that's how most courtin' couples could only hope to look. "

That's when it happened.

What Nate had been looking for, hoping for, praying for – what he'd feared might not happen.

Sophie looked at him, and her eyes said that she wasn't fighting him any more.

Oh, she was still fighting herself. But now it was like it was the two of them against that last bit of stubborn fear. And he figured he and Sophie together could lick anything. Even fear.

"Mr. Bracken, if you don't mind, if I could take Sophie inside for just a bit to talk private, I'd appreciate it."

From the sound that came from Bracken, Nate thought Edith poked her father in the ribs, but he wasn't sure because there was no way he'd risk taking his eyes off Sophie right now.

"Of course, of course," Bracken said.

"Use the parlor, Nate," added Edith.

He slid his palm under Sophie's unresisting elbow, and guided her up the steps and into the house, while Edith held the door open. He fumbled a bit finding the door to the parlor because he was still looking at Sophie, but he managed it, and drew her into the room, so they didn't break contact by touch or look.

For the rest of his years, he could recall the smell of wood polish, and it would bring a lump to his throat.

But at this moment the lump was from trying to find words.

"Sophie, I know you. Some from the letters, some from your time here, some from – I don't know – something inside us, I guess. Because you know me, too. I know you do."

He challenged her with the words, and his Sophie met the challenge.

"Yes."

"So I know why you decided against marrying String or Gunner. But Tinhorn, he'd have been just what you came here for. Yet when it came to it, you turned him down. Right there in front of the preacher and everybody."

"Yes."

"Because what he was offering turns out not to be what you really want when you could've had it."

Without breaking the look, she dropped her head and raised it again in a full nod.

"And me? You turned me down because I'm offering none of what you came here for – we wouldn't be in St. Louis. We'd stay right here. And you wouldn't be having your own establishment to run by yourself. We'd be together. Every way there is for a man and woman to be. You'd be a true wife to me, Sophie, and I'd be a true husband, truer each day by adding to what I learnt the day before."

Tears tracked down her cheeks. His muscles banded tense against the need to wipe them away.

"Is that why you said no to me, Sophie? Is that why you told everybody out there that you wouldn't marry me? Because I'm not offering you what you came here for?"

Her chin trembled slightly, but she gave one, sharp shake of her head.

"And I know you wouldn't've done what we did last night without … without having the feelings for me that a woman has for the man she marries.”

He thought he’d negotiated that rough ground pretty well. Then she pushed him off a cliff.

“You wanted to stop, so I would be saved for another man.”

“Hell no! I wasn’t thinking of any other man – not ever.” He stopped himself from saying he’d decided well before that point that they would marry one way or another. His Sophie wouldn’t take kindly to that sort of steering. “I just wanted to be sure you were sure.”

“I was sure,” she whispered. But she also dropped her head.

He changed his approach without stopping to think about it. “You have to stand up to what you did.”

“What did I do?” she demanded with more of that snap he loved in her, like the bite of the Wyoming wind.

“You made me fall in love with you. And you love me,” he added baldly.

She blinked fast against a fresh spurt of tears. “I don’t want to love you.” It was damned near pitiful.

“I don’t particularly want to love you, either, Sophie,” he said, a smile twitching his mouth. “But I do.”

She lifted her chin. “I most certainly don’t want a husband like you.”

“I didn’t want a wife like you, either. Another headstrong, opinionated female – it’s what I left Ohio to get away from, and here I am about to spend the rest of my life with one. But I’ll get used to not having what I thought I wanted, and so will you, Sophie.” He moved in close to stroke her cheek, the roughened tips of his fingers sensitized to absorb the amazing softness there, perhaps absorbing a few of those tears as well. “Because what we are together is a fair sight more than either of us thought to be solitary. You’re my Sophie. And I’m your Nate. Ain’t that so, Sophie?”

Head tilted back, she looked up at him. “Yes, Nate. That’s so.”

ophie Vandercook married Nate Abbott at the OS Ranch, with Edith Bracken as her attendant and with every cowhand lucky enough to be in the vicinity that day as witnesses.

The day was not at all as Sophie had planned, and neither was the marriage that followed it. And every night, she said a grateful prayer that that was so, just before she kissed her husband, and heard his whispered question:

"Sophie. Why'd you come here?"

"For you, Nate. I came here for you."

And then she felt his rough, wonderful hands reach for her as he said, "My Sophie."

EPILOGUE

St. Louis

"'And so,' " Alice read aloud from Sophie's letter that had come all the way from Wyoming, " 'I am married now to Nate Abbott. And I know that each of you was with me in spirit as we made our vows. It is not at all as I planned, but so much better. I wish the same for each of you, my dear friends. My sincere affection always, Sophie.' "

"Oh, that is the most romantic story I have ever heard," said Rose Kershaw, who had taken Sophie's post and now slept in Sophie's bed in the attic of Mrs. Forestell's Young Ladies' Academy.

Alice sighed as she folded the letter along the lines worn deep into the paper from the many times of being folded and unfolded in these past weeks.

"And how lovely that Mr. Bracken has now allowed the girl Edith access to her mother's trunks. It makes me weep each time you read that passage of Mrs. Abbott's letter, when Mr. Bracken finally opens his memories to tell Edith about her mother as they look through the trunks."

It did, indeed, make the younger woman weep. But since nearly any occurrence could accomplish that feat, it was not viewed as noteworthy by the two more senior instructors.

"It is my opinion that more happened in the cabin that night than she has confided in us," declared Louisa, who was regarded as an expert on such matters since she was a widow.

"What more could have happened?" asked young Rose, eyes wide.

The other two regarded her but said nothing.

Then Louisa heaved a sigh. "It's so unlike Sophie," she said, not for the first time. "How could she come to have abandoned her plan, Alice?"

"I don't know."

"And to live so far from St. Louis! How will she bear being away from here?"

"I don't know."

"And now, to become a partner with Mr. Bracken in the ranch, when she never breathed a word to us of such an inheritance. What can she be thinking?

"I don't know."

"It's really most extraordinary. There is so much unsaid in her letter. I wonder when she is going to write to us with a fuller explanation."

"I don't know."

"I don't know! I don't know! I declare, that's all you've said every time we've discussed Sophie's letter these past weeks. Why, it would seem that you just don't know anything these days."

Alice looked up, a new light her in eyes. "Yes, I do. I know that I'm going to Wyoming."

THE END

* * * * * *

A Note From PATRICIA McLINN

Hello!

I hope you've enjoyed Sophie and Nate's story, and will consider sharing your experience with fellow readers by posting a review online.

To be notified of my new releases, sign up for my book alert at www.PatriciaMcLinn.com. That's also where you can find a printable book list, excerpts, and lots more.

Here are a few of my books to check out:

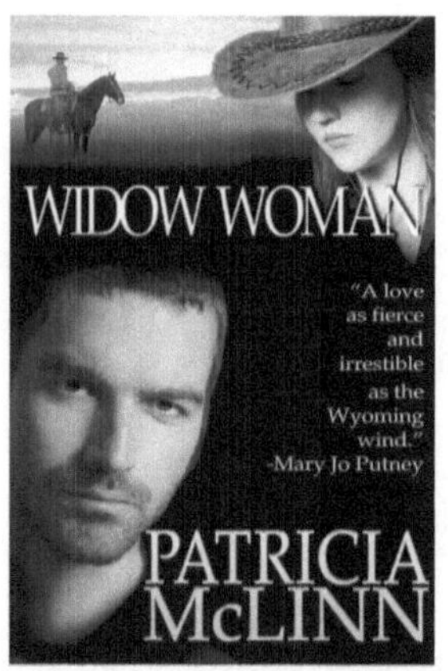

WIDOW WOMAN: Emotional western historical ". . .a strong woman, a dark tormented man, and a love as fierce and irresistible as the Wyoming wind. . . Splendid. . . Sizzles."

THE GAMES: Contemporary fiction "Fast-paced, vivid and true–to–life. . . . A gold-medal winner . . . Your ticket behind the cameras and inside the hearts of the Winter Olympics."

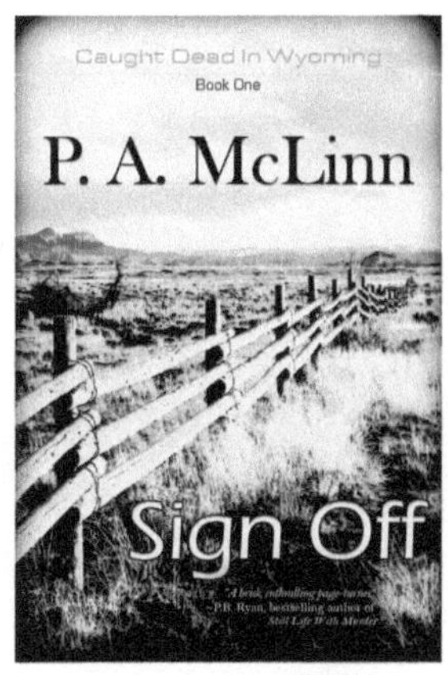

SIGN OFF: Murder mystery with humor, romance "Crackles with wit. . . Twists and turns. . . Dry humor…Fast-paced and intriguing. . . Will keep you guessing right until the end."

Happy reading!

Patricia

Patricia McLinn/P.A. McLinn

P.S. Hope you'll come connect with me on Facebook https://www.facebook.com/PatriciaMcLinn Twitter http://twitter.com/PatriciaMcLinn and Pinterest http://pinterest.com/patriciamclinn